Coconut Badger

www.coconutbadger.com

Mark MacNicol was born in Glasgow, Scotland in 1971

Published by Two Fit Poles 2011

First published in United Kingdom in 2011 by Two Fit Poles

A CIP catalogue record for this book is available from the British Library

ISBN 978-0-9567958-0-9

Papers used by CPI Antony Rowe are natural, recyclable products made from wood grown in sustainable forests. The manufacturing processes conform to the environmental regulations of the country of origin

Printed and bound in Great Britain by CPI Antony Rowe

Dedicated to my wee bro Jason

Special Thanks to:
My Mum, Elizabeth, Nana Cook, and Angela.

CHAPTER 1

Dalry's was unlike the other bars around Tam's office in that it was independent and not run by faceless number crunchers. An unassuming doorway flanked by bay windows opened into a lush visual splendour of dark panelling and leather upholstery. City workers were spoiled for choice when it came to post-toil drinks but Dalry's was for the more discerning among them. Tam's finances would normally preclude it as an option but as usual he was keen to impress Stella. As he struggled to attract the attention of frantic bar staff, he watched her chatting with people he vaguely recognised from the office.

An elbow squeezed against his ribcage, indicating the arrival of a man who had no intention of observing bar etiquette. This triggered a slight nausea as a familiar inner turmoil spread. An always silent part of Tam wished he could find the nerve to confront the stranger. Thankfully though, he had the excuse to justify inaction on this occasion. Remaining focussed on his mission to finally ask Stella on a proper date would take priority. To do this, he had to find a way of getting her on her own. He also knew that he could only afford this one bottle of wine. There was no way he could extend his meagre funds to a larger round including co-workers. On his junior wage this was often a source of discomfort to Tam, forcing him to avoid socialising with colleagues – a Glaswegian who avoids buying a round is regarded on a par with a necrophiliac.

After waiting patiently for the stranger to be served, Tam manoeuvred himself through the busy bar. To his relief, Stella was standing alone.

'Sorry it took me so long, total nightmare getting served in here so it is.' He made sure she saw him checking the glass was clean before handing it to her and then he poured carefully. 'Who was that you were talking to?' he asked.

'Oh just some people from the second floor, I don't think you know them.' She dipped her nose over the rim of the glass and sipped. He copied her.

'Mmm my favourite.' Her tone was enthusiastic, but Tam suspected she was in fact fully aware of this grape's lowly status. Nonetheless, he was grateful she had made the effort to spare his feelings.

'Please, will you let me pay half this time?' She reached down groping for her bag.

'No honestly I insist, this is my treat.' Despite being sorely tempted he couldn't bring himself to take a contribution. It was vital he display generosity as another of his many qualities.

'Not again Tam, you do this all the time, please let me give you something.' She held her purse open and Tam could see a faded photograph of a young girl with a woman in one hand and an ice cream in the other, a picture of Stella with her mother perhaps? He wanted to ask but while pondering on the boldness of such a personal question, the moment passed.

He gently pushed her hand back, committing the image to memory and she reluctantly pressed the purse closed. The edges of her mouth curled upward a fraction and Tam recognised a split-second prelude to one of her smiles. In the the six months they had worked together Tam found himself becoming covertly familiar with each of her smiles.

Soon after falling head over heels in what he suspected was a textbook example of lust at first sight, Tam had come to the realisation that Stella was out of his league. As a result, he had tried to avoid her as much as was possible rather than deal with the cocktail of heady excitement and stomach cramps her presence brought. Somehow though they had become friends. This was making things difficult. Despite Tam's best efforts, he had been unable to stem warm hope from seeping into the corners of his brain normally controlled by cold logic.

He surveyed the male faces in Dalry's, wondering how many had come here tonight as a result of their own hopeless infatuations. It would be funny if it weren't so pathetic. Tam knew the evening would rush past him in a blur. Stella would either leave too soon or his booze intake would accelerate him through Dutch courage and into pishdom. Alcohol was probably a useful vehicle if you knew how to operate the brake pedal – which he didn't.

'So, what exciting plans have you got for the weekend?' Her question pulled him back into the present and he quickly tried to collect his thoughts.

'Plans eh, eh.' He feigned a momentary bout of amnesia repeating her question and looking up at the ceiling in an attempt to buy some time.

'Oh eh that's right, I said I might meet a couple of friends later and go to a gig with them.' She giggled softly at his indecision.

'What, did you forget or something?'

'No sorry, I was miles away.' His cheeks burned as he gulped his wine, hoping that would be an end to the topic. He nodded at a random stranger nearby in an attempt to play it cool.

Stella followed his eye over to the man.

'So which band is it? It's ages since I've been to a concert.'

Tam wished he hadn't felt the need to lie. Realising she wasn't going to let him off the hook, he tried to establish some kind of composure. This wasn't easy with the distraction of pins and needles on the top of his scalp that often accompanied moments of anxiety. He knew they would soon be followed by a disagreeable hot flush spreading from his upper back through his neck and onto his face.

'I'm not really sure, one of my mates bought the tickets weeks ago for some band I've never heard of.' He hated himself for lying but regularly felt it necessary to fabricate weekend plans for Stella's consumption. He suspected the reality of flipping between blooterdom and hangover-induced wankfests was unlikely to impress.

'You're lucky, that sounds like it will be fun.' She looked directly at him and he froze with excitement and panic. It occurred to him that she might actually want an invite to this fictional concert with his imaginary friends.

'What about you?' He tried to change the subject.

'I've got a 10K on Sunday so I'll have to go after this bottle, don't you be trying to lead me astray.' His forced smile masked disappointment as this meant yet another opportunity would soon pass: he knew her running club was something she took very seriously. Just then he spotted Campbell and moved slightly in the hope he could avoid being seen. It was common knowledge at the firm that this guy was nursing a raging hard-on for Stella. Not only was he from a similar well-heeled background, he was disgustingly handsome and had charisma in spades. Tam knew his attempt to hide was likely to be futile and soon enough he could see his rival approaching. All the hope and enthusiasm of the night slid like acid into the pit of Tam's stomach.

'Stella! Tam! Over here.' Campbell could be heard clearly over the rabble and although Tam didn't flinch, Stella turned.

'Did you not hear me there, Tam?' Campbell smiled, gripping Tam's upper arm; there was no doubt Tam had seen him and they both knew it.

'No sorry I didn't.'

'Right, well anyway it's smashing to see you both.' Campbell stared intently at Stella, holding her elbows softly then leaning forward and kissing both cheeks – a move regarded as pretentious locally, one cheek being the norm. Tam studied Stella's face carefully, scanning for any sign of reciprocation. Although he could detect none, the lack of disinterest was a trouble to him. There was no getting away from it, Campbell was exactly the type of guy Tam could see Stella ending up with and this admission was a painful one. He knew his own pasty pink skin and fleshy soft frame were no match for such a tanned and muscular specimen. Campbell probably didn't even need to step foot inside a gym to maintain his perfect physique. His extensive collection of bespoke suits were in stark contrast to Tam's single high-street purchase with its well-worn shine. Tam sighed and looked down at Campbell's pig-skin Palermo loafers. Even they seemed to be sniggering, mocking his own scuffed and bargain-basement brogues.

Campbell turned from Stella to face him. 'You'll have a drink with me and Stella, Tam?'

'No you're alright thanks, I just came in for a quick one, I've got plans.' Tam tried to act as casual as possible in an attempt to conceal the truth about how he would actually spend the remainder of his evening.

'Oh I see, you've got plans have you. That's a pity I was hoping we could discuss some new accounts I could maybe get you involved in.' As a Manager with the brokerage Campbell could undoubtedly open doors for him. But it was obvious to Tam that he was most definitely not included in any of Campbell's plans. The show of influence and generosity was purely for Stella's benefit.

'Campbell I'm sorry but I've got a race on Sunday so I'm afraid I've got to leave after this one too.' Stella touching Campbell softly on the arm added to Tam's discomfort.

'That's fine no worries, we can do it another time, lunch perhaps?' Campbell's tone was confident, insistent even but also somehow relaxed and carefree.

'What do you think Tam, lunch somewhere nice and posh seeing as it's work related?' Although Stella was asking Tam the question, he could see she was teasing Campbell. She must have known very well that the invite didn't extend to him. Paranoia wrapped tightly around Tam's chest. He tried to disguise his discomfort and play along with the charade.

***

The street outside was dark and covered in a wet sheen, a looming purple sky pressing down impatiently on menacing clouds. Stella needed a taxi and Tam had lied yet again by insisting he would get the next one. Actually the bottle of Shiraz had wiped

5

him out, leaving just enough for his bus fare home. Tam held her umbrella and they huddled together sheltering from the steady downpour, each searching the opposite direction for an amber light.

'You don't have to wait with me Tam, I'm a big girl.'

'No it's fine, I'm not in any rush to get home.'

'What about your gig?' For a split second he had to remind himself of his earlier fantasy.

'Don't worry they're waiting for me in the pub, probably pissed on Petrus by now anyway.' She laughed. His comment was directed at Campbell who had made a show of buying an expensive bottle of wine. Stella leaned forward, continuing her search of the horizon. A sudden shudder of excitement jolted through him as the soft curve of a breast touched his forearm. He had thought of them so many times and in so many different scenarios. Cupped in his appreciative hands, suckling a hard nipple, swaying like hanging baskets with him pushing hard from behind. To be even inadvertently in contact with one of them triggered warm waves of renewed confidence and encouragement. He couldn't delay the analysis any longer and quickly weighed up the possibilities. Could the contact be totally innocent? Or was it an attempt to tell him she understood how he felt and wanted the same thing? Could there be a third option: was she getting a kick from leading a sad and pathetic loser up her beautiful garden path? He pushed this last thought from his mind. There was no doubting at the very least that they were friends.

'I should come over to your neck of the woods some time for a drink or something...' Her voice tailed off in a way he took to mean he should respond. There was now some fresh air between his forearm and her roundness so he was able to regain his composure. In his mind he tried to harness this second wave of confidence and searched for the ever-elusive 'right' thing to say. The sudden rush of excitement however, had triggered his old friend anxiety, manifesting itself in the form of mutant butterflies and light-headedness. He also wondered how Stella might react if indeed she saw his 'neck of the woods' as she had put it. He doubted she had ever set foot on a housing scheme, let alone one as infamous as the Monkford.

With his delayed response hovering dangerously on the edge of what might be perceived as a snub, Tam blurted out the first thing that came to mind. 'You're welcome any time Stella.' He hoped he had somehow conveyed what he really wanted to say. But he knew deep down it was another opportunity missed and felt an inward stab of anger. Their silence was filled by strangers' laughter as a taxi splashed in front of them. Its passengers were a handsome couple and Tam felt a raw envy being projected onto the man stepping out from the cab. Tam moved forward, claiming the door handle and passing Stella her umbrella.

'No you keep it you'll get soaked, are you sure you won't share?'

'Honestly it's fine, I'll get the next one.'

'Thanks Tam, you're such a sweetheart.' He allowed himself the luxury of melting into her auburn eyes, but couldn't differentiate between what could be a bright beam of passion, or just as easily a steady glow of friendship. Soon she waved through the back window as the engine stuttered, waiting for a gap in the traffic – and then she was gone.

As her cab turned the corner out of sight, the door of Dalry's swung open behind him with a loud bang. He turned to see Campbell thundering towards him.

'I've had enough of you taking the piss you little fucker.' Within a millisecond Campbell was inches from his face. 'I've heard through the grapevine that you've got the hots for Stella and I'm telling you right now she's out of bounds, spoken for, so far as you're concerned that's the end of it, comprende?' He poked a stiff finger into Tam's chest.'I mean for christ sake, get a grip, you have got no chance with someone like Stella, what exactly are you thinking about, seriously?'

Tam searched within himself, looking for a strength that he

knew simply wasn't there. All he wanted was to get away quickly, whilst maintaining whatever masculine dignity he could.

'There's nothing going on with me and Stella, we're just friends.'

His voice quivered under the words. Cowardice was just another item he could add to the growing list of reasons why Stella would never be interested.

'Well that's not what I've heard, the word is that you've got a soft spot for her.' Campbell's face was so close now Tam could smell the Petrus on his warm breath. Tam leaned back, trying to keep his balance until he was being pressed against Dalry's window. His knees weakened beneath him. A line was being crossed and Tam could sense that the time for dialogue would soon be at an end. He wanted desperately to run, but a life on the Monkford had taught him that people who run were as despised as those who neglect to buy a round.

Campbell was now pulling and pushing and Tam could sense the black mouth of the alley approaching from behind. He also suspected the shoves were an attempt to get some privacy and that the well-lit street might offer him some protection. But as he tried to clamber past, Campbell pulled him into the waiting darkness. Moving deeper now into the throat of the alley, Tam was overcome by a range of disgusting sensations. He could feel his rain-soaked clothing sticking to his skin and realised he was no longer holding Stella's umbrella. Hoping he hadn't lost it, an image came to him of her smiling back from the taxi. He felt an acute embarrassment; how could he ever have thought there was a chance for them?

A whistling was followed quickly by an impact around his ear and the dull thud of bone on bone. That seemed to trigger some kind of physical shutdown followed by an epidural release. The muscles beneath him relaxed, both of his tanks emptying simultaneously. He heard laughter and shouting but with a loud ringing inside his head he couldn't be sure what direction the noise came from.

After what seemed like a long delay the second and subsequent blows came in rapid succession. His legs were gone now and he dropped hard to his knees before falling forward onto the bed of moonlit cobblestones. Tam curled into as small a target as possible. For a period he couldn't distinguish between seconds or minutes, finding himself strangely yearning for each blow as he knew it would wipe out the sensation of the last.

After it stopped, all he had to focus on was a dull ache in his side. Then some more seconds or minutes passed but he had no idea how long or if he had even been conscious for all of it. Gradually he became aware of his surroundings. He was lying in the darkness with sharp edges of rubbish bags beneath him. He looked up at the now vibrating violet sky. The rain fell toward him backlit by a moon he knew was there but couldn't see beyond the top of the buildings. He felt the rain land on his face, but not for some reason in his eyes. Things didn't seem quite real and he liked that. After a while, he couldn't block out the reality any longer, the smell and warmth beneath him obviously hadn't been generated by the rubbish bags. A dry boulk aggravated his tender ribs as he became aware of two very different sensations. Comfort and torment ran through him seemingly in equal measure. The relief that his ordeal was over now covered by the dark and hopeless blanket of a coward's shame.

CHAPTER 2

Neither blue nor grey, the sky released a steady drizzle. A forceful breeze pushed its way into the busy taxi rank as Pat waited to return home to the Monkford. Another afternoon had gone, spent drinking among strangers in the quiet bars of the city centre. His late arrivals at the local pub were an attempt to avoid arousing Lina's suspicion relating to his drinking habits. Lina was the landlady and had been a good friend to him. She had also taken care of Betsy's funeral arrangements.

Betsy had always handled the household affairs. She had also attempted to ensure that whoever was left behind was financially secure. In this respect she had miscalculated; the life insurance along with Pat's own money equated to much more than he required.

The cab driver was friendly, but his attempts to engage were met with reluctant grunts from Pat. Looking out onto the glistening streets, Pat's main feeling was one of anger, as was usual. Betsy was much younger than him; he had always expected to be the first to go.

Entering from the darkening sky into the Public Bar he was greeted by the usual faces and his anger subsided. Lina struggled with a remote control attempting to find a channel; pool balls kissed among sporadic bursts of laughter. He perched himself on a stool waiting to be served.

***

After the dreaded closing bell, Pat had no choice but to go home. The rain had stopped, but the breeze had grown into a muscular wind. The walk from the pub had been made with her so many times it was often too much to bear. Tonight he chose a different longer route, but still his mind stabbed and goaded him with memories, the sound of her voice woven into the wind.

As a young couple, they had been among the first to move here. The scheme had been designed as an overspill for the inner-city slums and most of its inhabitants considered themselves lucky. Well-trimmed hedges and spotless windows framed by a genuine sense of community. Pat and Betsy's top-floor flat looked down from higher ground, an area known to locals as The Hill. The scheme was situated on the southern perimeter of the city with cold grey industry in its face and a patch quilt of green fields at its back. A sprawling myriad of breeze-block split in the middle by a bus terminus, metal shuttered shops and the Rannoch Moor pub. The Hill sloped down into the lower section of the Monkford known as The Valley. Packs of children and dogs ran unchecked among burnt-out cars and abandoned shopping trolleys. Betsy had always been terrified of the roaming mongrels; each time she left the house on her own she did so in fear. Her preference was to wait at her window until she spotted someone she could walk with.

As Pat fumbled with his key he could hear the dog inside clambering for a hiding place. Moving up the darkened hall and into the kitchen he picked up the whisky bottle and glass. He moved into the dark living room, ignoring the whimpers from behind the sofa. Placing the bottle and glass on the windowsill, he removed his battered tobacco tin. Betsy had forbidden smoking anywhere other than out of a window. He studied the dark and deserted street below, hoping to find something of distraction, but only memories looked back at him.

The once spotless windows of the street were slowly being replaced by council boards as more people decided to throw in the towel. A new generation were running the place into the ground, with spiralling drug use and soaring crime rates. Local gang the Monkford Bushwakas were generally regarded as the scourge of the community. Both The Hill and The Valley had sunk into a pit of hopelessness.

On the Monkford, as is the case on any scheme, one of the

highest yielding currencies is a man's reputation. Pat's was one of legend passed through the generations. His being a resident of The Hill had over the years diverted at least some of the undesirables down to The Valley. Although Betsy hated violence she understood that in this respect her husband's past had its advantages. Now she was dead, he no longer cared about the Monkford, The Hill or even the home that was once her pride and joy. His windows were no longer spotless and the once-polished cream and red stairwell was now covered in graffiti. Even climbing his stairs required hardy lungs to avoid the stench of shit and piss.

The weeks approaching the first anniversary of her death had brought with them an increasing sense of dread. Their home spewed forth volcanic rivers of rubbish, most of which consisted of empty whisky bottles and lager cans. Although a few well-meaning friends from the pub had called by, Pat never answered the door. He felt a sense of shame at the state of her once spotless home.

Pat switched on the dim standard lamp and dropped his suit jacket on the floor before falling into his armchair. He had been wearing the same suit since the day they burned her.

The dog's whimpering face poked out hesitantly from behind the sofa. It was starving.

He removed a fresh crossword page from the magazine rack. She had loved crosswords. Such was her consumption that he would always be on the look-out for discarded newspapers and magazines. He continued to collect them after her death and as with most things he did these days, he wasn't quite sure why.

Pat stared hopelessly at one across. After another day of heavy drinking it was a struggle for him to focus on the clues, let alone solve them. His eyes strained in the room's dull light as he waited impatiently for sleep.

***

Tam had been able to sneak up to the bathroom without being spotted by Lina. She would be suspicious if he didn't go in to say hi but he wanted to get himself cleaned up as best he could. Growing up above a pub had several advantages throughout his childhood. One of these was the safe and undetected passage he could normally be guaranteed via the back door, with his parents working in the evenings.

They had wanted Tam to join them on their retirement to Spain after the robbery. Finally, they had agreed that rather than take him out of school, provided Lina would look after him, he could stay behind. The brewery had been happy for Lina to take over the licence as it meant they didn't need to find a replacement. That might not have been easy in view of the pub's reputation and location.

With her long coal-black hair and smooth olive-brown skin, Lina's appearance was almost hispanic. Her undoubted beauty however, was of the type that attaches itself to someone who neither wants nor recognises it. During adolescence Tam had harboured pubescent hankerings toward her, frequently rifling her underwear drawer. But those feelings had subsided and were eventually consumed by a sibling-type affection.

Sitting on the toilet, he gripped his scraped knees to stop them shaking. He prepared himself for the task of moving the contents of his crotch into the pan beneath him. The only suit he had ever owned was now a piss-and shit-stained rag. He didn't really care though. He would never go back to the firm and never have to confront Campbell. The stupid feelings for Stella would be buried; he was finished with all of it. The thought of ever being goaded by her beautiful face again was more painful to him than any beating he would be given in her name. Campbell was exactly the type of boyfriend he could see her ending up with and Tam was a pathetic coward. With this thought, a heavier sadness than he had ever known in his life descended on the small bathroom around him.

Now that had been settled, the clean-up operation would take priority. He wanted to make sure Lina didn't worry but even if he did manage to dodge her tonight he would still have to come up with an explanation for the bruising to his face at some point. A good night's sleep would hopefully facilitate something believable. Just like his fictional concert for Stella, again he would create a fantasy, one in which he had at least put up a fight. While the Monkford code dictated you couldn't run away, it required at the very least having a go. His being bound by a straightjacket of paralysis would have been an embarrassment to any self-respecting Monkford man.

Tam diverted inward breathing from nose to mouth and using his hands began shovelling at the mound of discharge. The rancid odour had ensured the crowded bus journey home hadn't been pleasant for either him or his fellow passengers.

Finally he stepped into the shower and pulled the plastic curtain behind. Closing his eyes he faced upward toward the warm water but in the darkness was returned to the alley next to Dalry's and fear shook him by the shoulders. He opened his eyes but unlike the rain this water stung and he turned, giving the side of his head to the jet. A memory of childhood bathtimes with his mother; wearing a foam ring of bright yellow to protect his eyes.

'Tam a didnae hear ye comin in, ur ye no comin doonstairs fur a pint?' Lina knocked on the door gently. He had now soaped and scrubbed every inch of his aching skin. 'Kin ye no hear me in there Tam? You better no huv somebidy in there wae ye!' Lina over the years had invested a fair amount of time and energy matchmaking on behalf of a local girl Paula. She would have been unhappy if he had someone other than her in the shower. He looked down into the darkness of the plughole searching for an excuse.

'Am no feelin that great tae be honest, a think al jist hit the sack if it's aw the same.' Silence followed during which he hoped she would buy his story, allowing him to delay any explanations until tomorrow at least.

'Whit's wrang wae ye Tam? Let me in there.' As he suspected would be the case, it hadn't worked. She had known from his tone that something was wrong; that was how close they had become.

'Tam am no messin aboot, if ye don't open the door right noo al kick it in.'

'Awright awright, hing oan a wee minute eh.' He knew she meant it and pulled a towel around his waist before cramming his clothes behind the curtain under the sink. The small bathroom was tight even for one but with two of them it was a struggle. She somehow managed to squeeze herself in and close the door, sitting next to him on the edge of the bath. The silence between them wasn't an uncomfortable one. She lifted his arm, carefully surveying his ribs and the scratches on his back. Gently, she touched his chin turning his face to meet hers. Tam hadn't known much about Lina's past before she arrived to work for his parents, but he had always somehow known that she had been no stranger to suffering. He also suspected that the lack of words now came from someone who knew how futile they would be. She was all he had in the world and his earlier strategy of making up a story disintegrated. He would tell her what happened, not because he had to but because he wanted to. They held each other for a while longer as music and laughter rose up through the floor beneath them. Then, on the edge of their silence he told her everything.

***

Tam stared despondently at his first pint of the day, drawing stripes down its condensation with his finger. The Old Firm game wasn't due to kick off for a couple of hours but already the Lounge was filling with excited punters. Lina had made him promise not to resign. Instead, he agreed to take time off in order to think things through properly. He knew he wouldn't go back, but had agreed in order to keep her happy.

With more seating and screens than the Public Bar next door, the Lounge was popular for watching football. The decor was supposedly more comfortable, though in truth it hadn't had a makeover by the brewery since his parents' time. Faded upholstery peppered by pre-ban cigarette burns, garish wallpaper and framed prints of sky scrapers in mid-construction.

'Ur ye gonnae watch the game in here?' Paula had been sitting with friends, obviously waiting for him to speak to her. When he hadn't, as was usually the case, she made the first move.

'Aye that's right, a wis plannin tae.' She waited for an invitation to join him, or perhaps at least an offer to buy her a drink. He knew exactly what she was after but didn't like female company when watching the football, so remained silent. Although not looking directly at them he was aware of her piercing eyes. Whatever the light was doing at a particular time seemed to dictate whether they where blue or grey. Regardless of colour they had a constant sparkle to them, like precious stones he thought. He knew there was no doubting that she was attractive. Unlike Stella's long hazelnut hair, Paula's was golden blonde and cut into a modern bob. As a hairdresser, unsurprisingly she always seemed to sport the latest styles. She was of a heavier set and of course lacked Stella's abundant self-assurance and poise. She wasn't fat, but was certainly in the early stages of the fleshy upper-arm syndrome. With her defined triceps and high confidence levels, Stella had propelled herself out in front previously on his score card. Of course all that had to be forgotten now.

'So who ur ye gonnae watch it wae?' She looked at the vacant seat next to him.

'Am waitin oan wan a ma pals inta,' he lied looking at the door.

Tam and Paula had known each other since primary school. As teenagers their relationship had turned physical, after much badgering on his part. It had remained so over the years in what he conveniently took to be a casual one. Of course, he knew her perception of the arrangement to be much more serious and did occasionally feel pangs of guilt. But since meeting Stella he rarely spoke to Paula, unless pissed and horny. There was no doubting he had some kind of feelings for her, but he also knew that she liked him – a lot. Somehow that seemed to make it less of a challenge. Which impala tastes better: the one that you chase for miles across a dusty savannah, or the one that yields its throat after just a few yards? Now he had given up on the chase of one though, he suspected he would retrace the scent back to the easier target. These however were things he would rather not think of during the football and with perfect timing the considerable bulk of Wan Brick squeezed down onto the seat next to him.

'Maybe see ye later oan then Paula eh.' Tam nodded back over to her table indicating it was time for her to rejoin her friends.

'Aye whatever.' Her voice made no effort to disguise its annoyance; then she was gone.

'Sorry Tam a wisnae interuptin wis a?' Wan Brick placed a fresh pint for Tam on the table.

'Cheers big man, naw yer awright, done me a favour actually.'

'Aw a see, it's like that is it?' Wan Brick got his name as a bricklayer who over the years had developed a reputation for poor productivity. In summary, he was a habitual skiver who would normally touch on average one brick per day. Until his employers discovered this of course and gave him his marching orders. He had a wide almost oval face, unkempt yellow hair and as always was smiling.

A group of Monkford Bushwakas were in high-spirits at the next table. Sinking multiple chasers with every pint they had obviously been up all night, no doubt taking all sorts.

'Mixed company Tam, cannae huv that in here!' Wan Brick nodded toward the table as he supped on his pint. He had heard one of them make a partisan comment which he had taken offence to. Although the pub was mixed they were mostly local and supposed to know the etiquette, especially on a day as sensitive as an Old Firm one. Being the only pub on the scheme meant regulars normally carried out their own form of self-policing, to try and avoid any flashpoints. Other schemes with more than one pub would have the luxury of segregation, but that simply wasn't the case here so there were guidelines.

'A didnae hear them say anythin.' Tam had also heard the comment but as usual was keen to avoid any confrontation.

'He said chucky arla, that's bang oot ay order so it is.'

'Jist forget aboot it mate, no worth the aggro,' Tam tried to reason.

'Haw you, a heard that!' Wan Brick's tone was one of heavy censure as four baseball caps turned in unison, eyes on springs, jaws grinding on invisible gum.

'Heard whit yan auld tadger, mind yer ain business.' There had once been a hierarchy on the scheme and young men like these would have known their place. But a new disrespectful breed were coming up through the ranks. Wan Brick looked at Tam and raised his eyebrows, as if to say let's find out if this lot are capable and or willing. Tam immediately understood, blowing his cheeks out and looking at the pre-match build up on TV. He made it clear he had no interest in pursuing things further. After a frosty pause each baseball cap resumed the laughing and joking. Then one of them could be heard adding a final insult.

'Ach he's jist an auld shitebag.'

Just then Tam spotted Pat approaching from the bar. His stare was fixed hard on the table of Bushwakas. Tam couldn't be sure how much of the altercation he had heard. But from his stony grimace it was obvious it had been sufficient for him to get the general idea.

'Whit's goan oan here then?' They stared downward sheepishly into their drinks. Even the cockiest of them would cross the street before taking on a legend like Pat.

'Yoos ignorin me, a said whit's goan oan here?' The culprit turned in his seat with a high degree of trepidation. It was obvious Pat wasn't going to let him off the hook.

'Yees think yees ur big men aye, is that it?'

'Sorry a didnae know he wis yur pal, we wur jist cerryin oan.'

The volume in the Lounge dipped as the collective breath was held. Pat had a small man's frame but somehow carried the menacing demeanour of a giant. He also sported a year-round tan, which was unusual as he never went on holiday. On closer inspection, his ravaged capillaries could be attributed to the whisky. His bald head was smooth and had the shine of a snooker ball. Sagging bags under his eyes and prominent laughter lines gave his face a look of surplus skin: Tam had never seen so many lines on a human face. In a flash he had slapped the culprit's cap off his head and was pulling him hard and fast by the hair to the waiting pavement. Within seconds the youngster was joined by his friends, wisely departing the scene.

Tam could remember Pat from his childhood, but it wasn't until he himself had become older that he picked up on the reverence other Monkford men would show when he was around.

'Yer usual is it Pat?'

'Aye cheers Wan Brick.' Pat sat next to Tam who shifted uneasily. Tam was sociable enough, but Pat was much older than him so they had always moved in different circles. As usual he was wearing a black suit, which had that well-worn shine familiar to all Monkford suits and a white shirt with a high collar. He surveyed the patrons in the Lounge, acknowledging those of significance with a nod.

'A wis talkin tae Lina son and she wis tellin me yuv been hivin a wee bit a bother.' His gruff tobacco voice was that of a man who had smoked since teenage years. Tam looked over at the bar and could see Lina watching anxiously while dipping glasses into the washer.

'Aw for fucks sake, how many other people hus she telt?' Tam shook his head in frustration. 'How much did she tell ye, exactly?'

The older man rubbed the silver stubble on his chin

thoughtfully. He looked up at the pre-match build up on the screen as he spoke.

'Tell me if av goet this right. You've goet the hots fur some posh bit a stuff at yer work, some other guy found oot and gave ye a doin cos he fancies the lassie anaw. Noo you're thinkin ay leavin the joab tae avoid any mare hassle, sound aboot right?' Tam was confident Pat's deep voice hadn't been heard now that the room's normal volume levels had been restored. 'Ye know son, Lina wis a good friend tae me and ma Betsy, in fact so wis your Maw an Da. Whit am basically sayin is that Lina has asked me tae see if a kin help wae yer problem, an av agreed. So it's up tae you, dae ye waant ma help ur dae ye no?' Pat raised his eyebrows sending deep ripples upward onto to his forehead.

'Whit kind a help ur ye talkin aboot, dae ye mean settin aboot the guy that done it?'

'A wis thinkin somethin mare alang the lines ay me geein ye a few pointers like, tae help ye in the future wae these kinds a situations.'

Pat looked straight at him.

'But did she tell ye everythin that happened, durin the fight an that?' Tam was hopeful she hadn't actually told him everything and he could spare at least some embarrassment.

'Whit, thit ye pissed an shat yerself?' Immediately Tam's cheeks inflamed and his thoughts turned to running from the pub and the scheme never to return. Then the old man surprised him by gripping his forearm in a reassuring, almost fatherly way.

'Listen it's nothin tae be ashamed ay, believe it or no whit happened tae you isnae actually that uncommon. The boady behaves in strange wyes when dealin wae adrenalin so it dis. Physically we urnae that much different fae the cavemen who hud tae deal wae aw kinds a scary stuff, sabre tooth tigers an aw that.' Tam hadn't expected a lecture on prehistoric physiology from someone like Pat, but it would seem that was exactly what he was getting.

'The trick son, is learnin how tae hawnle the adrenalin. Maste people jist cannae deal wae it an they crumble as soon as it starts. But if ye kin jist ride that first wee bit, well wance it's in an workin yer awright efter that.' Wan Brick returned and carefully placed a pint and a half in front of Pat as though they were incendiary devices, before backing away slowly in an almost bowing motion.

'Ye really think a could learn that?' Tam was sure he was over simplifying for the purpose of illustration but nonetheless he made it all sound relatively straightforward.

'Well am no sayin it wid be easy, but am prepared tae gee it a go.' Both men stared silently up at the TV screen.

Pat spoke first. 'So, whit's it gonnae be?'

Tam remained silently thoughtful, weighing up his options. He was almost certain it would be a complete waste of time, but there would be no harm in having a go. Besides he did appreciate that Lina was only trying to help. There was also the chance that a refusal might piss Pat off, not something he or anyone else would be in a hurry to do.

Tam nodded in agreement, as Pat drained his pint in throaty gulps before wiping the foam from his top lip with the back of his hand. He downed his whisky and then hoovered the shorts left on the next table by the Bushwakas.

'Awright then young yin, nae time like the present, follow me.'

CHAPTER 3

The Gallowgate sits on the eastern perimeter of the city centre in one of its oldest sections. Seventeenth-century steeples nestle among shops, open-air markets and famously Celtic pubs. During the cab journey, Pat reminisced of his youth as a member of the infamous Hayfield Street gang in nearby Gorbals. Tam stared at the passing rain-soaked shoppers from the warm interior of the cab. He also pondered on the level of enthusiasm Pat seemed to be putting into his new mentor role. Although anxious and well outside his comfort zone, Tam had decided the line of no return had been crossed, at least for today. He would simply try to stay in one piece.

Their cab stopped outside McNairs and Tam knew it would be packed to the rafters with Celtic fans. His butterflies hovered on the verge of nausea with the worry of why Pat had brought him here. As a Rangers fan Tam would never dream of venturing into this area on an Old Firm day. He knew Pat was a Celtic fan though and tried to use this fact to reconcile his discomfort. The old man turned to face him before pulling on the door handle.

'Jist remember whit a telt ye aboot the adrenalin, awright?'

'Aye sure, but listen am no a fighter ye know that daint ye, so yer wae the wrang guy if there's gonnae be any bother in here.' A familiar quiver tickled Tam's throat as the trembling of his knees increased a notch on the severity scale. Pat's mouth opened into a wide tobacco-stained smile.

Immediately on entering they were met by a cacophony of wall-to-wall Celtic fans, their excitement levels ramping beyond frenetic. In view of his financial circumstances, Tam was relieved when Pat handed him a crisp cashline twenty. He was then despatched to the crowded bar while Pat searched out a spot with a decent view of a screen. Row after row of freshly poured golden pints like soldiers on parade had been set up in advance by staff. He was served quickly and returned to find his mentor.

'There ye go Pat.' He handed him a pint and a half as well as his change but the old man nodded indicating he should keep it. He was grateful and hoped he would live long enough to spend it. Unfortunately things in that regard straight away weren't looking good. Tam could see they were standing in a great spot, but obviously obstructing the view of at least one table behind them.

'Here mate, any chance a movin we cannae see the telly,' a stranger's voice bellowed from behind and Tam glanced sideways at Pat who continued to sup casually from his frothy pint.

'Ignore the cunt, shouldnae be sittin at a table when a games oan anywye, where dis he think he is the fuckin bingo?' Pat didn't turn but his voice was loud enough to be heard by the men whose view they were obstructing. Tam decided his best chance was to simply stare at the screen pretending to be deaf and dumb. So that was that, the table behind now had restricted views and were having to adjust their seating positions or in some cases stand. There were a few huffs and puffs but Tam was surprised by the fact the men hadn't even challenged them.

'Good game son eh!'

'Aye Pat yer right it is, fairly even.' But Tam hadn't been able to relax for a second of it. The only noises being made by the supposedly Celtic supporting Pat were sharp intakes of breath every time Rangers misplaced a pass. What Pat was playing at Tam had no clue, but it would seem he was in a pub full of like-minded Celts, pretending to be a Rangers fan. A niggling thought occured to him that perhaps on approach to the first anniversary of Betsy's death he was being ridden pillion into some kind of suicide mission. He stared hard at the clock in the top left of the screen counting every passing second appreciatively. With only minutes to go he prayed the score would remain goalless.

Just then his heart juddered with relief as the referee pointed to the spot – penalty to Celtic. The room erupted, a blanket of bodies flung themselves jubilantly in the air drinks spraying everywhere. Pat and Tam were the only two that remained motionless but no one seemed to notice or care. Tam had no interest in the game, his hope was that Celtic scoring a penalty would keep Pat and the rest of the pub happy. They might by some miracle make it back home unscathed.

Unfortunately the collective energy was sucked vacuum like from the room as a nervous striker sent the ball soaring high over the bar. The city seemed to see-saw on the earth's crust with the blue half airborne, while the greens remained welded to its surface.

'Serves 'em right, divin bastard if ye ask me.' Tam was as shocked as the rest of McNairs at this outburst. 'Whit yees lookin it? Come ahead then!' No one made a move as Pat calmly picked up an empty pint tumbler, smashing it on a table edge. He turned with the jagged stump to face the packed pub. Tam struggled to control his breathing in between bursts of acute panic. His immediate focus was trying not to empty the contents of his stomach on to his shoes. Instead he stared downward, attempting to visualise an escape route across the floor. As soon as the inevitable onslaught began he would hit the deck and try to crawl his way to freedom as though on a smoke-filled plane.

'Aye a thought as much, yer aw shitebags, so yees kin jist hawd yer weesht an let me an the boay watch the rest ay this poxy game in peace, unless that is wan ay yees fancy getting yer face ripped tae fuck in the meantime.' Tam was working hard now to control his bodily functions as they seemed to be shutting down beneath him. His initial feelings of terror were now shifting toward confusion. Not only was everyone in the bar motionless, they even seemed to be averting their faces. Not one person touched eyes with this ageing cyclone.

A small barrel-shaped woman with blonde streaked hair peered out from behind the bar: 'Mister, a don't waant any bother in here.' Her normally small voice was amplified in an echo that bounced down from the high ceiling puncturing the alien stillness of the room.

'Well that's awright hen cause we don't waant any bother eether so everythin should work oot jist fine. An by the way don't you be dayin anythin daft like phonin the Polis, cos al come back an go tae town oan this shoap, you mark ma words.' The woman disappeared back behind the pumps and after the longest period of stoppage time in Tam's life, the whistle was blown. Not one person made a move or spoke even a whisper. No one wanted to be singled out as recipient of the menacing vessel in Pat's hand. Then with a high degree of nonchalance, Pat walked to the exit and turned, signalling to Tam with a nod it was time to go. He picked up a newspaper from a table as he left.

Stepping from the silence into the noisy daylight, Tam's thought was of putting as much distance between himself and his current location as possible. He searched the street with desperate eyes for a taxi, perplexed by Pat's decision to stand right outside the pub seemingly in no hurry. Tam watched in amazement as Pat carefully tore a page out of the newspaper with one hand while holding the broken glass in the other. A stressed mother with shopping bags and two young children hanging from her arms looked first at Pat and then at the glass with a worried expression.

'Kin ye believe somebody went an left this oan the pavement when there's wains aboot, a wis just aboot tae put it in a bin.' She seemed half satisfied and offered an entry-level smile before hurrying past and round the corner. Tam was relieved to finally secure passage from the area and hopped impatiently by the open door of a cab. His mentor looked up and then slowly walked to a waste bin where he disposed of the glass and newspaper before folding the crossword page and placing it in his jacket pocket.

Neither man felt the need to speak once inside the taxi and Tam concentrated on trying to regulate his breathing and to get his heart rate back under control. The pep talk about adrenalin had made no difference and he had felt nothing other than extreme discomfort for the duration of his visit to McNairs. While counting his breaths he looked out on to the busy shopping street around them. The rain had stopped and thick bursts of winter sun shot down from the sky like giant columns. Tam studied the faces of strangers; none of them knew what he had just witnessed. He couldn't help but feel a very real sense of fear at what Lina and himself had started.

***

Saturday was Fat Boab's disco night in the Rannoch Moor Lounge. It had become so popular with Monkford residents of all ages that the DJ had invested in a new set of speakers, making their debut tonight. The main reason for the sudden surge in popularity had been Lina's decision to exclude all Bushwakas; they had been causing even more trouble recently than was usual. There had been some talk that she might make the exclusion a permanent one, but for now it only applied to Saturday nights. As a result of this, there had been some terse stand-offs at the door, which Tam had thankfully managed to dodge. However, with the help of Pat and a few of his enforcers, Lina had managed to uphold the ban. Now that the Bushwakas were having to venture further afield for their sport the regulars were thankful for some respite.

Fat Boab did a fair amount of perspiring even when motionless, but the exertion of carrying the new speakers from his van with Tam had resulted in a profusion waterfall-like from the tip of his nose. Soon after the cables had been run the sound tests became Boab's priority. Staff were under strict instructions that the doors were not to be unbolted until he was happy with the new hardware. As a result of this delay a small group had formed in the evening chill. This was the first time in his long career Boab could remember a queue outside one of his venues; he could barely contain his excitement.

After helping Boab, Tam was gasping and stood at the empty bar trying to attract Lina's attention next door through the connecting hallway. He needed a drink. In truth the experience in McNairs earlier had rattled him. He was hopeful that would be the end of it and that the old man would be satisfied with the afternoon's rush of adrenalin. Also while the Stella thing was still painful he had a feeling the best way to put it behind him, would be to get things back on track with the ever-reliable Paula. To that end he had purchased a pill of supposedly premium quality and was planning to half it with her.

Eyeing the row of shiny lager pumps, he licked his lips with anticipation. He would start off as usual on the milder UK models with good intentions, before ending up on the strong continentals later. Boab whistled loudly through his stumpy fingers and Tam turned to see that he was of a like mind and also after some refreshment. It was customary for Boab along with Pat's men on the door to be supplied with their drinks on the house. That was all the excuse needed and Tam lifted the hatch and set about doing the honours, along with one for himself of course.

'Hey you! whit dae ye think yer playin it?' Bad timing; caught red-handed.

'Sorry Lina, Boab asked me tae get him wan.' That was at least partly true.

'C'moan you, other side ay the bar, al sort them oot.' He might be a lodger but the rules were clear and both bar areas were strictly out of bounds. He was lucky though as he only ever paid for his drinks if it was one of her staff who served him. So needless to say he always made sure Lina poured his pints. He also knew that the rule was her way of trying to make sure he didn't get any more of a taste for the stuff than he already had.

'How's yer bruisin?' she asked.

'Aye it's fine, nae bother.'

'Did ye huv a nice hot bath like a telt ye tae?'

'Naw, a jist hid a shower.' Despite being reminded by the occasional ache from his ribs, this afternoon's performance had managed to put the whole business out of his head. He was keen to keep it that way.

'Honestly am fine so a um.' She seemed to understand from

27

his tone that he didn't want to dwell.

'Did ye know Paula was in earlier?' As usual, she was championing Paula's cause. Boab cranked up the volume during his sound tests and Tam felt his diaphragm shudder in a way it had never done with the old speakers.

'Whit's that yer sayin?'

Tam put his hand to his ear and she leaned over the bar shouting, 'A wis jist sayin did ye know Paula was in here earlier fur the fitba?' Lina of course knew very well that he knew, and was obviously trying to drill him for information. Possibly so that she could report back to her friend.

'Aye that's right, a wis talkin tae er fur a bit.' He could see Boab waving over at them excitedly, while pumping clouds into the darkened room from his surprisingly effective smoke machine.

'Nice girl Paula so she is, very pretty.' She looked back at him with a face that indicated perhaps he was taking Paula's interest for granted. Again he remained silent in an attempt to show he wasn't for being drawn on the subject. 'Here ye go, gee them tae the boays and tell them tae unbolt the door seen as Boab's obviously happy.' Tam spread his fingers around the golden vessels, distributing them as instructed before returning to the bar to collect his own. He held out payment but as usual she refused. 'By the way a meant tae ask, where did you and Pat disappear tae earlier?'

'Eh, we went up the Gallagate.' He briefly considered being truthful about what had happened, but decided she would only get herself worried about Pat having lost the plot – which he obviously had.

'So whit's a Rangers man like you dayin in the Gallagate oan an auld firm day?' It was a fair enough question; he hesitated over how he could answer it in such a way as to avoid arousing her suspicion.

'Eh, aye but Pat's a Celtic man intae, we wur fine a wisnae wearin any colours, met some ay his pals fur a bevvy.' He looked over at the door as the first of the punters entered, scanning for Paula's face but she wasn't amongst them.

'Listen he's hud a really hard time since he loast Betsy. Aknow he puts this hard man front oan but a think he's still hurtin really bad, kin ye keep an eye oan em fur me.' It was obvious she cared about the old man.

'Aye of course a will, nae bother ataw.' Tam paused while sipping on his pint, trying to get his head round who was supposed to be looking after who.

'Thanks Tam yur very considerate, that Stella's no good enough fur ye.' She reached forward trying to pinch his cheek as though he were a toddler but he managed to lean back just in time. 'So is Paula meetin ye in here the night?'

Tam knew she was more likely to know than him if Paula was planning to make an appearance. 'Aye a think so, a wis plannin oan huvin a wee word wae ur the night, tryin tae get things sorted between is.'

'Good boay, she's a wee stunner so she is.' Her tone was full of enthusiasm and Tam couldn't help but smile. It was nice to be in demand, even if it wasn't with the impala he had originally hoped it would be.

An hour later there was still no sign of her and the Lounge was heaving, almost at capacity. Tam stood just inside the door delivering more refreshments for Pat's men. He had just swallowed his half of the pill and was about to head back inside when he was told the old man was looking for him. Sooner or later he knew he was going to have to speak to him. There was also the danger that if he blanked him he might find out and Pat wasn't someone you blanked under any circumstances. As Tam walked outside the first thing that struck him was the freezing cold. Pat was in his shirtsleeves as though it were the middle of summer. Puffing on a roll-up, he saw Tam and waved him over.

'There he is there, how's ma protégé dayin the night?'

'Aye am brand new Pat, how's yerself?'

'If a wis dayin any better there wid be laws against it son, c'mere the noo a need tae talk tae ye.' He indicated for Tam to follow and they moved far enough away from the group of smokers at the entrance to be out of earshot. Tam accepted a roll-up; he rarely bought cigarettes as he only smoked when drinking, a social smoker. This pissed a few of his mates off, having to dish out fags constantly, but Pat didn't seem to mind.

'So whit did ye think aboot earlier then?' Pat cupped a hand around the small flame of his lighter.

'A don't know whit tae say Pat, it wis heavy duty so it wis.'

Tam's alcohol level was now sufficient for him to at least feel capable of expressing an opinion on the events of the day.

'But did ye see the point a wis tryin tae make tae ye aboot the adrenal dump?' Tam was as clueless now as he had been before they walked through the doors of McNairs.

'Aye a see whit ye meant, thanks fur yer help by the way a really did appreciate it.' He decided the less questions asked the quicker Pat would be satisfied. Then they could get on with their lives as far apart from each other as was possible. Pat seemed to be staring straight through him, exhaling upwards through a clicking jaw forming perfect smoke circles. He paused, searching for the right words of enlightenment.

'That's good son so it is, am glad it wis helpful. See the point is this, fear or whitever ye waant tae call it, isnae real, it disnae actually exist. It's jist the adrenal gland dumpin intae yer boady, maste people cannae deal wae it.' Tam nodded in agreement trying to disguise his bemusement, although in fairness the old man did seem to sound fairly credible. Tam didn't want to ask questions though, deciding he would get the encounter over with as soon as was possible.

'So ye think the next time somebidy gees ye any hassle ye could remember that how ye feel is nothin tae dae wae fear ur cowardice ur any ay that shite?' Tam knew the answer was a resounding no. But he also knew that being honest might initiate a second demonstration, and he might be less fortunate in escaping it in one piece.

'Aye, am pretty sure that a could.' Again Tam nodded as convincingly as possible while trying to stop his teeth from chattering, a mixture of nerves and cold. Pat eyed him in a way that made Tam suspect he wasn't buying it.

'That's good am glad tae hear that son.' Pat dropped his fag butt twisting it with the sole of a black leather shoe. It sported a large silver buckle on the front and somehow didn't look right to Tam. It was the shoe of an old man purchased in a young man's shop.

'Wid ye believe me if a telt ye that anybody, including you, could actually control the adrenalin, use it tae yer advantage?' Pat's fleshy face looked back at him mystically.

'Aye as ye said, yuv jist goet tae keep the breathin right hintye.'

Tam could sense they weren't even close to being finished and that Pat was in fact enjoying himself. The mentor put an arm around his shoulders and pulled him in so close he could smell the harsh edge of the whisky on his breath as he whispered.

'Shitey farts...' Tam couldn't help himself and let out a laugh at the strangeness of the phrase in the context of their discussion. In a flash the mood changed and Pat clamped Tam's face in his strong hands, leaning forward menacingly.

'Who the fuck dae ye think yer laughin it?' Tam felt himself being sucked into black deranged eyeballs but the fear, adrenalin, whatever it was called, quickly averted his eyes. The small group of smokers around the entrance had sensed the shift and watched back eagerly, hoping for a floor show.

'Am no laughin it ye Pat honest, nae offence intended.' Tam did his best to speak through the old man's gripping hands. The sickness rose up from his stomach and into his throat. It occurred to Tam that it might simply be another demonstration so he could feel his adrenal gland in overdrive once again. After a pause, Pat seemed satisfied and released his grip.

'That's awright then, nae harm done.' Within a split second things were back to normal, other than the numbness of Tam's face which now had a hand print over it. Tam was surprised by his own initial reaction. It wasn't purely relief that he was safe, he was also glad he hadn't offended the old man.

Pat paused, trying to re-establish his train of thought. 'Aye that's right, well when a wis a young boay in the Hayfield Street. Wan ay the main men took a likin tae me and kinda did whit av been tryin tae dae wae you. Took me under his wing a suppose ye could say.' Tam didn't like the sound of that. Being taken under Pat's wing indicated more longevity than he thought he could handle. The old man removed a tobacco tin from his jacket pocket, lighting two pre-rolled simultaneously before passing one to Tam.

'See in the early days a hud a similar problem tae you, ma bottle crashed wan night when things goet a bit heavy duty.' Pat nodded in acknowledgement at the look of surprise on Tam's face. 'Aye well, a did tell ye it's mare common than ye might think.' Tam rubbed on his jawbone, still numb from Pat's vice-like grip.

'Anywye, this aulder guy in the gang, he telt me thit as soon as a felt they first butterflies, in that split second, a needed a diversion. Specifically a memory, somethin tae take ma attention away fae the adrenalin.'

'Whit kinda memory?' Tam realised after the words left his mouth he had asked his first question.

'Somethin thit a could train maself tae remember so that ma focus gets diverted fur jist long enough that am no overcome, no paralysed by it ye see.'

'So where dae the shitey farts come intae it then?' Tam couldn't help himself as on the one hand he was petrified to get in any deeper but on the other, he was fascinated.

Pat smiled approvingly now that he could see the boy was taking an interest. 'He telt me tae think back tae somethin that hid happened tae me at some point in ma life, hud tae be somethin unpleasant, a bad memory. A should focus oan it as soon as a felt they first butterflies.' Pat paused, as though considering whether he could explain the concept without telling Tam everything.

'When a wis wee there wis an aulder boay who used tae bully me. Durty bastard used tae stick ees hawn doon ees pants an fart right intae it. Then he wid grab a hawd ay me an press ees hawn oor ma face. A could eether suffocate ur else breathe in his stinkin shitey farts.'

Tam could hear that even talking about this memory was making Pat angry.

'So did it work?' He decided it would be best to continue discussing the concept rather than the specific content.

'Did it work? Aye yer right it worked.' Pat's face was deadly serious.

'The boay that used tae bully me wis the first wan a used it oan, he ended up in a right state so he did.'

'Is that whit ye used earlier in McNairs?'

'Naw, efter a done it a few times it wis as if a goet desensitised tae the adrenal dump, ended up no actually needin it efter a while.

Nooadays the adrenalin kin pump in an oot ma system withoot it even really botherin me.' Tam was transfixed and although Pat could tell he believed him he suspected he wasn't convinced the method could be applied to his own problem.

'A like ye, ye know that daint ye son?' Pat pulled him closer into a conspiratorial huddle.

'Aye, a like you anaw Pat.'

'You need tae dae the same as whit a done. Think back tae the worstest maste upsettin thing ye kin remember and use it tae yer advantage.'

Tam knew in that instant.

CHAPTER 4

Tam's bedroom was directly through the wall from his parents. It would happen twice a week: Wednesdays after closing and Sunday mornings. He could hear everything.

First there would be a low mumble of voices, negotiations or instructions perhaps. Then the bed springs straining as bodies repositioned and aligned. This would soon be followed by a light tapping of the headboard on the adjoining wall. On Sunday mornings this light tapping would normally go on longer than in midweek. It would steadily grow faster and stronger until it was more of a banging than a tapping. Each time it happened he would cover his head with a pillow and try his best to block out the noise, but couldn't. Even as a child, without knowing exactly what was occurring, he knew from his mother's voice that she wasn't being hurt, she was compliant. Why couldn't they keep quiet? Or move their bed away from the adjoining wall at least. He considered they may be doing it deliberately; they wanted him to hear perhaps. But he had discounted that theory, unable to come up with a motive.

Their moaning and groaning was bad enough as it grew in volume along with the pace of the headboard banging. But that wasn't the worst of it. At the point of his father's climax, each and every time without fail, after the headboard was pushed into the wall with the final thrust, the alpha male of the house emptied his lungs along with his balls screaming the words COCONUT BADGER!

Pat seemed to somehow know that Tam had been thinking of his very own shitey fart memory.

'Don't tell me whit it is son a don't waant tae know, aw am tryin tae dae is explain tae ye when tae use it.' Tam simply nodded and smiled nervously. Pat made it all sound so plausible but he just couldn't believe something so simple could work. All these years he had been biting his lip, avoiding eye contact, backing down, crossing the street, anything rather than face the nausea and panic attacks associated with confrontation. Yet here was a man telling him there was an easy way to make it all go away. Pat held him softly by the elbows, his deranged eyes wrapped in conviction.

'Jist gee it a try son, whit huv ye goet tae lose? Next time ye feel the sickness rise up inside ye, gee it a try and see whit happens.'

'Any chance a kin a huv a quick word Pat?' They turned as TV John approached. Both men seemed to be lost in a mixture of shitey farts and coconut badgers.

'Aye, sorry John a wis miles away there, whit can we dae fur ye?' TV John was a tall rake of a man with a large head and sharp-edged jaw giving his face the square shape of a television. John smiled, looked at Tam and then hesitated.

'Nae fear John, anythin ye waant tae say tae me ye kin say in front ay the boay.' Tam's chest swelled with reluctant pride at this endorsement.

'It's tae dae wae ma boay, Martin.' A hopeless sadness fell over John's face. His son had been murdered by a Bushwaka recently in an unprovoked stabbing that even by their standards was shocking. The boy had never been in any trouble, a simple case of wrong place wrong time.

'Polis huvnae geed us the boady back, we cannae even arrange the funeral neer we kin.' The grief on John's face seemed to be merging into an actual physical pain.

'Aye a wis really sorry tae hear aboot yer loss.' Pat reached up, placing a hand on the tall man's shoulder.

'Aye me anaw John, a liked Martin.' The boy was younger and although Tam hadn't known him well, he did know he was a decent sort and didn't deserve to be cut down in his prime.

'It's they fuckin Bushwaka scum, they've goet the run ay this place am tellin yees. Not wan witness came forward kin ye believe that?

Broad daylight an not wan person seen anythin, cos they're terrified. An as fur the Polis! They urnae interested in the slightest, mare chance ay seein Haleys Comet roon here than a polis motor. They've jist waashed their hawns ay the place if ye ask me.' TV John was obviously riled and Pat nodded in agreement while avoiding eye contact in the way one does with the recently bereaved.

'Yer right John so ye ur, it's a disgrace whit's become ay the place.' Pat cast a glance of seemingly genuine sadness out over the bus terminus and beyond.

'See whit it actually wis Pat, a wis efter a wee favour.' TV John pushed both hands deep into his pockets in an awkward way. He looked over at the group of smokers by the entrance to ensure no one had moved within earshot.

'Anythin ye need John, whit can a dae?' Pat leaned in closer.

'See the guy that done it, any chance ye could get get him done in fur me?' Pat quickly stepped back lifting both hands up, palms outward.

'Hing oan a wee minute John. Ye don't waant tae be goan aboot the place sayin stuff like that, ye could get yerself intae aw sorts ay bother.' Tam stepped back also, he desperately tried to think of a way he could make his excuses and get back inside without offending Pat. TV John shifted uneasily, on the verge of tears.

'Tell me, whit other option have a goet? They've no even charged the scumbag that done it, an everybody oan the scheme knows who it wis.'

Pat placed both hands on his hips staring downward thoughtfully at his silver buckled shoes. 'Yer right aboot they Bushwakas right enough, somebody needs tae put them in their place. But that's no whit am aw aboot any mare John, av kept a low profile fur years since a merried ma Betsy.' Tam didn't quite understand how Pat could terrorise a packed pub that very afternoon, then later the same day claim to be a pacifist. But he certainly wasn't about to take issue.

'A jist don't know who else a kin turn tae, a huvnae slept since it happened, a cannae even look ma misses in the eye any mare. A need tae get some justice fur Martin, ma poor boay hud ees whole life ahead ay em so he did, an some low life just took it away, an fur whit? Nothin that's whit, nothin ataw.' The threat of tears was now realised as moist lines ran down his grey and gaunt cheeks. There followed a long silence as TV John looked at Pat waiting for a response. It was understood silently between the two men that Pat would decide what was to be done and that his decision would be final. Pat then reached an arm around John, turning him in the direction of the Public Bar.

'Let me think aboot it John, how aboot a buy ye a nice malt an we let the bold yin here get back tae chasin the montivani.'

***

Tam congratulated himself on the timing of his arrival back in the Lounge. It had coincided with 'age of love' one of his all-time favourite techno anthems. He knew this signalled a shift of emphasis in Boab's playlist and that the milder chart content was about to be steam-rollered by the classics, referred to by the DJ as his 'guns of navarone'.

Tam merged himself among the new arrivals on and around the dance floor (not an actual dance floor, just a large square tiled space in the centre of the Lounge). He estimated that the first of his rushes would be generated very soon. His plan was to leave all the Pat business behind. He just hoped he wouldn't be too far gone by the time he finally caught up with Paula. Tam searched for some elbow room as the track moved its way through the initial build up. Each week he would go through this same routine, building his internal excitement levels and entering an almost trance-like state. Eyes closed, shifting his weight slowly and taxying down his very own private runway. A mixture of sweat and Boab's smoke slid down the back of his throat as the base vibrations wanked the shaft of his tingling spine. The track's introduction was normally a slow one in any case, but Boab had reduced it to a crawl. As was usual, the DJ attemped to delay their climax, teasing the room with the pumping onslaught, accentuated even further by his new speakers.

Tam's patience was rewarded. A colossal cheer nearly blew out the windows with the arrival of the main base-line, like a jet engine scraping the roof over their heads. There was a sudden rushing forward of bodies as those cautiously dipping their toes in the water were now fully submerged. In unison the entire dance floor launched into one mass bouncing movement as Boab cut the lights. The monster of sweating heads and rubber necks lost itself in delirium. Tam's heart-rate accelerated way out of his control as the collective around him fed hungrily from the raw energy. Tam found himself becoming aware of a strange, almost primal hallucination. In a corner, over by the gents, a hazy vision of Monkford cavemen dancing around an open fire. Their bongo drums building them up to a crescendo, complimented by their ancient moonshine.

Some time later, he wandered through duty free and into arrivals. He had no idea how long he had been away for. Regaining sufficient control, Tam scanned the room looking for Paula. Unsurprisingly, he couldn't see her anywhere in the mayhem. He considered leaving the dance floor and going to have a proper look as the chemicals now seemed to be releasing their grip slightly. But just as he was about to execute this plan and with the big waves seemingly settling down into a swell, Boab pulled out his elephant gun despatching 'a must be dreamin' another techno anthem.

The collective erupted around him and Tam decided to revert to plan B, swallowing Paula's share of the pill. His mind did a U-turn from arrivals back into the departure lounge. He was then lost in bear hugs, rugby tackles, a brief snog and even had a pint poured over his head at one point. Finally he spun through a sweating fog into a vision he initially put down to another hallucination. It was the shine of a familiar bald head pogo-sticking towards him.

Pat must have ditched TV John at some point, along with his jacket and shirt. He wasn't the only one; Tam had never worked out why the majority of the older men did the same thing each week. Topless as soon as they started working up a sweat and they didn't cover up again until the lights went on. Pat reached forward grabbing Tam in a playful headlock, shouting at the top of his voice, 'A must be dreamin, a must be dreamin, send me to heaven baby.' Tam was surprised that he had the chorus down for an old timer. After some struggling he managed to extract his head from Pat's sweating flesh.

In the silent approach to the main base line during any track, it was common for someone to offer up a chant, provided it wasn't football related of course. These chants were normally fairly unimaginative. 'Here we, here we, here we fuckin go,' was a favourite. Pat had seized his opportunity, his timing impeccable. Standing in the centre of the dance floor he raised his arms crucifixion style and as a gap emerged around him he emptied his lungs.

'Tweet Tweet Hayfield Street!' In his Christ-like pose Tam was amazed by how puny he seemed. He couldn't believe that the scariest man he had met in his life, actually had saclets of loose skin under his arms with no muscle to fill them. At that point the collective took up Pat's chant with blind fervour. Despite being clueless about what they were actually shouting or even why, the chant spread quickly.

'Tweet Tweet Hayfield Street!'

'Tweet Tweet Hayfield Street!'

As the base line arrived, Pat seemed to be engulfed by the monster in a frenzy. He closed his eyes with a smile on his face as wide as the river Clyde and fell backward into the swarm of sweaty flesh. From the reminiscing earlier in the day Tam knew this to be a war cry that hadn't been heard in the city for many years. He had a feeling that someone was about to come out of retirement. It was also starting to look like he had unwittingly been drafted as a conscript.

***

It was Monday evening, the day had been a slow one. Tam phoned his boss citing a family crisis as his reason for non-attendance. He had no intentions of returning, but had promised Lina not to tender his resignation immediately. The afternoon had been spent lounging and channel surfing, doing his best to put all thoughts of Stella and Campbell out of his mind – he was unsuccessful.

Boab's disco had passed in a blur but Tam could vaguely remember Paula turning up later. He also had a patchy memory of what happened after she helped him up the stairs. He tried to convince himself it had been a dream but knew better. Paula was a nice girl and didn't deserve to be treated like that. He remembered being naked on the bed and kneeling behind her, pushing the back of her head downward. Her face was being squashed into the pillow and then there had been some confusion. Getting himself into the condition where he couldn't tell the difference was bad. But having such little respect for her that he had carried on rather than realign, well that was worse. She wasn't like some of the other scheme girls. He believed her when she had told him once that he had been her only lover. It was simply that when it came to Tam she would let him do whatever he wanted and he knew it. It was taking liberties and again he promised himself that he would square things with her. She was a nice girl and Lina was right, he could do a lot worse.

Having had his fill of documentaries, he stood at the living-room window looking out onto the bus terminus. A thick grey mist had appeared, covering the concrete landscape like a soft blanket. Two buses sat nose to tail in darkness, their engines running as the drivers smoked inside the bus shelter. He didn't know where it was but could hear his mobile vibrate on receipt of a text. This was a familiar routine. Paula would always leave it for a day or two before making contact. He would normally ignore her, but not this time. Perhaps he would ask her to meet him downstairs for a drink. Then he remembered his midweek rule relating to alcohol consumption – that was a slippery slope. Besides, Pat certainly didn't share the same policy and would probably be in the bar holding court.

His jacket hung over the door and he patted its lining to locate the handset. As he did so the thought of the young Pat being suffocated by a hand steeped in shitey farts made him laugh. Perhaps he would ask Paula to the cinema by way of an apology. He opened the flashing envelope and his heart almost punched itself from his chest. The text was from Stella.

Herd u have fam probs. Hope all ok and c u back soon. S xxx

He stared intently at the xxx. Surely that meant something? Three x's after all was associated with adult-type content. In a flash he had left the building and was standing next to the bus shelter waiting impatiently for a driver to finish his cigarette.

***

He knew which flat was hers from once having dropped her off in a taxi on pay day. She had pointed up to the top floor on the right and he remembered a feeling of disappointment at the time. The whole reason for dropping her off that night had been in the hope she would invite him in; hadn't happened that way of course.

Properties in this area didn't come cheap but he suspected it would be something her father had helped her with. Perhaps that was unfair, but she was a junior analyst so he knew there was no way she could afford the flat on her own. On leaving home, the jacket over the door had been closest but wasn't the one that would have afforded most insulation. As a result the cold was already biting hard on his bones. He didn't want to go straight up to her buzzer though – he had to be sure she was on her own.

He walked across the street, deciding to check things first from a school playground. He moved as far back into the shadows and darkness as he could and then cast his eyes over her block. Three flats on either side of the close, similar to the Monkford. But these weren't breeze-block efforts thrown up in days, they had been built slowly with care and attention to detail by master stonemasons. Turn of the century commissions from the days of wealthy tobacco merchants, when the dear green place had been the empire's second city and the river Clyde a conveyor of prosperity for the fortunate few.

She stood in the large bay window landscaped by a warm and soft light. Her lips moved silently into a cordless telephone and she seemed to be looking directly at him. Tam panicked momentarily but soon satisfied himself the darkness shrouded him sufficiently. If she spotted him she would surely think he was a psycho stalker. He found himself worrying about who she was talking to as she smiled and laughed into the handset, could it be Campbell? Even from this distance his eye could follow the line from sternum outward to nipple. It occured to him that the thin black robe she was wearing may be one used around bathtime. Her hair looked to be dry so perhaps steaming water ran in an unseen bathroom. As the hesitation began to take a foothold he found himself trying to fend off second thoughts. He knew well enough from living all these years with Lina that bathing was something she certainly put a lot of time and effort into. In fact, Lina had a whole routine around bathtime. Perhaps Stella had a similar ritual and his arrival unannounced would totally spoil it for her. Too polite to tell him, she would reluctantly offer tea or coffee while an awkward silence surrounds them – all the while her bathwater dropping in temperature. Or even worse, her surprised face would be all he would see behind the door chain, the rest hidden from view with no invitation to step beyond the threshold.

His snottery nose brought him back to the present and he rubbed it vigorously, realising the tip had been numbed by the sub-zero conditions. He wasn't sure how long his eyes had been melting into the warm window above; he hadn't even noticed she was no longer standing there. Was she now being consumed by a soup of bubbles, he wondered; surely it would be even worse if he called during rather than prior to her soak. The resolve that had surged through him unchecked on receipt of her text drained away, leaving only a dull sickness low in his stomach and a sharp pain in his chest. He had been fooling himself again. The subtext of the message had obviously been that of a concerned friend – why did he keep doing this to himself? Nothing but his own wishful thinking was building these elaborate but wasteful structures on sand, waiting only for the inevitable tide of reality to wash them away. He shuffled dejectedly toward the bus stop, not looking back once.

CHAPTER 5

On his arrival home, Lina asked him to go and check on Pat as he hadn't arrived in the bar. This was unusual; she was concerned. Initially, Tam had objected, saying he would rather keep his nose out of Pat's business. Lina had responded with the whole 'lonely old widower' spiel.

Climbing the stairs to Pat's, it occurred to Tam that another advantage of living above the pub was not having to live in a close where six tiny flats were crammed on top of each other. However, he knew from conversations with older regulars in the pub that when the scheme had first been built the conditions people left behind were much worse. To the scheme's first residents, indoor toilets were considered a treat and the novelty of a private veranda pure luxury.

The close lights were long gone so in darkness he carefully felt his way, sliding his hand up the cold walls. After a couple of sharp rattles on the letterbox there was no sound of any stirring inside. He considered leaving it at that but knew Lina would only continue to worry.

'Hullo Pat, it's me Tam ur ye in?' He didn't shout too loudly for fear of arousing the suspicion of neighbours. A shadow moved through the frosted glass. There was a pause and then the door opened a fraction, as though in the darkness he wasn't sufficiently satisfied and wanted to scan Tam's face.

'Sorry son a didnae know it wis you, in ye come.' Pat seemed content and the door was opened fully.

'Lina wis jist wonderin how ye didnae come doon tae the pub the night that's aw it wis.' Tam could make out Pat's outline in the darkness but no facial features.

'Aye a hud a wee bit a business up the toon the day, hud tae pick somethin up.'

'Right nae bother, well al maybe see ye later on then eh.' Tam was already backing away toward the stairs.

'Whit ye no comin in fur a bit?'

In truth he wanted to simply go home and work on feeling sorry for himself after his wasted trip to Stella's, which he knew technically to be tantamount to stalking. But Tam found he couldn't bring himself to just leave. Perhaps an audience with Pat would act as a distraction, keep his mind away from Stella.

'Aye awright then, al come in fur a wee bit eh.' After following the old man down the darkness of the hallway, he was led into the living room where Pat switched on a standard lamp. Tam tried politely to avert his eyes from any specific object for too long.

'Sorry aboot the mess son, the cleaner's hud the past eleven months aff.'

Tam was unsure whether to laugh at such dark humour, so erred on the side of caution remaining silent.

'A don't get too many visitors up here in the penthouse, fancy a wee dram, tae heat ye up?' Pat clapped his hands together, rubbing them excitedly. Despite Tam hating whisky and also his midweek no alcohol rule, refusal didn't feel appropriate.

'Aye cheers.'

'It's good timin actually cos a waanted tae huv a wee word wae ye, there ye go.' Pat passed him a generous measure in a Glasgow Celtic mug.

'See av been hivin a think aboot whit TV John was oan aboot the other night.' Tam felt a familiar twinge of anxiety in his abdomen.

'Is that right,' he replied with an air of detachment as Pat motioned him to sit on the low threadbare sofa. There was a duvet and pillow on the floor next to it and Tam realised that this room must also be where he slept. As Tam sat, the sofa made a whimpering noise.

'How well did ye know ma Betsy son?'

'A didnae really know her that well, but a know everybody liked er.'

'Aye yer right they did that, she wis very popular so she wis.' Pat paced the carpet in front of the window and then stopped, leaning on the windowsill and staring down into the darkness of the street.

'A telt ye a used tae be in a Gorbals gang in ma younger days dinta?' He didn't turn but Tam could see his face reflected back in the window.

'Aye ye telt me, the Hayfield Street, that's where ye learned aboot the adrenalin thing.' The old man had now told him about the gang on several occassions. Tam wondered if his psychosis was perhaps aggravated by a dementia of some sort. It occurred to him that would be both an unusual and dangerous combination.

'Aye that's right, well before we goet merried she gave me an ultimatum. It wis tae be her ur the Hayfield Street, simple as that.' Tam was struck by the tenderness in Pat's voice whenever he spoke of his wife. Even in such a short time, Pat had become a man of stark contrasts to him.

'So ye chose her then?' he asked. Pat's neck twitched in a way that made Tam think it best not to turn this into a question and answer session. The older man would distribute information as and when he saw fit.

'Sorry a didnae mean anythin.'

'Naw it's awright son, fair enough question.' Pat had the ability to fill Tam with terror and yet within a heartbeat he would find himself at ease again. Tam decided that perhaps it would be best to show an interest, but only speak when spoken to.

'The truth is son Betsy hated violence, she hud loast her wee brother tae a gang fight a few years before we met. She made it clear tae me that if a waanted tae huv a future wae her, well a hid tae make the choice.' After a long pause, Tam wasn't sure if he had finished: should he say something? Finally, Pat continued.

'Well as ye said yerself a chose her obviously.' Pat's voice seemed to tremble ever so slightly. This was sufficient to accelerate Tam's abdominal twinge into borderline nausea. Pat turned to face him, leaning back on the windowsill arms crossed, an expression of bleakness.

'But she's no here any mare, kin ye believe it? A always thought it wid be me first. A mean am a drinker and a smoker fur fucks sake, yuv goet tae hawn it tae the big fella upstairs he's goet some sense a humour his he no?' Tam winced hard after gulping on his whisky.

'Aye yer right Pat, he hus.' Tam was unsure where this was all heading.

'Oan the wan hawn she always went oan aboot how much she hated whit the Bushwakas hid done tae the scheme. But oan the other hawn any time a suggested hivin a word she made me promise no tae get involved.' Pat continued to observe Betsy's house rule and opened the window before removing his tobacco tin.

'Well she's no here any mare is she?' Again Tam was unsure if he should respond. 'A said is she?'

'Naw thats right, she's no.' He spoke fearfully as the old man ran his tongue along the rim of a cigarette paper.

'So whit's stoapin me fae helpin TV John am askin maself.' Pat looked upward to the black sky as he spoke while Tam considered whether it was a rhetorical question.

'You deef son?' Obviously it wasn't.

'Naw sorry a wis jist thinkin aboot whit ye said.' Tam desperately tried to come up with a credible argument for him not having a word with the Bushwakas, he feared what that might mean. 'Well ye don't waant tae be gettin yerself intae trouble wae the Polis.' It was the best he could come up with under the circumstances, and Pat laughed heartily.

'Yur kiddin me oan right? A wis runnin circles roon them back in the day when the Polis wur a force tae be reckoned wae. No like nooadays, nae wonder the scheme disnae feel safe, TV John's right ye don't see them that often but when ye dae it's wee boays an lassies, ur fat cunts that couldnae fight sleep. Naw al no be gettin lifted son, but that's besides the point, these Bushwaka tadgers need tae be shown they don't run this place. That young boay Martin didnae deserve tae die, he hud ees whole life tae live, but no noo thanks tae that evil bastard that plunged him fur nae good reason.' Pat lit the roll-up, blowing smoke out the window.

'Nah stabbin innocent young boays is way outta fuckin line in ma book. In the auld days even the wans that were lookin fur bother rarely cerried weapons. It would be a square go, in fact some guys used tae frown oan it if ye used yer feet durin a fight. Absolute worse anybody goet wis slashed, an even then there wid huv tae be a good reason.' Tam's abdominal anxiety had now ramped up in severity from borderline nausea into palpable cramps. He speculated in his mind where this was all going.

'See there wis rules back then. Innocent people like that boay jist never goet touched, or else there wid be consequences.' Pat placed his roll-up carefully in the ashtray on the windowsill, walking to a side cupboard. Tam thought it must have been used as a drinks cabinet at one point in its life. But not now, he could see it was stuffed with unopened mail and other junk. Pat removed a small black leather box and placed it on the sofa next to Tam before moving back to his cigarette. Tam stared at the box. It was finished to a high standard with the initials JSN embossed in silver across the front. It looked like it contained an item or items of value. Tam was totally clueless as to its contents or why it was sitting next to him – medals, perhaps? Had Pat been in the forces and was about to show him some recognitions from a far-off battlefield, he wondered.

'Whit ur ye jist gonnae stare at it?' Tam sat his now empty mug on the floor and Pat immediately refilled it halfway; the whisky was certainly helping with his stomach cramps. He carefully unhooked the small latch on the front of the box and lifted the lid slowly. Not medals then. He wasn't sure exactly what they were but on first impressions thought perhaps a couple of old-style fountain pens side by side. Identical; silver with elaborate and detailed engravings he couldn't quite make out in the room's dim light.

Pat reached down, picking one up as if he were a child holding a hamster. He stared at it almost lovingly for several seconds and then split the handle in two. Tam realised with horror that what he had thought were harmless fountain pens were in fact two open razors. As soon as the mirror-like blade stretched out from the old man's hand, Tam's body began to shake gently with terror.

'Beauties int they... A saw them in a pawn shop windae oan Argyle Street when a wis jist a boay. A remember thinkin tae maself, if yer gonnae dae it Pat then ye might as well day it in fuckin style ma man.' He extended his arm straight outward, looking at his reflection on the blade. 'A wis the envy of every wannabe in the Gorbals. The boay in the shoap telt me they belanged tae some auld barber who hid fell oan hard times. That wis back in the days ye could get a shave anaw, nearly a weeks wages they cost me.' Tam was still shaking. Although he felt relatively safe he had never actually seen an open razor let alone someone like Pat holding one. The old man seemed to be lost momentarily in distant memories but quite suddenly snapped back into the present.

'So here's the wye a see it.' Tam had a sense of not being in control, events unfolding around him but outwith his grasp.

'The Bushwaka that stabbed TV John's boay, that Tommy Tattoo yin. Well he needs tae get the message alang wae aw ees wee tadger pals. Fae noo oan if a hear uv anybody oan this scheme cerryin a knife or takin any liberties – they're gettin slashed.' Pat dropped the razor into his trouser pocket, handing the other to Tam.

'Take it.'

'Oh no, a cannae take that.' Tam was surprised by the weight of the thing as it sat in his sweating palm.

'Whit dae ye mean ye cannae take it? It's a present.' Pat's face hovered between hurt and puzzlement.

'Eh, it's too valuable.' Tam of course cared nothing for its value, his only priority was to find a way of giving it back without causing offence.

'Nonsense, it's a gift fae me tae you, an al no be happy if ye don't accept it.' Each man stared and Tam searched for the appropriate words of polite refusal but could find none.

'Thanks.' He slipped it uneasily into his jacket pocket and the now empty leather box was returned to the side cabinet.

'So whit dae ye think then?' As Pat asked the question, Tam struggled to get to grips with what was actually happening.

'Whitever ye think's fur the best Pat.' Tam could feel his intestines churning themselves inside out. He wasn't sure exactly why he was being asked for his opinion. Inwardly, he cursed the part of himself that had a policy of trying to say what he thought the other person wanted to hear.

'That's good son, a wis hopin ye would say that.' Pat now put his jacket on and eyed himself in the mirror above the fireplace with an approving nod.

'Why wur ye hopin a wid say that?' Tam's voice was wrapped in trepidation.

'Cause you're comin wae me.' Pat smiled back at him in the mirror as Tam's shaking intensified.

'Naw Pat c'moan, ye already know this isnae ma cup a tea. A mean fair play tae you fur waantin tae help TV John, but ad jist rather no be gettin involved if it's aw the same.' His voice quivered with the fear, or adrenalin, or whatever Pat wanted to call it – it was more like an acid running through his veins. Gripping hard on his knees, the only hope he could cling to was that this was just Pat's idea of a joke.

A fatherly arm was slid across his shoulder. 'It's awright son calm yerself doon, am here tae look efter ye, a promise ye al look efter ye so a will.' Tam felt completely incapable of being anything other than extremely agitated.

'This is exactly whit we spoke aboot. See whit your feelin right noo, it's jist the adrenalin bein pumped intae yer system that's aw it is.

This is it, this is yer chance tae dae whit a telt ye, ye'll be fine.

Focus oan yer memory jist long enough fur the sickness tae pass. It will pass son, italways dis.' Pat sat in silence as though giving Tam an opportunity to use the strategy but he simply couldn't focus.

'Besides am no askin ye tae actually dae anythin, jist stawn back an let me get oan wae it.'

Pat gripped him firmly around the shoulders. 'Dae ye trust me Tam?' Again that voice, full of tenderness and understanding. Tam couldn't quite work it out but he somehow knew that he did trust him, that when he was with Pat he felt safer than he ever had in his life. To be so close to psychosis and yet feel so safe was a strange sensation. The old man was only trying to help and besides he was right, his argument did make a lot of sense. Tam had always somehow known that his problems with confrontation existed inside his own head, that they were not real. Pat stood and extended his hand.

'Ye promise a wulnae huv tae dae anythin?' Tam's voice was still quivering.

'A promise ye son, jist come alang fur the ride an practice whit a telt ye when ye feel the sickness.' Tam took a deep breath to steady himself and then rose to his feet. He could feel a cocktail of warm whisky mixing with the adrenalin.

***

The walk from The Hill to Tommy Tattoo's flat down in The Valley was taken at a brisk and deliberate pace. They twisted and turned through the dark and cold streets, at one point passing the Rannoch Moor. Although Tam had been tempted to bail out he simply couldn't do it. It was as though an invisible rope tied him to the old man. He felt somehow obligated to see this business through.

As they approached the close, Tam could see an almost physical transformation taking place in Pat. A rigidity seemed to be running across his shoulders, down the arms and even up into his neck which looked to be thicker than normal.

Going up the first flight of stairs, Tam tripped and cursed, wondering if any closes on the Monkford actually had lights that worked. He continued to climb in the darkness behind Pat, who was soon rattling insistently on the letterbox.

'Hullo, a need a word wae Tommy is he in?' Pat's voice was devoid of emotion.

'How, who is it?'

'It's Pat fae The Hill.' The motionless shadow of a head behind the frosted glass considered the next move. Pat was well known by everyone on the scheme including the Bushwakas. Tommy Tattoo calculated that if Pat had business with him, it would probably be better to get it over with sooner rather than later. Some rattling of chains and bolts and then the door was swung open.

'Awright mucker whit can a dae fur ye?' Tommy Tattoo's voice was full of pleasant surprise, as though greeting a long-lost friend. He was also attempting to focus on the figure behind the older man.

'A need a quick word Tommy, is it awright if me an ma pal come in fur a wee bit?' Pat paused in a mannerly way on the threshold, waiting for confirmation to proceed.

'Aye nae bother, in yees come.' The door was opened wider and both men were shown like royalty toward the smoke-filled living room.

Tommy was topless, wearing only a pair of grey joggy bottoms, and in his bare feet. Obviously Tam had always known where Tommy got his name, but now for the first time he could see the extent of work he had put into his life canvas. Moving up the hallway behind them Tam peered over Pat's shoulder at a large snake's head staring back at him from between shoulder blades, its long fangs exposed. A line of Chinese letters ran straight down his spine out of sight between buttocks. These were surrounded by a matrix of skulls, numbers and names, but Tam averted his eyes in the interests of staying focussed.

Tommy was entertaining some fellow Bushwakas, along with groupies that Tam didn't recognise as being from the Monkford. This wasn't unusual as although males tended not to venture into rival schemes, the same rules didn't apply to females. The depth of cloud and overpowering stench of the skunk confirmed to Tam that they must have been getting high for some time.

'Kin a get yees a wee drink ur a smoke or somethin?' If Tommy was in any way nervous, Tam thought he was doing a great job of hiding it. Either that or he was simply too stoned to do the necessary calculations in terms of risk management. He was treating Tam and Pat like a couple of his own.

'Naw we're awright Tommy, thanks but, very kind uv ye tae offer so it is.' As Pat spoke he scanned the room, as though going through some more efficient calculations of his own.

Pat addressed the collective. 'Listen am actually glad there's a few mare ay yoos Bushwakas here cos av goet somethin tae say tae Tommy that concerns yoos lot anaw.'

'By the way am sorry aboot that cerry oan in the pub wae yer pal Wan Brick, al huv a word wae them, that wis oot a line.' Tommy fell back into the low armchair, picking up an empty plastic bottle being used as a makeshift pipe. He sucked the white smoke hard into his lungs.

'Naw it's nothin tae dae wae that Tommy. It's this business wae TV John's boay, young Martin.' Tam stood to the side of the sofa and in his peripheral vision could see one of the figures sitting on it shift uneasily. He felt it right then – the twinge, the butterflies, the nausea, the cowardice. He knew under normal circumstances these sensations would become his focus and consume him entirely. He also knew somehow that it had to be done now and it had to be done with nothing less than complete conviction. He would throw himself at it and give Pat every opportunity to be proved right or wrong. Reaching backward into his childhood he located his father's voice and played it on a loop inside his head, as load after load was dumped into his mother.

Coconut Badger! Coconut Badger!

'See in the past when ma Betsy wis alive, a let yoos lot get oan wae it, kept maself tae maself.' Pat half turned so he could address the others while inconspicuously moving closer to Tommy's armchair.

'But sadly, she's no aboot any mare. So things huv chynged and am tellin the lot ay yees, if a here uv anybody cerryin a blade oan the Monkford, or any mare takin of liberties like whit happened wae the young boay—' He smiled turning to face the others, while standing over Tommy's armchair.

'—Al be comin lookin fur yees wae a wee pal a mine.' They looked at Tam.

'Naw no that pal, this fuckin pal right here.' Tam hadn't seen it being removed from his pocket, but the blade was primed and fully extended. It was being held not by the handle but by the metal rim that fixed the blade in position and with pincer-like fingers. The next series of movements seemed quicker than a light switch. Firstly, there was a thrusting of his arm and an entry around the upper jaw, midway between eye and ear. Then his wrist made a twisting motion, which opened up the skin like a ripened peach. The left side of Tommy's face fell downward onto his shoulder giving his head a distorted and damaged look, like a watermelon that had fallen from a moving lorry.

Pat tilted his head as though an artist in front of an easel admiring a previously troublesome brush stroke. He was distracted by the work and hadn't noticed the Bushwaka on the sofa attempting to stand. The Bushwaka's intention may have simply been to make a run for it, or then again he could have been carrying a weapon of some sort and been about to retaliate. Either way, something strange happened. In a seemingly automated movement, Tam's leg snapped out, kicking the man square in the face. The connection was one of perfection and the Bushwaka's nose burst like a balloon full of ketchup as he fell backward. Pat turned and when he realised what had happened looked at Tam with a told-you-so smile.

'Ahhhh! whit huv ye fuckin done tae me ya mad bastard?' Tommy screamed the words in disbelief. He was gradually beginning to realise that part of his face was missing, hanging precariously over his blood-soaked chest.

'Whit dae ye mean whit huv a done tae ye? Is it no fuckin obvious ya stupid cunt? That's fur takin liberties wae that young boay. Noo stoap yer fuckin greetin an take yer punishment like a man.' Tommy's screaming was hampering his attempts to push the large hanging flap of flesh back into place, as well as undoubtedly increasing the workload of the surgeons he would soon become acquainted with. A deep red jam-like substance slid down the left hand side of his torso. Pat was now holding the razor by the silver handle, doing figure of eights, like a deranged swordsman. The other Bushwakas were obviously shitting themselves and completely speechless. Their chalk-white faces indicated that they were in no way interested in getting involved. The Bushwaka with the burst face had assumed the brace position and looked to be in a fair amount of discomfort. Pat dropped the razor back into his trouser pocket and nodded to Tam.

Stepping from the mouth of the close onto the cold pavement, an orchestra of screams provided the soundtrack for their exit. They would soon be in the welcoming warmth of the Rannoch Moor. Tam's heart raced with euphoria not just at what he had witnessed, but what he had been a part of. Yet again he had been transfixed by his mentor's awesome display. But more importantly, he had taken Pat's strategy for a test drive and it had worked perfectly. For the first time in his life, Tam felt like a real man. Putting himself right in the firing line, not only had he managed to come out in one piece, he was about to leave the battlefield with a commendation from his commanding officer.

'See whit a telt ye son, it works dintit?' Pat slapped Tam's back hard, flinging an arm around his shoulders and pulling him tight into the closest thing a man like Pat could offer up as a warm embrace. They laughed their way back to the Rannoch Moor to celebrate.

***

Tam had been a child on the night of the robbery, and he was thankful that his memories over the years had been so elusive. They had been buried at the far end of a dusty corridor, deep in the recesses of a protective brain. It would seem however that something somewhere had been disturbed. For reasons he was unsure of, recollections of that night and its events were being offered to him for the first time.

A childhood summer and the excitement associated with extended daylight as he chased a football with friends on the grass next to the bus terminus. Although called home later than was usual, still there was a feeling of frustration. His father's voice had called out much earlier than his friend's parents. Tam was reprimanded by his father for not having changed out of his school clothes before playing. He didn't normally see his parents much in the evenings. Mother always prepared his meals and both took turns to come upstairs periodically and check on him. That night he ate his dinner while watching TV, pretended to do some homework and then played with action man figures. He was tucked in at bedtime by his mother.

The noise of smashing glass woke him but he wasn't startled. Stragglers at chucking-out time were often noisy and glasses were frequently smashed while cleaning up. So it wasn't of concern and he slipped back into a slumber. Then he was jolted upright and knew immediately something was wrong. His mother was screaming. He carefully opened his bedroom door; the upstairs rooms in complete darkness, he crawled along the hallway on his belly. Heart like a drum in his ears, Tam reached the banister at the top of the stairs, gripping it tightly.

The voices of angry men drifted up from below; such was Tam's grip on the banister it would leave a bruise across his small chest. He remembered the pyjamas he wore that night, white cotton with blue and red racing cars. Just wait for the voices to go away, it will all be over soon. For a long time he sat there, waiting for the uninvited to leave his family be, but they didn't. The warmth started between his legs and worked its way gradually under his buttocks onto the floor beneath him.

CHAPTER 6

Tam's desk was situated on the end of a long row in a forgotten corner of the office. By straining his eyes he could just make out the grey morning light through the large windows at the far end of the floor. New business hunters in the high net-worth section effectively cold-called full time and didn't get much in the way of variety. As a result staff turnover was very high and budget for furniture and stationery practically zero. All of their equipment was either broken or had been paseed to them from other departments.

Last night's sleep hadn't been a good one; he had spent the time going over all of the things he had learned from Pat. Looking across at the glass-fronted offices, he could see Campbell hadn't arrived yet. While waiting for his desktop to flicker into life, he glanced across at Stella's section. She was on the phone staring at her bank of monitors; she either hadn't seen him or he was being ignored. For now though he tried to ready himself, concentrating instead on the lines he would deliver to Campbell. No more being pushed around by him, or anyone else for that matter. After the Tommy Tattoo slashing, Pat had convinced him that his performance proved he was capable of returning to work. Pat had also seemed confident that Tam's nemesis wouldn't pose any challenge. He could use his newfound skills to resume his pursuit of Stella. There was hope.

Tam continued trying to catch Stella's eye but his boss was heading straight for him. Simon was known behind his back as Shergar. This was due to his severe strand of halitosis being similar to a horse's breath. His substantial shoulders looked wasted on a white-collar position, more suited to the blue variety. His short curly black hair was, as always, caked in handfuls of thick gel. Tam could imagine him hanging off the back of a dodgem, fag perched expertly on bottom lip, chatting to inappropriately young girls.

Simon controlled the new business section with its high staff turnover and senior management had seemingly turned a blind eye to his infamous bullying antics. Tam knew the best way to avoid him was to ensure your face was permanently welded to a handset. Shergar monitored the call logging software hawkishly and was very much of the opinion that quality was of secondary importance to quantity. A numbers game, as he would always say. He leaned over Tam's shoulder in his usual sneering manner.

'You've got a lot of catching up to do after your little holiday.' He suffered from a light lisp and his words were delivered inside a spray of saliva.

'I explained to you when I phoned, it was a family issue, unavoidable.' Tam leaned over in his chair as far as he could without falling off.

'I don't really give a shit to be honest, your numbers weren't looking great even before that so you're on a shaky peg. Have you got any idea how many people out there would jump at the chance of working for this firm?' The sensations came to Tam like a disliked acquaintance of old, starting with a numbness around the throat and then a warm flush across his shoulders.

Coconut Badger! Coconut Badger!

Simon remained silent – he was waiting for an answer. Tam would normally have capitulated into standard submissive responses. Something along the lines of I'm really sorry Simon it won't happen again. Shergar didn't seem satisfied with the silence and leaned in even closer. A tiny droplet of saliva landed on the side of Tam's face.

'Are you ignoring me? I'll have you out that door quicker than you can say Kappa Tracky.' Tam swivelled his chair to face him: he could see they were alone and that no one was within earshot. A clarity washed over him as though the storm had been weathered and he was being rewarded by delivery into the eye of the tornado. He felt every sensation in his body and rather than the paralysis of before, it was as though something formidable had just had a saddle thrown over its back.

'Ever seen wan ay these ya baw bag?' Tam had slipped the razor from his jacket pocket, it sat motionless on his left palm. Shergar stepped back, eyeing it with child-like curiosity while trying to define the change in his subordinate's tone and manner.

'What is it?'

'Oh al dae better than tell ye whit it is ya fuckin tadger, al show ye.' Since Pat had given the unusual gift to him he had been fascinated by it and was now surprisingly adept at splitting the razor from the handle one handed, zippo like.

Simon immediately leapt back, pressing himself against a wall and stammering: 'I'm sorry Tam, I didn't mean any offence just my little bit of fun that's all.' Simon's face flushed emergency crimson, his eyes darting around their deserted section desperately looking for help.

'See aw that schemie talk, makin oot you're better than me. That's the kinda talk that get's people a sore face, dae ye understawn whit am sayin tae ye?'

'As I said, it was just a joke Tam I didn't mean anything by it.' The moisture that had swelled in Simon's lower eyes spilled over on to his cheeks.

'Aye very good, jist fuck off an leave me in peace, an don't even think aboot tellin any cunt aboot this ur al take yer face aff fur ye.'

'Whatever you say Tam, no harm done.' Simon slowly backed away as though retracing his steps through an office peppered with landmines. Tam could feel yet another surge of euphoria building inside him. It was like a drug. This had been his first solo mission and it was a resounding success. He hadn't even planned for Simon; it was Campbell he was preparing himself for. Pat was right – this was a doddle. He looked over again at the closed blinds of Campbell's office in the knowledge that would be the real test. Unlike Shergar he had witnessed first hand the pitiful cowardice of the old Tam, pre Coconut Badger.

***

Tam stood next to the coffee machine, looking out the floor to ceiling windows across the lower rooftops around their building. On a clear day you could make out the Monkford in the distance, but not today.

'Wow, have you won the lottery or something?'

'Had a wee bit of a makeover Stella.'

'Well you certainly look the part.' Her auburn eyes expanded wider than he had seen before.

'Buy you a coffee?' He was joking as the machine was free. It tasted like sand and hot water but the view was worth it.

During negotiations with Pat in relation to his return to work, Tam had explained that his only suit was a piss and shit stained mess. Pat insisted on a visit to the city centre to buy a new one. The sales attendant could have been forgiven for thinking he had walked onto a scene from a mafia movie. A Capodecina taking his Soldato for a rig-out. Pat had insisted they be shown to the premium racks where he approved the purchase of a grey wool DKNY single breasted suit. This was swiftly followed by black leather ankle boots from Bond Street, sheer linen white shirt and understated tie and cufflinks. Tam felt like he had just stepped from a glossy magazine. He had tried to steer Pat toward the cheaper racks but his mentor had been insistent.

God she looks so good, power suit, ready for business, jacket off, pencil skirt, silk sleeveless blouse, fuck a can see her bra, that pearl necklace oh god. Pearl necklace mmm...

He carefully passed her the hot plastic cup and they moved away from the spluttering of the machine closer to the window. She looked down at the street but as was usual her vertigo forced her back.

'I sent you a text.' She said it lightly, as though him not having responded were no big deal.

'I know I'm really sorry, meant to phone you back but I had so much on.'

'No it's totally fine honestly, I was just worried about you, is everything alright?'

'Yeah it was nothing really, I fancied a few days in the sun so went to see my parents. The whole family issues thing was just to keep Shergar off my back.' When it came to Stella he still felt the need to create a parallel reality for himself. His enrolment at psychopath boot camp was unlikely to cut the mustard he suspected.

'They live in Spain don't they?' He couldn't remember telling her that and was hopeful she had been doing some research on him, asking around.

'Yeah that's right, they retired there from the pub game when I was young.'

'Lucky them, wish I could get away, I need a fucking holiday from this place.' He thought that might have been the first time he had heard her swear. It was weird the way she said it, fucking rather than fuckin. He liked it.

'Where's Campbell this morning?' He nodded toward the glass-fronted office doing his best to remain calm.

'He's not been in all week. I think he's taken an unscheduled holiday as well.' Tam's heart skipped a disappointed beat. All those scenarios he had replayed over and over would now have to be put on hold. His hand fingered the razor in his pocket thoughtfully. If he had pulled it out on Campbell, like with Shergar, there was no way he would have used it. Prison food wasn't something he was keen on sampling any time soon. But based on Simon's reaction it seemed all he would have to do was give it some fresh air to achieve the desired effect.

'He's such a fuckin tosser.' Stella raised her eyebrows as he had never vocalized his opinion of the man directly to her.

'He's not that bad, what's he ever done to you?' Tam wished he could tell her about what had happened.

'I don't have a problem with people like you Stella—'

'—People like me?' she interrupted with a slight annoyance.

He touched her forearm gently. Her smooth skin was wrapped

in soft wisps of dark hair he had never noticed – that could mean only one thing...

'—It's people like Campbell who think that because they went to Uni and were born with a silver spoon up their arse that makes them better than me.' Tam was trying to make her understand what Campell was really like, without having to spell it out.

'You could have gone to University Tam, It's nothing to do with where you're from.' Her smile indicated to him that she sensed a slight chip residing on his shoulder.

'All due respect, that's bollocks. It's everything to do with where you're from. At our school we had class sizes probably three times bigger than yours. Careers advisers only interested in steering us into trades. If you applied yourself at your studies you were beaten up for being a square. Besides all that, your parents paid a lot of money for your schooling and wanted a return on their investment, so you had no choice but to step up. Hardly a level playing field.'

'Fair enough, I suppose, but Campbell's a nice guy, a bit arrogant at times but he doesn't mean anything nasty by it.' Her tone was soft and sympathetic, but not in a patronising way. Tam could see the smokescreen Campbell had created was an effective one – she simply couldn't see the truth.

'He's a snob Stella, that's my opinion anyway.' He watched as she twirled a pearl thoughtfully in her fingers, her eyes were fixed on something in the distance, across the rooftops and beyond the river Clyde, under the cloud.

'I'll tell you something else for nothing, guys like Campbell...' He finished the last of the brown liquid, letting the grit slide down the back of his throat. Then he threw the empty cup, from a fair distance, into the waste bin next to the machine. She smiled at his bulls eye, looking from the bin back to him with a bet you couldn't do that again face.

'What goes around comes around Stella, that's all I'm saying.' He knew he had to do it now. The one thing he had been putting off for so long. His sphincter vibrated aggressively and his bowel squeezed downward with an urgent and acute impatience.

Coconut Badger! Coconut Badger!

As they silently surveyed the city sprawling around them, Tam waited, repeating the mantra of his father's voice on a loop. Soon enough the same calmness he had experienced with Shergar arrived. His sphincter, bowels, and frantic blood pumping all seemed to appease simultaneously. As though he had ridden the storm and was placed back in the peacefulness of the tornado's eye.

'So, are me and you going out on a proper date then?' Tam felt incredibly relaxed, in control, as though he were enjoying himself even. If his ego were a car he had just crossed three empty lanes from a slip road and was now hugging the central barrier, thundering down the fast lane. Boldly, he placed a hand on her shoulder feeling a lacy ribbon or bow on an unseen strap. His increased blood distribution had begun to concentrate its delivery on one specific area. If she was in any way uncomfortable she wasn't showing it – she didn't even acknowledge his hand, which he kept on her shoulder. He could see a slight flush in her cheeks, but this simply made his twitch even more aggressive.

'Yeah sure why not, that would be nice.' Not only did he not move his hand, he slipped his thumb under the strap rubbing her shoulder bone.

I have no fuckin clue what I'm doing here, but I like it.

'Maybe get something to eat later on?' He tilted his head in an attempt to read her eyes, but couldn't see them.

'Yeah, food sounds good.' She half turned toward him, smiling coyly like an awkward teenager. For the first time since meeting her, he could see the chequered flag in the distance – surely there was enough fuel in his tank to reach it. Mission accomplished. He turned on his heels, returning to his desk as the DKNY wool chafed his bulbousness with each step.

***

If he had written the script he couldn't have planned it any better. Everything during their date had gone exactly as he had hoped it would. No running club excuses this time meant he could steer her to a second bottle of Shiraz. Rather than becoming a hindrance as was usually the case, the alcohol seemed to be complementing his newfound confidence and he certainly looked the part. He had money from Pat in one pocket and a razor in the other; each seemed to be helping him in different ways.

His initial understanding of the strategy had been that it was for use in violent confrontations. Thankfully, it would seem the pursuit of a beautiful woman was an additional application. Tam felt as though a cosmic shift of some kind was taking place. One by one, the planets were moving into some kind of alignment – now was his time.

As they left Dalrys in a taxi he didn't once look at the black mouth of the alley. That had been someone else, not him. Just as her hand closed the door he leaned forward, gripping the back of her head firmly. As he pulled her face towards his there was a resistance in her neck. He took it to be more shock than refusal and covered her lips quickly with his own. Within a few seconds her muscles relaxed into compliance and he pushed his tongue hard and deep into her mouth. He had been tempted in the bar to kiss her but managed to restrict himself to semi-obvious touching and stroking. He deemed that she was way too classy to be sucking face in full public view, tipsy or not. But now all they had for company was a pair of seen it all before eyes in the rear-view mirror. Those came with doctor–patient type discretion of course. Nonetheless, he wasn't going to make the mistake of going too far in the cab. The taxi would be purely kissing and provided she asked him in for the cliché refreshment, that was when the real fun would start. Stella placed a hand on his chest and pushed, signalling a timeout was required and he slid over to his side of the cab.

'Where did that come from?' Her hair and make-up were confused.

'What, you didn't like it?'

'It's not that I didn't like it, just a bit of a surprise that's all.'

Then some silence as though two chess players pondered their next moves.

'What was that all about in the bar earlier by the way?' She changed the subject, bringing up an incident in Dalrys in which Tam had become embroiled.

'Some flash harry giving the girl behind the bar attitude because she got an order wrong, bit over the top if you ask me.' He looked out at the passing landscape, calculating from their location on the Kingston Bridge they would arrive at her place within five minutes or so. He also found himself distracted, thoughts of the freezing river below and its infamous currents carrying jumpers out to the Firth of Clyde. He remembered once being told of nets in place further down the river, positioned to try and catch the bodies like little fish. Thoughts of bringing Campbell here and forcing him over the fence startled him.

'So what's that got to do with you?' she asked.

'How do you mean?'

'I said what's that got to do with you, the girl working behind the bar, why should you care, do you know her or something?' Tam sensed she was jealous; he liked it.

'No, I don't know her but the guy was out of order – the girl just made an innocent mistake, no need for him to go shouting and balling at her. Suppose I got fed up taking a back seat all the time, do you never feel like just putting people in their place for a change?'

'Yeah I suppose, but I've never seen you getting involved in anything before.'

'Well maybe I shouldn't have let things go in the past, the girl was almost in tears, somebody had to say something – right?' Tam looked back at her.

'Fair enough, but you need to be careful you know, all you hear on the news is people being attacked for no good reason.' He liked the protective edge to her tone, it was the first time he had noticed it.

'Aww that's sweet, were you worried about me Stella?' He smiled.

'Yes of course I was.' She turned away, embarrassed.

'So does that mean you'll be inviting me in for a coffee then?' After considering the moves open to him he calculated that it was possible, although not necessarily probable, that she may be too shy to ask him. So in the interests of maintaining the momentum, he had decided to seize the initiative himself. She laughed at his cockiness.

'Tam what's happened to you?'

'How do you mean?'

'You've become very...' She paused, searching for the appropriate word. 'Assertive... that's it, you've become very assertive. Did you go on some kind of personal development course when you were in Spain?'

He couldn't stop himself from laughing.

'What is it, what's so funny?'

'Nothing – I told you, I went to see my parents.' If only she knew, he thought.

Another silence ensued, each player pondering the board in front of them.

'So you like my assertiveness then?' The cab was now stationary and the driver switched on the interior light, turning to face them. They were just a few feet from the darkened playground across the street. He refused to look at the spot his sails had so recently floundered without a breeze – again that had been someone else.

***

The first thing that struck Tam was the sheer size of the square hallway, with its high ceiling and numerous doorways leading off to a surprising number of rooms. The interior was lit only by moonlight so he could make out nothing more than shapes and outlines. Her heels echoed on the wooden floor after she bleeped in her alarm PIN. Following her he calculated the timing and location of his attack. If he let her move into one of the rooms with its light switch, wasteful small talk could result in a stalling of his engine. Momentum was key.

'So, did you really want a coffee, or can I get you something stronger?' He instinctively knew that in this moment his priority should be the kill and imagined an impala having its ankles swiped. He had to take her down. As she moved toward a doorway he took to be that of the kitchen, he moved in close behind, sliding an arm around her waist and pulling back firmly. She reached out, grabbing the doorframe with a nervous laughter, half-heartedly attempting to prise herself from his grip.

'I thought you wanted a coffee?'

He heard something in her tone that he couldn't quite read but continued regardless. Gripping her waist tightly, he pulled her backward so she could be in no doubt. He knew she would feel in her buttocks the blood that had already poured out from him. Leaning forward, he inhaled a deep breath from the scent on the back of her neck. Slowly, he ran the tip of his tongue up from behind her collar across the pearls and beyond into her hairline. His hands moved up from her waist, cupping her roundness in a slow but firm caress. Licking on the back of her neck he continued to grind himself into her. Something primal and deliberate had taken control of him now. Wrapping the fingers of his right hand around her throat, he put the left to work on disabling her zips and buttons. Within just a few seconds her blouse had fallen open and her skirt was pushed downward. Her arms tensed at the elbow and she gripped the doorframe tighter. He dropped to his knees behind her and hooked his fingers over the elastic of her cotton briefs. Sliding them down over the mound of her cheeks he pushed his nose and mouth into the warm and wet darkness. He gripped her ankles, shuffling them wider. Then he worked his tongue deep, tasting the bitter sweetness of her essence mixed with traces of her waste. He worked until the back of his neck hovered on the verge of a cramp and unable to deny himself any longer he opened his trousers and stood erect.

'Wait! Wait!' she panted.

'Have you got a thingy?'

Motherfucker, bastard, cunt.

'It's fine, I'll pull it out before I come.' He could feel her wetness on the end of him and knew the chequered flag was within millimetres.

'No Tam I can't, I'm right in the middle of my cycle.' He had no idea what a cycle was. All he felt was anger at being unprepared. Effectively he had come to a gunfight armed only with a knife. The thing was, with someone like Stella, he wasn't sure he would get another chance. With scheme girls like Paula there would be an understanding, another opportunity would present itself. But women like Stella were an unknown quantity to him; he simply wasn't sure if the same rules applied.

***

Tam's skull was being pummelled by legions of tiny hammers. He waited for a gap to appear in the busy road and then crossed. The anger of the previous night ensured he hadn't slept a wink. After the whole condom thing, the rug had been pulled out from under him. She had tried to make a joke of it while he waited for his taxi. But she didn't say the words he wanted to hear, something along the lines of him getting another crack at the title. He did his best to play it cool though.

Even after climbing into bed and giving the wee fella a major slapping session, he simply hadn't been able to douse the flames of longing and lust. His palm was simply too loose and dry, all he could do was lie in bed staring at the ceiling, thinking how he could redeem things. He couldn't remember the last time he had seen a Monkford sunrise, but it was while watching one creep up from behind the Campsie Hills that he came to his decision. As the lack of a condom had been the only issue, that could be resolved easily enough. He would get back over to her place early doors, accompanied by the best hangover cure known to man – square sausage, oven blasted rolls and chilled Irn Bru.

Butcher, baker, slippery balloon maker.

So here he was at 08:55 on a Saturday morning in a busy street near Stella's flat, hopping impatiently outside a chemist. The key-holder was in her early twenties, a similar age to Tam. As she approached, he could see from her look of disdain that she thought he was after methadone. Soon enough, she discovered his anxiety was caused by another equally urgent need. She blushed, which Tam found amusing.

Now accompanied by butter croissants and skinny americanos, unable to find anywhere that sold his preference. Again he went over it in his head; all made perfect sense as only seven hours ago he was literally millimetres away from sliding inside her.

'Hello Stella, it's me.' It had taken a couple of blasts on the door entry and he could feel the doubt bubbling upward along with a nasty despatch of butterflies.

Coconut Badger! Coconut Badger!

His looped mantra again did its job, diverting his attention away from the nausea. This seemed to reach a peak in the background, independently of him, and then subside. Again, he was left with calmness.

'Is that you Tam?' He lowered his head to look directly into the camera and smiled.

'Yeah, brought you some breakfast.' He held up the bag and after an extended pause the door buzzed open. Pushing through, he raced up the stairs, carefully trying not to spill any more coffee.

'I was sleeping Tam.' The nature of her tone was a concern to him. Peering out from the door, she clutched her dressing gown closed at the neck. What she was all about he had no clue – after all just a few hours ago he had his tongue in her arse.

'I like my long lies on a day off Tam.' Fair enough he thought, but why wasn't he being shown inside at least; this was just rude, surely.

'Listen Stella, eh I picked a wee something up.'

'That's really thoughtful of you, thanks.' She looked at the breakfast, breaking a forced smile through her sleepiness. It was evident to him she definitely wasn't a morning person. She could get back to sleep soon enough though as he was certain it wouldn't take him very long to empty his load, then they could spoon the morning away.

'No, I don't mean the breakfast.' He decided a picture speaks a thousand words and pulled the small box from his jacket pocket, smiling expectantly. Her face flushed with embarrassment.

'Oh, eh, Tam, listen I've arranged to do a training run with one of my friends and they're due quite soon so...' This wasn't how things were meant to be going.

'I'm sorry Stella, I didn't mean to be presumptuous or anything but I really enjoyed last night and just wanted to kind of pick up where we left off.' The calmness was being jeopardised by an embarrassment attempting to force its way to the surface.

Coconut Badger! Coconut Badger!

Something inside was trying to suck all of the progress he had made from the previous evening like marrow from a bone.

'Me too, I had a great time Tam.' She reached out of the doorway, gripping his forearm reassuringly. 'We'll do it again sometime – I promise.' She smiled in a way that encouraged him and the marrow was immediately pumped back. He was beginning to get a handle on the situation and the calmness returned.

'Listen it's fine, no worries, here take breakfast for you and your friend when she gets here.' Stella hadn't actually specified the friend was female and he knew that was simply wishful thinking on his part. For a split second he imagined Campbell inside under the duvet, but he discounted that; not her style.

'You don't mind?' Her face held a look of regret, as though hoping not to have hurt his feelings.

'No not at all, as I said it's totally fine I've got something on at

71

lunchtime anyway, rain check for sure yeah?' It most definitely wasn't fine. He wanted to be inside now, prospecting in search of undiscovered resources, not being held at the door like a fuckin Jehovah Witness. Looking her straight in the eye, he pictured the needle of a lie-detector machine.

'Yeah that sounds nice, thanks for breakfast Tam, I'll give you a phone.'

Soon after, Tam was back on home turf munching on an oven-blasted sausage roll, brown sauce dripping down his chin. He walked slowly as he ate, considering all the possible permutations of what had occurred that morning. Weighing up the arguments for and against the case of whether or not he had just blown it.

CHAPTER 7

Tam sat next to Pat in the Rannoch Moor's Public Bar, watching him stare down at the table in yet another futile attempt at a crossword. The mood both here and next door in the Lounge was upbeat, almost celebratory. In the days after Tommy Tattoo's slashing, it had seemed the Bushwakas were keeping a low profile. Tommy was out of hospital, still heavily bandaged but seemingly uninterested in any acts of revenge – at least, for now.

Monkford residents were now returning to the Rannoch Moor. This was pleasing for Lina; the brewery had been giving her a hard time over the takings. There was something else though, something bigger. A new feeling of optimism, as though there was a chance they had taken their community back. The entire scheme seemed to be nurturing a new belief, that the Bushwakas weren't the ones in charge after all.

'So how did ye get oan at yer work?'

'Pat am tellin ye, it wis amazin so it wis. A wis like a completely different person. A put wan ay ma bosses right in he's place so a did, ye should've seen ees face it wis a dillion. An Stella wis blown away fur sure.'

Pat folded the crossword page putting it in his jacket pocket. 'Whit did a say tae ye, a told ye dint a.' Pat reached under the table, gripping Tam hard above the knee in a firm shake.

'Aye ye did tell me, an ye were right anaw. Ye should go intae business ur somethin, people wid pye money fur that kinda knowledge.'

'A think am a bit auld fur new business ventures. So tell me whit happened?' Pat picked up a fresh pint from the table full of drinks, purchased by appreciative patrons.

'It wis jist like ye said, same as whit happened oor at Tommy Tattoo's. As soon as a felt the butterflies a jist started tae concentrate oan ma worst memory.'

'That's good son, as a telt ye, efter a while it gets so ye don't even need tae use the strategy.' Tam nodded his head while considering what it would be like to live a life without fear.

Lina had just taken a long overdue break and slumped into the chair across from them looking even more tired than was usual. She was understaffed but couldn't afford to take anyone else on. Tam had even been considering offering to do some unpaid work to help out but just never seemed to get round to it.

'Awright, how yees dayin?' She forced a tired smile.

'If we were dayin any better there would be laws against it sweetheart.' Pat smiled enthusiastically as he gave the retort Tam now knew to be one of his favourites. She looked from Pat to Tam with a worried expression.

'An whit aboot you?' Tam could tell immediately that she must have heard something of concern.

'Am brand new.' He wasn't lying, as with the exception of a slight anxiety surrounding the prospect of a Bushwaka revenge attack, he had never been better. Now he had Coconut Badger he felt almost capable of taking on the lot of them single handedly.

'How's things wae you sweetheart? A think yer workin too hard, ye know that.' Pat reached forward and took her hand gently as he spoke. Tam could tell the old man was well gone with the drink as such public displays of affection were unusual for him. He also seemed to be lapping up the adulation from the punters in his new position – saviour of the scheme.

'Well al be honest Pat am a wee bit worried aboot some ay the stories av been hearin.' She withdrew her hand from his, leaning back in her chair, eyeing them both suspicously.

'Whit huv ye been hearin like?' Pat straightened in his seat as though his spine were linked in some way to his virtue.

'Well a heard yoos were involved in whit happened tae that Bushwaka.'

Pat laughed. 'Yer kiddin me oan Lina, that wis nothin tae dae wae us hen.' Tam had to give him credit for what was a very convincing response. But Lina crossed her arms and stared hard at Pat, indicating she was still to be sold.

'Look, TV John asked me to huv a word wae the boay, which a did cos it wis bang oot a order whit he did tae John's boay. Awright, a maybe gave em a wee slap but that wis it honestly. A didnae slash em that must a been somebidy else later oan, tryin tae make it look like me ur somethin.' Pat managed to cover his face with a seemingly genuine incredulity. 'Listen hen am an auld timer av no goet the energy tae be takin oan these young yins. Av heard whit's been gettin said aboot me slashin the boay, an well, av no been denyin it cos the wye a see it things aroon here huv been settlin doon a wee bit huv they know?'

She looked over her shoulder at the briskness of business. 'As long as yoos didnae huv anythin tae dae way it that's aw am sayin, you're supposed tae be lookin efter Tam, a don't waant him gettin intae any bother.' Her guardian role was one she took seriously. Looking at Tam, she smiled the softest most beautiful smile. Pat decided she would have to hear it from the one person she knew would never lie to her; he nudged Tam in the side.

'Oan ye go, tell er son.'

'Tell er whit?'

Pat didn't appreciate his tone and only had to twist slightly in his chair in order to convey it. Lina of course was blind to such subtlety.

'You were there wae me when a spoke tae the cunt, sorry pardon ma french hen, go ahead an tell her whit happened.' Pat turned his face away to illustrate to Lina he was in no way being coercive. He nodded back at a patron, confirming he and Tam would be glad to accept another round of drinks.

'Cheers pal, pints wae hawfs eh!'

She looked straight at Tam. He hated himself for what he was about to do. In truth, he felt an obligation to them both and lying kept everybody happy. Besides Pat was right, since the slashing incident the place was completely different – like a shadow had been lifted.

'He's right aboot whit happened that night Lina. We went intae the boay's flat an Pat told em exactly whit he thought aboot him stabbin young Martin. He wis completely oot ees nut oan skunk so Pat slapped him oan the face a coupla a times tae get the message acroase.' Lina nodded her head sufficiently to indicate she believed him, and then looking at her watch decided the short break was over.

'Aye but tell er whit ye did.' Pat slapped his palms together, rubbing them excitedly.

'Och gonnae jist leave it Pat eh.' Again the twist in his seat to face him; Pat was the boss and Tam knew it.

'Naw, a wulnae jist leave it, a said tell her.'

Lina tilted her head inquisitively as Tam blushed.

'Al tell her then if your gonnae go aw shy oan us.' Pat leaned forward in his seat as though about to tell another parent about his child's glowing report card.

'A wis huvin a word wae the Tattoo'd yin, wan ay ees pals stawns up tae huv a go. The bold yin here boots the guy in the face, it wis a beauty so it wis.' Pat beamed with satisfaction. 'Dae ye no get it hen? You came tae me no that long ago cos the boay wis gettin the pish ripped oot em. No any mare! Naebody's taken the boay fur a ride any mare Lina, ye get it?' Pat leaned back in his chair, satisfied he had demonstrated his pedigree as a tutor.

'That's ma boay eh!' Pat grabbed Tam's head in one of his playful headlocks, scrunching hair with his wide cube-like knuckles.

'You were supposed tae be helpin him wae ees confidence Pat, no turnin him intae some kinda hooligan.' She seemed to be taking issue with his methods; Lina or not, Tam could see Pat didn't like it.

'Here hawd oan a wee minute. See in ma book, the number wan priority is loyalty tae yer pals, goet tae look efter yer pals, otherwise whit's the point? That night the boay hid ma back covered, who knows whit might a happened tae me if he hidnae stepped in when he did. This boay here, well ees becomin a real Monkford man Lina, not to be fucked with.'

Her face softened and she reached over clasping Tam's hands in hers. 'OK but listen, yer Maw an Da asked me tae look efter ye, an a jist waant tae make sure yer awright, that's aw, so jist be careful ye hear me?'

'Aye a wul be.' He would do anything to keep her happy, and if that meant shielding her from the truth then so be it. She reached over and took Pat's hand also, the three of them linked around the table like a prayer meeting.

'Both of you be careful.' Pat smiled back at her, nodding reassuringly to indicate he understood what she was saying.

'A know whit am dayin pal, nae need tae worry aboot eether uv us, honestly.' She seemed appeased, at least for now, and was soon back serving behind the busy bar.

'Ye don't huv tae sit wae me aw night neer ye dae son.' Pat poured yet another whisky into yet another pint. Tam had by now given up trying to match him for pace.

'How dae ye mean?' Tam asked.

'That young burd oor there's nearly sliding aff er stool is she no?' He was right, Paula had recently arrived to meet friends but seemed more interested in staring across at him.

'Naw yer awright Pat, she's no goan anywhere.' Now that he was making progress with Stella, Paula had been nudged back down the pecking order. No point having her completely disappear though, things with Stella were by no means a cast-iron certainty.

'So whit aboot that posh burd, whit's the plan of attack?'

'Och am no sure if she's intae it tae be honest.'

'How dae ye mean?' Pat asked as Tam sipped on the foam from a fresh pint. The word on the scheme was that they were a team, so now Lina wasn't the only one he could rely on free drink from.

'Well last night we hid a wee bit ay a kiss an aw that, well in fact, it wis quite a bit mare than a kiss actually.'

77

'That's ma boy!'

'Aye but things didnae go the wye a hoped they wid.'

'How no, whit happened?' If it had been someone his own age perhaps, but it wouldn't have felt right divulging the details to an elder like Pat, so Tam extracted the graphics.

'Well, she widnae huv sex wae me, cos a didnae huv a condom.' Pat looked back confused. 'Son a might be an auld timer but a know that safe sex is a big thing nooadays.'

'Aye a know that, that's fair enough.' Tam glanced at the next table leaning forward in a hushed tone. 'So a went back early doors in the mornin dinta, wae some condoms. But she still wisnae up fur it.'

Pat burst into laughter, attracting the attention of a few punters, obviously keen to share the joke. 'Uv course she wisnae up fur it ya fuckin dafty.'

'Keep yer voice doon!' Tam didn't want anyone in the bar, especially not Paula, to get the gist of their conversation.

'Sorry son.' Pat lowered his voice as he took on a more serious demeanour. 'I might've been oot the datin game for a zillion years but it disnae surprise me she wisnae up fur it the followin mornin. See womin ur different fae us, they cannae jist turn it oan an aff like we kin. Naw, they need tae build therselves up tae it, ye need tae get them in the mood like. So when you've jist turned up oot the blue an goet er oot er scratcher, well, even a could've told ye that widnae work son. Besides there's also the danger that yer geein the impression yer desperate, an that's the worst thing ye kin dae wae a lassie.' Pat smiled at Tam's youthful exuberance.

'Ah right enough, a see whit ye mean noo.' Tam looked over at Paula while considering his fundamental mistake in going back to Stella's.

'Naw yer makin good progress there son, jist keep at it. Ye'll get there, especially wae that posh cunt that battered ye oot the road.' Tam nodded thoughtfully, of course he was right. All he had to do was play it cool, no more slip-ups like the croissant condom combo and he would be fine.

'Am proud ay ye son, yuv come a long wye so ye huv.' Pat flung an arm behind his neck. 'That's ma boay eh!' As was usual when Pat raised his voice, the majority of the bar turned to see what was going on. Tam put the older man's excitement levels down to being pissed. His enthusiasm to see the Stella thing work out was endearing. It was like he was Tam's towel man and with a world champ like Pat in his corner anything seemed possible.

'A toast, tae Tam!' Pat stood with imbalance and raised his glass.

'Yoos lot fuckin deef, ah said a toast tae Tam!' He increased the volume into a three-line whip that was immediately understood.

The entire Public Bar turned and raised their glasses. 'Tae Tam!'

Tam's chest and throat swelled and he felt a deep pride at being associated with a man like Pat. After the toast a few punters brought Tam yet more drinks. They thought it might be his birthday or something. The number of untouched drinks on the table was getting ridiculous and Tam tried to keep up but couldn't. Slowly he slipped deeper into pishdom.

At some point, Tam became aware that Pat had left and Paula was sitting next to him. It was a one-sided conversation. She was going on about some promotion she had been given at the salon. Tam briefly considered being honest and coming clean about Stella but it also occured to him that conversation would be best conducted while sober. In any case, what if things didn't work out with Stella? In fact what if they did work out, but he decided it was Paula he wanted all along. After all, she was beautiful. Her blonde hair had a shine to it that reminded him of buttercups. No, he would say nothing until he had established which of the two impalas represented the best choice in terms of his long-term happiness.

CHAPTER 8

Pat stepped from the pub into the evening cold, with whisky warming his bones. He was headed for the derelict tower block up on The Hill. The boy hadn't had the best upbringing, what with his parents fucking off and leaving him. Besides, Lina was like a daughter to him so when she asked for his help it was a given. As far as Pat was concerned the boy was now firmly planted inside his inner circle. If there were anything within the scope of his powers he could do to help him, he would do it.

As he walked, Pat could see two Monkford mongrels heading menacingly toward him. He laughed, wondering if this antagonism may have been generated out of sympathy for his current house guest. Maintaining his pace and direction as they approached, he could see they were coming in for a sniff. The timing was perfection as he gently hopped into a small skip before delivering the silver buckle on his right shoe directly under a soon to be shattered jaw. This sent both dogs scurrying into the distance.

'Too many ay yoos cunts aboot here fur ma likin,' he snarled after them. If anyone had been within earshot they would have agreed with the sentiment, though probably not his methods.

Hope the boay appreciates this.

The tower block shooting upward into the black sky was one of three on the Monkford. The others were still occupied, located down in The Valley. This one stood redundant; it had been earmarked for demolition to make way for a new twenty-first-century housing strategy. Eventually this was to result in the flattening of every tenement on the scheme. For now, the tower's twenty-five floors stood silent. Perimeter security fencing indicated that no one had any business here, apart from Pat of course.

Reaching inside a plastic carrier bag, Pat removed a black

rubber torch and stepped over the debris around the main entrance. He picked up a yellow plastic bucket and began his ascent in the darkened stairwell. He had selected a flat high enough to be out of the way, but low enough to be within the respiratory capabilities of a chain-smoking alcoholic in his fifties.

He arrived at the metal door, pausing for breath. After fiddling with the padlock, he opened it into a narrow hallway. None of the rooms had doors. Placing the yellow bucket on the floor, he moved up the hall. He adjusted his eyes to the pitch black of what would have once been a family living room, a metal shutter covering the glassless windows. Pat imagined a family eating a TV dinner together, before the residue of children's laughter was erased by a muffled groan.

He pointed the torchlight to the figure tied to a kitchen chair, heavy rope around his legs and upper body. The man had fallen over onto his side. A segment of an old shirt blindfolded him with the remainder being used as a gag. Squatting down, Pat grabbed handfuls of shoulder and neck and the groaning intensified. He pulled upward hard, losing his grip a couple of times, eventually Pat managed to get him upright.

'Make sure ye don't faw oor like that again cos al no be liftin ye. Next time al jist leave ye an the rats kin eat yir face aff.' Pat spoke as though he were scolding a five year old.

'Av brought some mare grub fur ye. Ye know the rules, any mare screamin an yer gonnae get another sore yin – awright?' The man nodded his head and Pat removed the gag. He opened a small supermarket quiche. 'Never let it be said a don't look efter ma guests.' Pat poured tap water from an Evian bottle into the man's dehydrated mouth. He then untied him, leading him down the hall still blindfolded to the toilet with its yellow plastic bucket. He had considered getting him to use the bucket in the living room, but that didn't seem right.

Pat would take the yellow bucket downstairs with him and dispose of it outside. But first he needed to return the man to the living room. As Pat tied the man back into the chair he began to sob like a child. This was distasteful to Pat and he snapped at him.

'Get a fuckin grip ay yerself ye hear me, stoap yer wingin like a wee baby. Yer supposed tae be a big tough guy ur ye no?' The man's tears and snotters combined, making a thick drip from the tip of his nose on to his shirt. Pat felt a hungry urge to use the heavy torch on the side of the man's face.

***

Tam knew it was wrong of course. To be pursuing Stella and allowing Paula to 'help him up the stairs' at shutting time. That was always going to end up going only one way. She had never once put him to bed and then left it at that.

His bedroom was in darkness but the street light afforded sufficient illumination for him to see her outline as she undressed. She was definitely well put together and had more in the way of feminine shadows and softer edges than the athletic Stella.

Paula climbed naked onto the bed. Tam was on his back and she moved immediately into the sixty-nine position. As her head moved up and down he stared at her entrance. He was too pissed to lift his mouth, besides there would be no need to work on her in order to facilitate the necessary lubrication, she was doing that all by herself.

Slurp. Gasp. Breath.

This would happen occasionally if he had drunk too much, she would simply take over. In fact, since Stella's arrival on the scene, their sexual encounters would normally conform to Paula being in control and Tam being inebriated. There would be times when she would get him hard, like now, while on other occasions he would simply sleep.

Deciding she had stiffened him sufficiently, she slid herself into a reverse cow girl position (facing away from him). She then began with her rocking-horse manoeuvre. Her pace was a slow one but he felt a queasiness bubbling up from his abdomen, the evening's drinks swirling inside him. Reaching behind, she grabbed his wrists, pulling hard – a giant slug grinding a trail over him – all the while steadily increasing the pace. His nausea was ramping up with all the movement and a dash to the toilet was becoming a priority. But he didn't want to seem rude and interrupt her, besides he knew from experience this shouldn't take much longer. Right on cue, she lifted herself from her knees to her feet, like a jockey. Leaning forward she grabbed his ankles pounding him hard before turning into the home straight.

The constant movement was simply too much for him and he projectiled up and outward, covering her arse cheeks in a warm splash. Incredibly, she appeared not to notice. Her focus was the finish line and she thundered down the home straight before claiming first prize in the one-horse race. Stepping down from the saddle with weakened legs and panting heavily, she lay on her back next to him.

He decided rather than visit the toilet now and have to accept responsibility he would simply slide into a slumber. That would avoid any embarrassment and in any case he knew she would be gone by morning. With any luck, she would clean him up before leaving.

***

As Pat approached The Rannoch Moor he watched the pink sun slide behind the Campsies until morning. As was usual he had spent most of the afternoon in various city-centre bars. They were always quiet in the afternoons after the lunchtime rush; he was simply a nameless stranger. The young staff never eyed the clock with accusatory looks. Lina wouldn't actually say anything of course but that slightest of glances at her watch was always sufficient to get the point across. He would have much preferred to do his afternoon drinking on home turf in his local, but he couldn't endure that glance at the watch.

The Lounge was normally quiet at this time of the evening

so he entered the Public Bar instead. He could tell something wasn't right straight away. The atmosphere was different; he felt it as soon as he passed through the creaking of the swing doors. Tam was propped on an elbow at the corner of the bar.

'Two pints an two hawfs pal.' One of Lina's staff took Pat's order. Tam was thankful, the money the old man had given him was gone and he had been nursing his pint.

'Cheers Pat.'

'Whit's the matter? Somebidy kicked the bucket ur somethin?' Pat looked at the other patrons whose volume had dipped with his entrance even more than was usual.

'There's some guy in the Lounge askin fur ye.'

'Don't worry yersel son, dae a look worried?' Pat moved up to the end of the bar curiously. He looked through the adjoining hallway into the Lounge but couldn't see anything other than empty seats. He returned to Tam, handing him a cashline twenty.

'Dae me a favour son, square er up an ask er tae pass them through, then you come and find me.' Tam was worried and his face showed it. 'Yer awright son, am here so there's nuthin tae fear eh.' He smiled over his shoulder as he left; patrons weren't allowed to cut through the adjoining hallway, not even Tam or Pat.

Tam had a strange feeling. Like a teenage girl unsure of a boyfriend's intentions. Pat seemed to be drawing him further into his world with each passing day. If Tam wasn't working, Pat seemed to expect him to be by his side. Although fond of the old man, Tam's preference would have been for a little more in the way of distance. He was grateful of course, his confidence levels had propelled from zero to hero. But still, he was unsure why Pat was insistent they spend so much time together. Part of him thought the old man was simply lonely with Betsy gone.

There were a few patrons in the Lounge but not many and Tam made his way toward the table occupied by Pat and the stranger.

'Gonnae dae me a favour son, stick some Deano oan eh.' Tam slid some shrapnel into the jukebox, selecting the first track he came to.

The stranger looked like he was on his way to or from a funeral, wearing an ill-fitting grey suit, its buttons long term redundant due to a protruding girth. A dark crombie overcoat lay on his lap. His frame at first sight looked to be obese but on a second take Tam suspected he had more the look of a scrum-half about him. Silver hair matted with sweat; red cheeks; relaxed and confident eyes – too confident.

'This is DCI McGregor son.' Pat appeared as unruffled as usual, but Tam's thoughts turned to the contents of his stomach and his shoes.

'Ah, you must be Tam.' The detective didn't stand but extended a hand as big as a baseball glove and Tam shook it limply.

'Ye jist gonnae stawn there? Take a seat son.' Pat smiled as he spoke and Tam sat next to his mentor. The DCI's large frame was taking up almost two seats across the table from them. Tam could feel his heart pounding through his chest: how did he know his name? Even being with Pat on the night Tommy Tattoo was slashed made him an accessory. On top of that there was the guys face he himself had kicked – that was assault at least.

Oh Shit.

'McGregor's fae Pitt Street son, kin ye believe that?' Pat looked at Tam with an amazement wrapped in a thin veil of sarcasm.

'We're lucky if we see local Polis but a DCI, fae headquarters uv aw places, well that's jist unheard of, am a right son?' Tam knew the old man was cool but he was playing a blinder, unlike himself. His own eyes were darting from the door to the windows, awaiting the arrival of flashing blue lights.

'A wis kinda hopin tae keep this private between urselves.' This statement by McGregor immediately threw Tam into a state of even more confusion. Thoughts of alibi came to him, or specifically who would be most likely to agree to give him a false one, Paula or Stella. He soon realised the answer to that question was an obvious one.

'Anythin yuv goet tae say tae me can be said in front ay the boay.' Pat slapped Tam's upper leg under the table in endorsement. He then shouted over to Lina who was eyeing them suspiciously from the bar.

'Three mare lagers pal wae malt chasers, wur new buddy here's pyin!'

'As long as she kin gee me a receipt.'

Tam's previously panicky thoughts were replaced with amazement. Why was a DCI sitting with them at all, never mind buying them a round of drinks. There followed a long pause. Pat's folded arms and vacant smile conveyed he had no intention of breaking it, or allowing Tam to – not that Tam had the inclination. Instead Tam averted his eyes from his companions scanning the small number of faces seated around the Lounge.

'Awright then, a kin see ye urnae a man fur the small talk so al jist cut tae the chase. It's obvious that since yees slashed that Bushwaka they've been keepin a right low profile.'

Pat held both palms outward as he spoke. 'That wis nuffin tae dae wae us big yin.' Again, a very convincing tone Tam thought.

'Listen boays, av been dayin this joab fur aboot a hunner years an a make it ma business tae know everythin that goes oan in this city. The Procurator Fiscal might no uv charged Tommy Tattoo fur murderin the young boay Martin, but that disnae mean a didnae know it wis him. Or that the victim's Da asked you fur help. As a said, a know everythin that goes oan in this town. Noo am no gonnae take yoos fur a couple a dafties, but ad appreciate yees extendin me the same courtesy.'

Lina arrived at their table with the drinks and McGregor extended a rumpled twenty in his thick fingers.

'Ye kin keep the chynge sweetheart if yee gees a receipt.' Something in McGregor's smile told Tam he knew her, or perhaps simply wanted to know her.

'Besides, if yees were gettin lifted it widnae be a fuckin DCI pyin yees a visit a kin assure yees. Naw am no interested in chargin yees, if it was doon tae me ad gee yees a medal.' Pat looked sideways at Tam, his expression conveying he was satisfied with the explanation, for now.

'Awright, so whit dae ye waant wae us then?' Pat lifted his freshly poured pint, draining half of the golden nectar in two long gulps. McGregor looked at a table nearby and paused.

'Here son, gonae put somethin a bit mare lively oan, a don't waant any cunt hearin ma business.' Tam selected the first techno track he came to, returning quickly to the table.

'So here's the wye a see things. It's nae secret this city's always hud a very specific gang problem. We're a sixth the size ay London an wuv goet aboot the same number a gangs, kin ye believe that? The problem isnae gonnae disappear no matter whit a dae. But there used tae be some ground rules. No any mare though, an a lot ay innocent people like that young boay ur sufferin. Wance in a blue moon we manage tae loak wan up, but don't get me started oan prisons. Nae fuckin deterent. Aw their pals in there waitin fur them wae widescreen tellys an creative writin classes.' McGregor's previously rosy cheeks were now a throbbing red.

'Aye awright big man, keep yer shirt oan.' Pat reached over, lifting McGregor's whisky signalling him to drink it – which he did in one gulp. This was followed by a ferocious wheezing from his chest and then a spluttering cough through which he struggled to spit out more words.

'Since yoos slashed the Bushwaka they've done fuck aw in terms ay reprisals. Av goet tae sit up an take notice ay somethin as unusual as that.' Tam was concerned at his continual references to 'yoos', he wanted to correct him and say it was Pat who did the actual slashing.

'Naw, they fuckin know better.' Pat laughed as he spoke and, smiling, looked at Tam with a reassuring wink.

McGregor's coughing had subsided by degrees and finally the

scorching redness in his cheeks settled to a healthier shade. 'A love whisky boays, but it fuckin kills me.' McGregor stared at his empty glass as he spoke.

'Aye very good, but whit's the point ay aw this, whit's it goet tae dae wae us.' Pat's voice was underlined with an impatience Tam couldn't quite get his head round. Even a loony tune as bold as Pat surely wouldn't talk to a DCI like that?

'Awright then, the point is this.' For the first time since the meeting had begun, Tam sensed a slight frostiness in McGregor's voice. Perhaps he had just remembered Pat was on the opposite side of his professional spectrum.

'Av goet a list a tadgers like that Bushwaka as long as ma erm, aw runnin aboot plungin and terrorisin cunts. Fiscal isnae interested cos naebody'll testify – too scared, an wae good reason anaw.'

Pat spoke without frustration this time, calmly looking directly at McGregor. 'Fair enough big yin, but as a say a don't see how any uv this hus goet anything tae dae wae me an the boay.'

McGregor looked again at the nearby table but Tam had selected the techno track on a loop. The detective seemed satisfied they couldn't be heard, but leaned forward in any case.

'Well av goet a wee proposition fur yoos boays. A waant tae send a message oot tae other scum like that Tommy Tattoo.' Tam was struck by the irony of a DCI discussing anti-social behaviour with an out and out sociopath like Pat.

'Oh aye, so whit's this message ye waant sendin then?'

'Well the message is quite a simple wan. If yur takin liberties an we cannae prosecute, then there's a chance yer gonnae get yer jaw ripped. It's obviously done the trick oan the Monkford hus it no?'

'Aye but dae ye no think that's tae dae wae Pat's reputation here oan the scheme?' McGregor almost spluttered in surprise when Tam spoke, seeming to have calculated that the meeting would be concluded without a word from the younger man. Pat smiled proudly, indicating Tam hadn't spoken out of turn.

'Fair comment son, but this city kin be like a village at times, other gangs hiv already heard aboot a vigilante attack oan the Monkford. If it wis tae happen oan other schemes, well a think it's possible that word wid spread an they might think twice aboot liberty takin. Even if we stoap wan young boay gettin plunged it's worth it as far as am concerned. An if we don't, well at the very least another family gets the retribution that we couldnae gee them.' Pat was very quiet and Tam felt he was somehow monitoring him, as though this were a test of his progress. For some minutes, Pat simply stared at McGregor, stroking the silver stubble on his chin. The DCI broke the silence.

'A wid be the only person in Pitt Street that wid know anythin aboot it so yees wid be handled by me alone. A wid gee yees the names, but a kin gurantee ye immunity fae prosecution if ye dae end up gettin lifted fur whitever reason. That shouldnae happen but, because al make sure things ur sorted oot ma end.'

'That's aw very well, but wid we be expected tae be dayin it fur nothin?' Tam didn't even realise he had spoken until the words left his mouth. He was tired of accepting the money from Pat, he liked the idea of having some of his own for a change. Pat turned in his seat and raised his eyebrows creasing a fleshy forehead into lines of surprise.

'Naw he's right enough Pat, business is business as they say. The answer is yes, yees wid get pyed. A wid certainly make sure it wis worth yer while.' Tam calculated how some decent money would mean he could compete with the likes of Campbell. He could treat Stella the way someone from her background would be used to. You can't take a girl like her tenpin bowling, he knew that much for sure. An injection of cash could get her exactly where he wanted. An image flashed into his mind of a four-poster bed in a plush hotel, framing her perfectly toned and widely spread legs.

'So where wid you be gettin the names?' Pat asked.

McGregor paused, sensing the gravity of the question. 'Well as a said, there's guys we jist cannae pin anythin decent oan, but everybody knows they're liberty takers. Am no interested in ned oan ned stuff they kin stab fuck oot each other fur aw a care. Naw it's the wans that involve innocent people, they're the names yees wid be gettin passed.' The DCI drained his pint before wiping his mouth with the back of his hand. Lina placed a tray of drinks on the next table, swapping the empties with freshly poured. She paused, waiting for payment, not looking at anyone in particular and no one moved. She could tell McGregor was Police and wasn't pleased he had business with Pat or Tam, her own questions could wait.

'Yoos ur good by the way.' McGregor's thick fingers slid another rumpled twenty from his wallet as he spoke. 'Need another receipt sweetheart.'

'Aye nae bother.'

'Cheers, keep the chynge then.' As soon as she had moved out of earshot, McGregor continued. 'It's no like yer huvin tae kill them, see, the razor's unlike the knife in that respect. The guy's mare valuable tae us alive anwye.'

'How's that?' Pat had made short work of his half and was straight on to the pint.

Mcgregor smiled, lifting the whisky glass up to his face and dipping his nose over the rim, eyes closed. He spoke prior to drinking in anticipation of the impending whisky cough. 'Well the guy becomes a walkin billboard dintae.'

After downing the malt the DCI's cheeks turned emergency crimson and he gripped the edge of the table tightly. Pat and Tam sat silently considering the offer, each in their own way.
'Me an the boay'll huv tae discuss it.' Pat lowered his head to look into McGregor's bowed face, the wheezing and spluttering fit was much worse with this second whisky.

'Nae bother, here's ma cerd, don't take too long.'

'Here big man a think you waant tae be layin oaf that stuff dae ye no?' Pat nodded toward the empty whisky glass.

'Ye ever get that wye wae somethin where ye know it's gonnae kill ye, but ye jist cannae stoap yerself?' McGregor held his card out with one hand, trying to control the wheezing by gripping the table with the other. Pat nudged Tam, indicating he should take the card. As he put it in his jacket pocket, Tam glanced at the famous crowned thistle logo, Semper Vigilo, he couldn't remember how he knew the translation, Always Alert.

***

Tam was unaware that after McGregor left another meeting was about to take place upstairs. Paula had asked Lina if she could have a word. This in itself wasn't unusual, but on this occasion Lina could sense something was different. From the moment Paula entered the kitchen the older woman could see she was carrying a heavy burden. Lina was very fond of the young girl and had made no secret to Tam of her thoughts regarding their future. Paula had all the qualities that would make her the perfect partner, not least the obvious depth to which her feelings for Tam extended.

As the two women sat together, steam rising from their coffee, Lina could see from the redness around Paula's eyes that she had been crying.

'A jist don't know whit mare a kin dae Lina, honestly a don't.' The older woman slid her chair closer. 'A know sweetheart, a know how tough it must be fur ye.' There was no need for Lina to ask what she was talking about.

'Aw these years av been waitin. It's no as if there's been any shortage ay offers, you know that. But it's always been him, a jist always knew he wis the wan fur me.' Paula's cheeks glowed as a fresh supply of tears began to seep onto their surface. Passing her a hanky, Lina felt an ache in her chest. She suspected she was in the presence of each ingredient required to serve up the one dish no one wants to order, a broken heart. Lina knew that Paula loved Tam deeply and was convinced he had feelings for her also.

'It's ever since he started in that joab, that's when things

91

chynged. A could feel em slippin away fae me somehow. Dae ye think he's maybe seein somebody else at ees work?'

'He's no said anythin tae me pal.' Lina avoided eye contact for fear her inner thoughts would be visible. Instead she looked out the kitchen window as the last of the pink bled from the sky over the bus terminus.

'A don't know whit mare a kin dae Lina honestly av tried everythin. He knows exactly how a feel, am always there fur em whenever he waants me. Sometimes when am wae em a feel like a million dollars, but recently it's like ees been avoidin me. Makes me feel rotten that, when he disnae waant tae be seen wae me, a say tae maself whit huv a done wrang? Whit huv a ever done tae deserve this?' Her tone was riddled with hopelessness, Lina reached across the table, clasping her hands tight.

'Tell me whit a kin dae tae make things right between is Lina, al dae anythin ye tell me tae, whit is it a need tae dae tae make things right?' A deep and mournfoul sob shook the young woman as she blew a cocktail of tears and snotters into a crumpled hanky. Lina considered her response carefully. Her dilemma was that she had the interests of two people she cared about to consider. If it were someone other than Tam she would simply tell Paula to move on, that she deserved better. But she was sure Tam did care for the girl. To Lina the Stella situation seemed more about the value attached to things of an elusive nature by the complexities of the male ego. She was experienced enough to know that if a man is made to walk a long distance, his appetite is likely to be more significant than after a leisurely stroll.

'Don't take this the wrang wye hen.' Lina spoke before biting her lip thoughtfully. She had all the words ready; it was simply a case of delivering them in the right order, without adding in any way to her friend's already significant upset.

'Aye whit is it?' Paula had regained her composure slightly and was staring back at her, sensing a lifeline.

'You've never made any secret uv how ye feel, right?'

'Naw av no, well av never actually came right oot an said a

love ye but whenever he's waanted me av always been there fur em.' It occurred to Lina that her strategy of sleeping with Tam whenever he wanted was always unlikely to have been an effective one. But that was the way it had been done so now they must try to retrieve the situation.

'Well maybe ye could try playin things a wee bit different tae see if it works oot any better fur ye.'

'How dae ye mean?' Lina stood, taking the empty mugs to the sink and rinsing them, looking back at Paula's sad reflection in the darkened window.

'Well if ye were tae maybe make things a bit less...' Lina paused, deciding she shouldn't use the word easy.

'Whit a mean is, ye could maybe try and make things a bit mare uv a challenge fur em.' She desperately didn't want to offend but there was only so many ways she could spin the message. She also knew that Paula's sense of objectivity had evaporated.

'So, ye mean a should blank em?' Paula was confused; she simply didn't seem to get the concept that so many of her peers were using to such potent effect.

'Naw, am no sayin that, jist well...' Again Lina proceeded with caution.

'Play it a bit mare hard tae get, aye that's it be a bit mare hard tae get.' Lina smiled hopefully, turning from the sink and drying her hands on a dishtowel. She searched the young woman's face in the hope she wouldn't find any sign of fresh upset.

'Ah, right a see whit ye mean noo.' Paula said the words in such a way that Lina could tell her mind was working frantically in an effort to get a handle on things. Her smudged and teary face had a look of desperation, but the hope associated with an as yet untested strategy was providing a diversion. Lina didn't want to give her false hope, but she did believe Paula had a fighting chance of getting things on track. She also knew she couldn't get too involved and had to simply watch things play out from the sidelines. But she did hope that through a change in tactics Paula's stock could somehow be rejuvenated.

'A think ye might be right actually, maybe that's been where av been goan wrang, he takes me too much fur granted.' Lina finally allowed herself to relax in the knowledge that not only had she delivered the message with sufficient tact, it had seemingly been understood.

'Yer right, that's whit a need tae dae, al be mare uv a challenge fae noo oan.' Paula moved forward, hugging her friend with such enthusiasm she was pushed back leaning over the sink. Soon after she was gone, leaving Lina in a fog of gratitude. There was hope.

CHAPTER 9

Stella had agreed to meet Tam in Dalry's after work. He was hopeful he could orchestrate another invite back to her place to pick up where they had left off. The box of condoms remained unopened in his jacket pocket, despite his being tempted by the novelty of a posh wank on a couple of occasions.

Looking out the taxi window, Tam wondered if he was making a mistake. She had been insistent that she wanted to go back to the Rannoch Moor rather than her place. He hadn't wanted to agree but suspected refusal may result in some kind of patronising comment about there being no need to be embarrassed.

'I'm a bit nervous about meeting your friends. Do you think they will like me?'

'Of course they will.' He knew any guest of his would be welcomed warmly. Tam considered how far he had come. Only a few weeks ago he had struggled to find the nerve to ask her on a date. He looked down at her long legs in black silk wondering if she was wearing stockings. His mobile vibrated and he read the text from Pat informing him that Paula wasn't in the Rannoch Moor – the coast was clear.

'Who was that?'

'That was my other girlfriend.' She laughed.

'How many have you got?'

He wondered if she actually considered herself to be his girlfriend, or even if he himself thought of her as one. He certainly felt that he couldn't possibly consider her for the position prior to penetration. He also knew it was unlikely he could communicate that to her without potentially fucking things up.

'Well I've got a scheme girlfriend, a middle-class one and then there's one who is just a pure animal and can't get enough of me.' The eyes in the rear-view mirror looked back at him – what a lot of shite.

'So which one am I then?' He decided not to point out the obvious. She certainly wasn't from a scheme and they hadn't had sex so it wasn't difficult to work out.

'Who says you're one of them?' The butterflies wrapped around him like a corset. This was the exact crossroads he would have previously had trouble negotiating; with a stammer and stumble his engine would have spluttered into a stall.

Coconut badger! Coconut badger!

'Oh I see it's like that is it?' Her tone was playful. His heart raced but the strategy was working as his abdominal discomfort soon subsided. He continued with his mantra until the discomfort passed completely, leaving him with nothing but the calmness along with a strong sense of heightened awareness. He decided to proceed with the image in his mind, kissing her ear while placing a hand strategically on her knee. She wriggled and giggled softly. He slid his hand slowly up her skirt and his fingers advanced across a sea of silk onto a secluded beach of flesh.

Her eyes were closed and her knuckles white as she gripped the door handle. The movement from the exposed skin above the stocking to the target area couldn't be done with any subtlety. He made the move a quick one and began rubbing the unseen lacy material with a finger while continuing to corkscrew his tongue into her ear. He couldn't be sure if it was his tongue or the rubbing hand but something was having a big impact as her breathing quickened and she opened her legs wider. He slid the damp garment to one side and crudely pushed his middle finger inward as far as he could.

'Rannoch Moor, right yees are.' The interior light was switched on and the driver turned so quickly he could have pulled a muscle, but she had managed to cover herself just in time.

As soon as Tam entered the Lounge he could see the curious looks. Who was she? What about him and Paula? He had already decided that when Paula found out, which of course she would, he would explain Stella was simply a colleague. They were working on an important project together, which was at least partly true. Tam made a few brief introductions while practically pushing Stella up to the bar. Unluckily, as they approached he could see Lina was serving.

'Stella meet Lina, Lina meet Stella.' Tam knew she would be too polite to say anything rude in front of a guest.

'Pleased to meet you Lina, I've heard a lot about you.' Lina wiped her hands on a towel before reaching through the pumps.

'Aye likewise.' There was no way she would betray Paula by being anything other than purely civil of course.

'We've got some work to catch up on so I suggested we could finish it off upstairs rather than working late.' As Tam spoke he knew it was unlikely Lina would buy this. He also considered that Stella might be suspicious of why he would lie. Nonetheless the work-related premise offered his conscience some protection.

'Nice place you've got here.' Stella was making an effort, which Tam liked.

'Aye right very good, whit kin a get yees?' Lina smiled knowingly at the blatant but well-meaning lie.

'Can I have a red wine please.' Stella had enough about her not to ask for a specific grape or wine list, best to just take what she was given.

'I'll have the same thanks.' Lina raised her eyebrows, having never served him anything other than lager or spirits in the past.

'So do you know all these people?' Stella leaned back with both elbows on the bar in a way that pushed her chest out to Tam's liking. Her body language was always so relaxed, so confident.

'Most of them yes, I've lived here all my life.' Tam returned a series of nods. There seemed to be a lot of approving male faces staring back at him.

'There yees go.' Lina passed two well-polished wine glasses over the bar along with a newly opened bottle. Stella picked up her bag.

'No, not on yer life, ma treat.' Lina was shaking her head in a firm refusal.

'Cheers Lina.' Tam was relieved, having just exhausted the last of his money on the taxi from Dalry's.

'That's very kind of you thanks.' Stella smiled warmly back at her as she positioned herself on a tall bar stool. Lina cast an eye over her in the realisation that Tam's description of her hadn't in fact done her justice. Her heart was on the side of her friend and fellow Monkford girl who she knew was attractive for sure. But she also knew Paula lacked the boldness and posture of her unknown rival.

Despite having his story for Paula already planned, Tam wasn't keen on bumping into her. So as Lina moved away to serve a customer Tam decided finding a vacant table wouldn't be a good move. No, they would stay at the bar and as soon as was feasible he would suggest they move things upstairs. In all the time he and Paula had been seeing each other she had never once come upstairs without an invitation. He could be assured of the required privacy. Surely he and Stella could pick up where they had left off. Tonight was to be the culmination of everything he had been working towards.

'Lina seems really nice.' Stella managed to sit on a bar stool with nothing less than sophistication, even in such a short pencil skirt. She expertly moved her legs inward toward the bar, adjusting her position as she spoke.

'Yeah, she's great,' Tam replied.

'Are you related?'

'No, she's a friend of the family, been looking after me since—' Tam paused, there was so much she didn't know. '—When I was a wee boy; the pub was robbed and my parents were attacked. They tried to put it behind them but they were never the same after that. Anyway, they decided they'd had enough and moved to Spain. They wanted me to go with them but I kicked up a fuss as I didn't want to leave my friends. Lina was a barmaid at the time and she was close to my parents, she offered to take over the licence and also to look after me. I don't get out to see them as much as I should to be honest.'

'Are you not close then?'

'Not really...' She touched his arm softly.

Tam heard the opening lines of a Dean Martin track and knew it could mean only one thing. Turning from the bar, he scanned the faces. He hadn't spotted Pat when they had arrived, but knew he must be here somewhere or next door in the bar. He didn't want anything or anyone messing up his chances tonight.

'You okay?' Stella asked.

'Sorry, yes I'm fine.'

'You seem a bit distracted.'

'I thought I saw someone; it's no big deal.' Tam continued to scan the room.

'Is it your scheme girlfriend, is she in here?' Stella laughed and he wondered if she actually suspected Paula's existence.

'No she's at the opera with her pals tonight.' He regretted this comment almost immediately. It felt like a betrayal, joking about Paula behind her back.

He spotted the bald head standing at the end of a table obviously pissed, gripping the back of a chair for support. He was surrounded by a small group of regulars listening to his rendition with the appearance of wide-eyed enthusiasm.

'I just need to powder my nose.' Stella slipped from the stool to her heels without effort.

'Sure, no bother, it's over there next to the jukebox.' Tam pointed. As soon as she was out of sight he moved quickly to the table. He stood back slightly as Pat finished his song. After an applause from most of the patrons in the Lounge, Tam moved forward, leaning into Pat's ear for privacy.

'Ye don't mind me no introducin er dae ye? Am tryin tae get er up the stairs before Paula appears, ye know how it is.'

'Nae bother, don't you worry yersel aboot me am brand new so a um.' Tam could tell from the slurring he was even further gone than was usual.

'Chynged days eh son.' Pat moved his weight from the back of the chair onto Tam's shoulder.

'Jist a few weeks ago ye couldnae ask er oot oan a date, noo yer takin er up the stairs tae ride the arse aff er. Aye, am proud ay ye son.' Tam could see Stella moving back to the bar as he re-positioned Pat's grip onto the chair.

'By the way we need tae decide if wur gonnae agree tae help that copper ur no.' Pat dropped his voice so he couldn't be heard by the others – he was pissed but not that pissed.

'Aye yer right enough, al come oor tae yours the morra an we kin huv a chat eh.' Tam was keen not to offend the old man but Stella was now looking over.

'Nae worries son, come oor tae ma place the morra an we kin discuss it, a think ma fan club here ur waantin a wee encore.'

'Who was that you were talking to?' Stella nodded in Pat's direction who was raising a glass to her with one of his wide, tobacco stained signature smiles, he seemed to be aware he was being discussed.

'Oh, it's just a guy who's asked me to do some part-time work.' Tam finished the wine in his glass preparing himself to ask her upstairs. As soon as he made the decision, a familiar and unpleasant warmth began to bubble in his stomach.

Coconut badger! Coconut badger!

'What does he do?' she asked.

'Eh, he's a kind of security consultant.' Tam considered the improvised title, realising he wasn't that far off the mark.

'And what do you know about security?' She moved backward slightly, just about to climb back up onto the stool.

'Not a lot, he just needs someone to help him with a new project, like an assistant.' He wanted to ask her before she got back up on that stool. 'Listen you want to finish the bottle off upstairs?'

'Will she not mind?' Stella nodded toward Lina who was busy serving but still casting the occasional disapproving look in their direction.

'It's none of her business I live here, besides I'm not a teenager anymore she'll be fine.' He knew that with her loyalty to Paula she would be far from fine, but at the end of the day it was his life and he was confident Lina would respect that.

As he wasn't allowed behind the serving areas he had to enter upstairs via the back door. They moved out into the frosty air and around the side of the building. He opened the door letting her enter first and as she walked up the stairs he flicked the light switch. This was for no other reason than to watch from behind as her perfect form moved with each step. After a brief tour they entered the living room, where he ignored the light switch and simply pressed play on the CD player. He knew that with Lina being the only one of them who used it the contents should be a safe bet. Sure enough it was one of her numerous love compilations.

Stella moved to the window. The orange glow of a street light illuminated the room and he moved in silently, standing close behind her.

Coconut badger! Coconut badger!

It was evident to him from their first encounter that she liked it when he took control, even forced the issue somewhat. He licked the back of her neck softly just below her hairline and immediately every muscle in her body seemed to contract. But she didn't stop him. He gently slid his hands under her oaxters and began working on her blouse like a blindfolded soldier dismantling a gun. Her head flopped backward onto his shoulder and he resumed the corkscrew licking of her inner ear from earlier. Again her breath quickened, and with all the buttons now loose her blouse cooperated by falling open. He gripped her upper arms with an urgency, turning her to face him. Her eyes were closed as he leaned forward, opening his mouth over hers. She opened her lips slightly, affording him sufficient space to force his tongue inward. He reached up, grabbing hold of her face roughly, knowing he was being aggressive but sensing she liked it that way. He began to move her from the window toward the couch, still kissing her hard. The room and its contents were unfamiliar to her so she moved with caution, both hands

101

reaching out into the air around her. While she was distracted and concentrating on her surroundings, he worked quickly on the skirt zip and also her bra strap. By the time she lay on the sofa she had lost her blouse, bra and skirt.

From Stella's quick breathing and moans of arousal he was sure she was enjoying herself, but still he sensed she hadn't fully submitted. Eyes closed, she lay there wearing only her black hold-up stockings, black thong and patent black leather heels. He kneeled on the carpet between the sofa and coffee table with the street lamp lighting his path like a runway. His face dropped from the clouds toward her tarmac and the tip of his tongue made contact with a hard nipple. Soon he massaged his hand up her inner thigh and then slid his fingers under the lace, relieved to find her welcomingly moist. If he were satisfied she had submitted totally, perhaps he could slow things down a bit and savour the journey, but she hadn't and so he couldn't. He knew nothing was guaranteed, so his movements were deliberate and wrapped in an urgency that stemmed from one single motive. While working on her wetness with the middle finger of his right hand, he reached up with the left to his jeans and within a heartbeat he was exposed.

She must have heard his belt buckle and there had been no objection. He managed to remove the condom from its wrapper and slide it over himself using only one hand. His lips moved in a triangle from nipple to nipple to mouth with his finger not leaving her warmth for a second. He then moved himself upward and onto the sofa, kneeling between her open legs.

Just a few seconds now, millimetres, there it is there.

'Tam I'm sorry I can't!' She pushed him hard in the chest and spun round into a seated position. He was still on his knees. Motionless he tried to go back over in his head what he had done leading up to that point. Had he offended her in some way?

'What's the matter?' He heard his voice, it sounded like that of a five-year-old child.

'I don't have any solution for my contacts.' He was

dumbfounded. He didn't even know you needed solution for contacts but even so, didn't see what that had to do with anything.

'If I don't have solution I can't stay over, and if I can't stay then we can't do anything. I'm not a slut Tam, I'm not one of those girls who has sex with a guy and then gets a taxi home with her knickers in her handbag.' She climbed back into her skirt, clipping her bra strap and buttoning her blouse with an urgency equal to their removal. It occurred to him he could perhaps suggest going home with her and staying the night at her place. That way she would have her contact solution and they could continue. But he also knew the passion had been sucked from the room and besides, that suggestion might have an air of desperation to it. As they waited for her taxi, the silence was periodically punctured by her unsuccessfull attempts at small talk.

'I'll see you at work then Tam yeah.' He couldn't believe how normal and matter of fact her tone was, as though this were no big deal.

'Aye very good.' He made no effort to disguise his annoyance as she leaned forward kissing him on the cheek, and then she was gone. His mind went over and over what had happened but he just couldn't get a handle on it. What the fuck was going on? Why had she let him get so close on two separate occasions? Was she just a cock tease after all? Or was she still a virgin with hymen retention issues? Had she suffered some kind of abuse? Was she religious and wanted to wait for her wedding night? In the absence of information he was struggling to come up with an explanation and jumping to all sorts of conclusions.

He sat on the sofa with his old friend hardness, replaying the events over in his mind. He heard her taxi door close and then the engine fade into the distance. He considered the way in which women tended to bring a whole lot of complications to sex that did nothing other than get in the way. His urgency stemmed from the realisation that he might only have a small window of opportunity with Stella, he just wanted to climb through it while he had the chance. He opened the SMS screen on his mobile without a trace of guilt. His current condition may have been facilitated by the confusingly elusive Stella. Hopefully though, it would be welcomed inside an ever-reliable alternative.

CHAPTER 10

Now that Tam had an understanding with Shergar, he felt sufficiently confident to take a day off without making the required phone call. Since the razor incident his line manager seemed to be on the verge of a seizure whenever Tam approached. In effect, he had been extended carte blanche to do as he pleased.

Rubbing the early afternoon sleep from his eyes, he looked over to an empty pillow. He had texted Paula after Stella's departure but she had been unreceptive. As he suspected would be the case, someone had told her he had brought a woman into the Lounge. As planned, he explained she was simply a colleague, that they were working on a project together. In any case, Paula had refused his invitation to join him. In view of this latest development his position with both Stella and Paula was precarious to say the least. Just a few days ago his mind had skipped between them, in anticipation of having to make a difficult choice. Was it possible he would be left with neither as an option?

Turning his head to the window, he attempted to gauge what the weather had in store. Assorted shades of grey and not a drop of blue – ominous. He contemplated sinking his head back into the warm pillow in order to continue his slumber, but knew it would make sleep difficult that evening. He also remembered the discussion with Pat relating to DCI McGregor's proposal. Snapping back the duvet, he dressed quickly.

***

Climbing the stairs in Pat's close he diverted the breath through his mouth in order to avoid nasal contact with the stench. Pat had given Lina a spare key, asking her to pass it to him. She had done so, along with a bag of groceries and her gratitude, for everything

Tam was doing to help the old man. Tam carefully placed the bag on the battered Home Sweet Home mat and opened the door, listening for any signs of movement. Only silence came back and he moved into the hall, taking each step on tiptoes. He wasn't sure why he was being so quiet, but there was something strange entering a home other than his own with a key.

The small kitchen had piles of dirty crockery and a rubbish bin spilling over onto matted linoleum. He placed the grocery bag on the worktop, wondering where he should make a start. Moving slowly down the hall toward the living room he could hear Pat snoring. Two doors across the hallway were closed and he knew they must be bedrooms. Such was the mystique surrounding Pat he couldn't even begin to imagine what was behind each door. Torture chambers perhaps or storage for body parts. He tried to put the grizzly thoughts out of his mind and continue toward the living room but couldn't resist a peek. Opening the first of the doors as quietly as possible he could see it was a mess but not in a dirty sense like the kitchen. It was packed full of cardboard boxes and bags, thirty years of bric-a-brac. He closed the door carefully, moving to the second. Such was his surprise he had to catch his breath. It was beautiful.

From the blanket of dust he suspected Pat hadn't been in here for some time, perhaps even since her death. How could someone like Pat ever have slept in such a feminine bedroom? Tam paused to wonder how many more of the city's hard men slept in bedrooms furnished by their wives. The thought made him smile. He remembered Betsy's visits to the Rannoch Moor. Elegant and sophisticated, Tam had often thought she looked like a movie star. Lina put her own extensive cream usage on her skin down to advice gifted her by Betsy. She would often give the younger woman pointers on the importance of looking after oneself while youth is an ally. The dressing table in the corner was covered in creams, scents, cosmetics, brushes, all sorts of files and strange implements. This must have been where she spent her time, looking after herself.

He backed out, carefully closing the door and moving into the living room. Pat had fallen asleep fully clothed in the armchair. The window must have been open all night as the room's temperature matched that of the street; Tam closed it quickly. He couldn't remember seeing a dog on his previous visit, and Pat had never mentioned having a pet, but a sleeping tail protruded out from behind the sofa. Tam scratched his head while looking at the mess: should he make a start here or in the kitchen? Pat's head had fallen back on to the chair exposing his mouth wide. Tam wondered how long he had been sleeping in that position, his jaw would surely be painful when he woke. A crossword page waited on his lap, a glass lay where it had fallen at his feet, and an empty whisky bottle looked down from the mantelpiece.

Tam decided to tidy the kitchen first and then make the breakfast, leaving the living room till last. Hopefully Pat would be stirred by his noise and wake naturally. To try to wake someone like Pat from a deep sleep would be a procedure riddled with unknown hazards.

Some time later, thankfully and as anticipated, Tam heard movement from the living room as he completed his tasks in the kitchen.

'Av made some breakfast fur ye.' Pat straightened himself in the armchair, opening and closing his mouth like a goldfish in an attempt to grind away the ache.

'How did ye get in?'

'Ye gave Lina a key fur me dae ye no remember?' Tam felt a slight anxiety that he might have over-stepped the mark.

'Oh aye that's right so a did.' Pat folded last night's crossword page, placing it in the magazine rack at the side of the chair. Stretching his arms above his head in a waking yawn, he rubbed on his stiff jawbone.

'There ye go.' Tam handed him the warm plate with a cushion for his knees.

'Tell ye whit son, a could get used tae this.'

'A hud somethin tae eat earlier, so am jist gonnae finish geein the place a wee tidy up eh.' Tam wasn't altogether sure if Pat would be pissed off with the enforced housekeeping. He was however confident that their relationship had reached a level where he could get away with being so familiar. Had anyone else pulled that kind of stunt he suspected the reaction would have been a different one. Pat didn't seem angry though.

'Thanks fur this son, av been meanin tae get roon tae it, but ye know how it is.' Pat's tone held just a hint of embarrassment.

'It's nae bother ataw, a quite enjoy the novelty actually, Lina dis everythin in oor place disnae let me lift a finger.' He was lying of course, not about Lina doing all the housework that part was true, but she moaned at him constantly to help. He hated housework, but simply couldn't stand seeing someone he cared about living in this mess.

'Aye she's good tae ye that lassie, good tae baith uv us.' Pat munched into his traditional breakfast of potato scones, black and fruit pudding, square sausages and fried eggs.

'This is lovely son, sure ye don't waant some?' He spoke with a full mouth as a shiny line of grease ran down his stubbled chin. Tam continued to clear away the bottles and cans, even giving the surfaces a polish while Pat continued enthusiastically with his breakfast, eventually lifting the plate to his face and licking it clean. Tam worried how long it had been since the old man had taken nutrition from something other than malted barley. Pat sighed with satisfaction, opening his tobacco tin.

'Did ye get any Bru?' he asked.

'Aye a put it in the fridge, al goan get it.' Any Monkford breakfast of that type had to be accompanied by a bottle of chilled Irn Bru.

'Tell ye whit son yer too good tae me so ye ur.' Pat struggled to remove the bottle top with his greasy hands and Tam assisted, twisting it with the bottom of his shirt. He passed it back to the old man who drained the bright orange liquid in long throaty gulps.

'A didnae know ye hud a dug?'

'A don't,' Pat replied. Tam nodded toward the back of the sofa.

'Oh that yin, nah that's deed.'

'Fuck, am sorry tae hear that Pat, a didnae even know ye hud wan. When did it die?'

'Never mind that, we've goet important business tae discuss, take a seat.' Pat motioned toward the sofa.

'Eh right, so whit huv ye decided tae dae?' Tam sat awkwardly, thoughts of the unseen corpse behind him. How long had it been lying there, he wondered?

'That kinda depends oan you son.' Tam was confused.

'A don't understawn whit ye mean.' He also felt the twinge in his abdomen normally associated with the rapid transit of faeces through his intestines.

Coconut badger! Coconut badger!

'Well am no dayin it oan ma tod, al need a number two, somebody a kin trust tae watch ma back.' Pat ran his tongue across a cigarette paper and turned from the window, staring at him.

'Besides a know ye could probably use the money tae show that burd fae yer work a good time. She's a classy filly yer gonnae need some serious dough ur ye no?' Tam's anxiety eased, backup man didn't sound all that dangerous. Besides, surely a legend like Pat wouldn't even need such a thing. Tam suspected it was simply that he enjoyed his company, was looking for an excuse to get him involved; that's it, he was lonely. There was also the fact that Pat's coaching had been responsible for pretty much turning his life around. Tam was indebted to him. There was no doubting the cause was noble and Pat was right about the money being attractive. Pat lit the roll-up, leaning back on the windowsill.

'McGregor's right son. If we kin stoap wan scumbag fae takin a liberty like whit happened tae that young boay Martin, then it'll be worth it. Ye already know how a feel aboot these cunts, it jist widnae a been allowed tae happen in ma day. If Betsy wis still aboot obviously a couldnae get involved, but she's no here, so...'

'But ur ye sure ye wid waant me as yer backup man?' Tam felt a mixture of pride tinged with uncertainty.

'A like ye a lot son, besides as far as am concerned ye demonstrated in Tommy Tattoo's hoose that yer mare than capable a watchin ma back.' Pat licked a middle finger, rubbing egg yolk from the corner of his mouth and looking back at Tam with the happiest of smiles.

'Me an you son, whit dae ye say?'

***

The following night was to be the first of the McGregor attacks. Pat and Tam began the evening with drinks in the Rannoch Moor. Tam could sense from all the wise cracks that the old man was in his element, even looking forward to the state-sponsored carnage ahead.

They had taken a taxi into the city centre where they met McGregor at a rank behind Central Station. It was in no one's interest for the detective's visits to the Monkford to become a regular occurrence. It was also agreed that all future rendezvous would be of a covert nature. When McGregor's car pulled up, Tam climbed into the back and Pat the front. They were driven to the Clarendon area, a scheme to the north of the city. Tam had never been, but had certainly heard of it.

Tam thought of Glasgow's schemes as self-contained villages in some respects, each with its own shops, pubs, sports fields and play areas. Some residents would rarely venture beyond the perimeters, and men would often think twice about entering a scheme other than their own. McGregor had picked them up in his own personal car and Tam had to slide over to the passenger side as the area behind the driver was a mess of empty coffee cups and sandwich boxes. McGregor gave them some background on the target as he drove. Soon enough the car manoeuvred out beyond the busier roads, moving slowly into the quieter streets of the Clarendon. Tam could see how similar the layout was to the Monkford with row after row of identical tenements and their white railing verandas. As the car pulled in across the street from the Clarendon Bar, Tam felt the sickness rise up.

Coconut badger! Coconut badger!

He had been assured by Pat there was nothing to worry about and that his involvement would be minimal. They had discussed his role in detail earlier and it all seemed very straightforward. It hadn't escaped Tam's attention that only weeks ago he was terrified by his own shadow and here he was acting as a backup man to a Glasgow legend.

'Right yees are, he's in there wae ees croanies.' McGregor nodded across the street at the windowless ramshackle on a neglected corner. The Clarendon was an older scheme than the Monkford and this pub would have once been surrounded by old style tenements above and on either side. They had long since been demolished and Tam wondered why they hadn't flattened these types of pub at the same time. Perhaps a town planner with a romantic streak had wanted to leave a piece of the culture untouched. Or had it been simply been in an attempt to keep the locals on the piss? Either way most of the older schemes like the Clarendon had them as testament to a forgotten era.

Tam leaned forward as McGregor opened a brown manila folder. It contained a large surveillance photograph, some papers and a thick envelope. There was no light inside the car other than that from the street as McGregor held out the envelope to Pat.

'The boay handles that side ay things.' The detective raised his eyebrows before passing the envelope to Tam, who in truth was equally surprised as he slid it into his jacket pocket.

'Right then, the guy in the photograph is Blondie McAvoy, a right evil bastard jist like yer pal Tommy Tattoo. He murdered a young boay fur nothin mare than wearin the wrang colours oan an auld firm day.' McGregor turned the folder in such a way that Tam and Pat could both see the surveillance shot.

'Nae chance ye kin charge em then?' Tam suspected he knew the answer to the question but wanted to be seen to be getting involved by both men.

'Na naebody'll testify they're aw terrified, an wae good reason anaw, the guy's a loony tune.'

'You goet a good look at em?' Pat turned in his seat to face Tam as he spoke. It was Tam's job to enter first and wait for Blondie to go to the toilet. He would then phone Pat's mobile who would head straight for the gents where he was to do the business, discreetly.

'He runs wae the Clarendon Monks, jist like the Bushwakas oor at your place they've made a right nuisance ay therselves here so they huv.' McGregor passed the folder back to Tam so that he could get a closer look at the soon-to-be opened face. Blondie had close-set eyes and a pointed nose. He seemed to be looking after someone else's lips as they were too fleshy for his small face. His hair, like coal and heavily gelled, was swept back from a face of deep olive brown. The name Blondie had been an attempt at irony that had stuck. He wore two large gold loop earrings in his left ear. Pat moved the rear-view mirror so that he could converse with his assistant without turning.

'Awright son ye know the drill, any questions?'

'Naw yer awright, a know whit a need tae dae.'

Coconut Badger! Coconut Badger!

Minutes later, Tam was standing at the bar ordering two pints of lager. As expected, his unknown face had drawn some enquiring glances. If anyone asked he was to say he was waiting for a cousin called Jimmy, hence the ordering of two pints. He discreetly surveyed the room for Blondie and with no Lounge and only a Public Bar the search was an easy one. The long gantry stretched down the centre of the room like an island. It was surrounded by punters on all sides. A red upholstered bench ran round the yellow-stained walls and the room was flooded in an overly bright fluorescent shower from the long strip bulbs of the high ceiling.

Tam spotted him sitting at a table with another man and two women. He wasn't exactly hard to pinpoint, that face of his looked like it would be more at home in the exotic breezes of the Mediterranean, rather than the harsh winds of northern Europe. Tam's heart rate picked up a notch accompanied by a slight anxiety. He noticed however that it wasn't wrapped up in dread like the old feeling, this one had an excitement running through it. Tam could see Blondie was drinking spirit chasers as well as pints so suspected he wouldn't have too long to wait. Again he found himself delivered into the calmness. Staring at the healthy brown skin of the target, he became excited by the fact he was the only person inside the pub who knew what was about to happen. Thoughts of the boy whose life had been cut short also came to him and he hoped he was looking down from wherever he was and would approve. Perhaps young Martin would be there also; he imagined them both peering over the clouds smiling. The moment of retribution came nearer as Blondie unwittingly entered the gents. Tam removed his mobile casually. He even felt confident enough to stray beyond his brief with some acting, looking at his watch and shaking his head in frustration.

Pat must have been standing directly outside, as only a few seconds passed before the doors that Tam had entered rattled back against the walls. Every head turned.

'So... this is where the famous Clarendon Monks drink.' It was obvious immediately to everyone that this guy was trouble. A couple of figures near the door moved toward Pat in what looked to be a pre-emptive stike.

'Whit yoos gonnae dae ya couple a fannies?' Pat snapped his arm forward, extending the mirror-like blade and they immediately retreated.

'Aye a thought as much.'

Tam was confused. The plan discussed with McGregor had been to carry out the attack discreetly in the gents. Pat was very much his own man though and it seemed indiscretion was to be his preferred method of delivery. The faces of the older

113

patrons reflected memories of their youth and the younger ones confusion. The razor after all had been forced into retirement by the knife. Pat moved casually to the bar, lifting a pint and drinking as though it were a glass of water and he were about to engage in some public speaking.

'See it's like this folks. Av been hearin a few things aboot these Clarendon Monks. Av been hearin that wan ay them recently took a liberty wae a young boay that didnae deserve it.' Tam could sense from the majority of facial expressions that the silent consensus were in fact frustrated by the Monks. But they had to live here and no one was going to speak up against a local gang member.

'Am here the night tae deliver some justice oan behalf ay that young boay. An am tellin yees right noo that if there's any mare liberty takin, al be comin back.' Pat walked to the door of the gents and leaned a shoulder against the wall as though waiting at a bus stop. His audience were captivated. He was making a much more significant statement than would have been the case had he used the privacy of the gents. This type of behaviour was rare. It required a degree of insanity that few people in the city, modern or old, possessed.

On pulling open the toilet door, the first thing Blondie noticed was the squeak of a hinge, he had never heard that before. Then a surreal and silent room full of faces staring back at him. His immediate thought was - but it's no ma birthday?

'Hey blondie! Whit ye fond ay?' The words were being shouted from his left. He turned but didn't recognise the small bald man. Nor did he see the hand rising to his face. He certainly didn't understand why his earring was being yanked from his ear. At first he put it down to a prank of some kind. Friends had often poked fun at his gold hoops, but surely this was a bit OTT?

***

The car journey back to the city centre was a silent one. It was evident that for reasons known only to Pat he had deviated from McGregor's requested discretion. Tam was anxious at how McGregor would react. But he also considered that Pat's decision to make it so public was likely to be much more effective at making the message a fast and wide reaching one. He leaned his head backward closing his eyes, fantasies of being inside Stella washed over him. His share of the money would be used to facilitate a bridge between those hungry thoughts and the real world.

***

The security guard was trying to strike a balance between keeping his job and avoiding the wrath of Pat. Whoever was checked in upstairs had been making a lot of noise. It was another guard who had noticed while doing his rounds in the evening darkness, but Pat's insider had volunteered to investigate further. Rather than enter the tower block, he headed straight for the Rannoch Moor. The guard returned to his colleague, saying the noise was down to a loose board over a window banging in the wind; he would report it to the Housing Association in the morning.

Pat stood back from the tower, watching. The unsuspecting guard was due to finish, as soon as he had left Pat was to be given confirmation. His mobile rang.

'Awright, an remember yuv seen nothin.' Pat entered the living room by torchlight and could see his guest had manouvered his chair in such a way he could reach the board over the window with his feet.

'Here pal, huv you goet some sort a fuckin death wish, is that whit it is aye?' Pat slid the chair back into the centre of the room and positioned slabs of concrete he had found in the hallway around its legs.

'There ye go, that should dae it.' The man mumbled desperately into his gag.

'Naw, am no gonnae take it oot, ye need tae learn thit there's consequences. Your wee performance, makin aw that racket, that means losin certain privileges.' Pat removed a plastic bag from his jacket, kneeling behind the man. With his captor out of sight the man's neck and head twisted from side to side frantically, as though expecting an impact of some kind.

'It's awight settle doon am no gonnae hurt ye, it's jist some antibiotics, tae make sure ye don't pick up any infections aff the rats. Never let it be said a don't look efter ma guests eh.' Pat rustled in the bag before opening his zippo. Burning the brown powder in a spoon, he watched the tiny globules become liquid. Removing one of Betsy's insulin syringes from his pocket he hoovered the substance up and into the chamber. Pointing the torchlight on to the inner arm, he located a prominent vein just below the elbow. The tip of the hypodermic lifted the flesh effortlessly and he emptied the chamber with a knowing smile.

CHAPTER 11

Tam hadn't expected to keep all of the cash from the attack but that's exactly what happened. Pat said that with Betsy's life insurance he had more money than he knew what to do with. Despite Pat's best efforts it would seem the heavy drinking hadn't made much of a dent in the account balance. Initially Tam had been thinking of booking something along the lines of a decent city centre restaurant. But the contents of the envelope had surpassed even his most optimistic expectations. His endeavours were subsequently propelled into the dominion of expensive hotels and convertible hire cars.

Buying his own set of wheels had never been an option since passing his test. Lina had paid for the lessons in the hope it would help him secure a job, but the position in the bank was desk-based so the driving licence had been a wasted exercise, until now. The journey northward out of the city toward the picture postcard Loch Lomond area would be a short one even adhering to the speed limits. Opening up the throttle however facilitated a rapid transit and soon the still waters of the Loch were looking back at them.

Several times during the journey Stella had asked him to slow down, but he took her tone to indicate the comment was a clichéd and half-hearted one. He had to remind himself more than once during the drive that he wasn't actually dreaming. The aroma familiar to all new cars wafted up his nostrils even with the roof down. Although their ceiling of late afternoon sky was grey, going cabriolet was a novelty he simply couldn't deny himself. He had also switched the seat heating on, his back and legs were being toasted more than adequately.

'Your seat's not too warm is it?' Tam asked.

'No it's quite nice actually.' She wriggled as she spoke. Looking down from the road he could see their black metallic reflection bouncing back up to them. He manoeuvred carefully along the precarious bends. There was a newer more popular alternative but this road was very quiet, and it seemed more authentic as he traversed the spectacular natural beauty of the Loch's west side.

'Remind me how you said you could afford all this?' He hadn't actually told her for obvious reasons but she wasn't stupid and would know that on his pittance even a Travelodge would have been a stretch.

'Remember the wee bald guy you saw me speaking with in the Rannoch Moor?'

'The one singing Dean Martin?'

'Yes him. Remember I said I was helping him with some of his security work.' Tam thought it best to lace his lies with a modicum of the truth.

'What kind of security work?'

'I told you that already, he's a consultant.'

'Who for?' When he offered up the information he hadn't considered that she would want him to elaborate further.

'Strathclyde Police.' Fuck it he thought, why not.

'You're joking right?' She twisted in her seat leaning back against the door to face him. He ignored her, using the narrowing and winding road as an excuse, masking his face with concentration.

'Why would Strathclyde Police need a consultant to help them with their security? That just doesn't make sense.' She wasn't letting it go and he was panicked slightly by her reaction. On reflection, he realised the concept he was attempting to sell her to be a ridiculous one.

'Listen, I've already told you more than I should have, they made me sign the Official Secrets Act.' He couldn't actually remember if it was only the armed forces who signed that or if it included the Police. Nonetheless he was impressed with how quickly he had come up with the excuse.

'Pat has got some specific expertise that I can't talk about, his work is covert so anything I see or hear while assisting him, I'm not allowed to tell anyone.' There was a pause.

'I'll get your tongue wagging later when I get you pissed.' After she spoke he lost himself in thoughts of how he hoped his tongue would be put to work. Not, he suspected, in the way she was thinking. She responded to his silence by offering a small smile of reassurance he managed to catch in between bends on the road. He heard her give what sounded like a gasp as he turned a corner into a truly stunning landscape. He himself had to do a double take at the sheer immensity of the mountains looming over them like colossal skyscrapers. He was glad their arrival had been prior to sunset otherwise the scene would have been swallowed by the darkness. A small road led to an even narrower one as they passed the huge sign for the Ardlui House Hotel. Formerly the 19th century retreat of an English Duke, now favourite wedding spot for celebrities and home to its very own helipad and celebrity chef.

Their arrival at the main house had been like nothing Tam had witnessed, although from Stella's casual manner it was obvious she was in familiar territory. There was a crunching of the gravel under the car as they pulled up, and then two men in maroon waistcoats hurried from the hotel to open their doors and carry their bags. Tam passed each a tip but then realised he should probably have waited till they had been shown up to reception. He was determined that would be both his first and also his last slip-up. Under no circumstances would Stella, or anyone else, suspect him to be out of his depth. The thickness of his wallet along with the backup envelope were reassuring to him as he followed their bags through the manicured lawns.

The facia and turrets disappeared high above as they stepped onto the lush carpet, its colour matching the maroon waistcoats. An early evening dusk suspended itself just over the surface of the still loch behind them. As he approached the desk he found himself sucked into a smile even more striking than that of his companion.

'Hello Sir, Madam, my name is Lisa we have everything ready for you.'

'Glad to hear it Lisa.' Tam returned her smile while wondering if she infact actually knew who they were, how could she? Perhaps all the other guests had checked in and she had deduced via elimination. Her face, still framing that smile, moved down toward an unseen screen.

'Ah...' Now this Ah... of hers was at the very least an Ah... of approval but Tam thought it might even have been an Ah... of arousal.

'I see you've reserved the Inchmurrin suite Sir.'

'Yes that's right Lisa, I've heard it's very nice.' He hadn't heard any such thing of course and they both knew it but he was thoroughly enjoying himself. He glanced at Stella but could see no reaction, she seemingly hadn't registered that he had upgraded to a suite. Lisa looked straight at him and then at Stella who was leaning back on reception in a cool manner that he suspected pissed the staff off. Then Lisa looked back at him and his heart literally shot up into his throat. She had somehow managed to expertly convey to him in that instant that she wanted to fuck him.

Lisa was much better looking than her job warranted. He thought she must surely be model material with skin like satin and teeth like headlights. The girl was on another level even from Stella.

'Would you like me to see if I can get you a reservation for the restaurant tonight Sir?' Those headlights of hers made him feel like he was just about to be run over.

'Oh sorry Lisa I didn't realise I would have to make a reservation.' Stella had now moved to the side of the desk and was standing in front of a display cabinet of predictable tourist fodder, pretending to be thoroughly bored. It occurred to Tam that Lisa probably had that same affect on quite a few of the female guests.

'Since Pierre got his third star things have gone a bit crazy.'

'Oh I see, is that him a Major now?' She laughed, and he was as sure as he could be that it was sincere and not out of professional obligation.

'Actually I'm sorry Sir all of the standard tables are gone, we only have Pierre's table left.' He knew very well that Stella was listening to every word and although he didn't actually know how Pierre's table differed to the others he was determined not to embarrass himself.

'That's fine, sit us at Pierre's table then, I just hope his English is better than my French.' The idea of sitting with some French bloke wasn't overly appealing but with nothing for miles it was either that or raid the mini bar. Also, not that money was an issue, but he would certainly expect a table used by the staff to be cheaper than the others. He might be flush but he wasn't for being taken advantage of.

'Very good sir, I'll take care of everything.' Tam suspected that with their location being so close to a heaving metropolis like Glasgow, Lisa would have frequent dealings with guests of his type. Winnings at a bookmaker, drug-money, inheritance, a multitude of scenarios all boiling down to the same thing. People who had come into some money and wanted a taste of the high life, even if just for a weekend.

By now he was easing himself into the wealthy playboy role with nothing less than panache. He returned her smile, managing to reciprocate her earlier unspoken signals and was even able to initiate a blush, which pleased him. He took her to be early twenties like himself and calling him Sir, whilst sounding strange, was definitely turning him on.

'If you follow William Sir, he will show you up to your suite and I'll arrange for your bags to follow shortly.'

'Thanks Lisa.' He wasn't a complete numpty of course, even he knew the receptionist didn't get a tip.

After William had shown how the various electronic gizmos worked, Tam tried to play it cool, resisting the temptation to let his excitement out into the open. He had never set foot in a hotel like this, let alone stayed in a suite. Nonetheless, it was vital he impress Stella and as she hadn't shown any overt signs of excitement he would do the same. Thoughts of Paula came to him. If she were here rather than Stella they would both be jumping up and down, intoxicated by the luxury. There would be no need to play it cool or pretend he wasn't excited.

'Come and see the view.' Her voice came from an adjoining room. When he entered there was no sign of her, but the slightest movement of a thick curtain indicated an unseen balcony. He pulled at the heavy material, searching for a gap and then his face moved out into the freshness of the air. The collar of her blouse fluttered with the wind which was stronger up here than it had been on their arrival.

'You certainly don't see this every day of the week.' As she spoke he decided her own enthusiasm for the view signalled a green light for him to lower his casual pretence slightly. It would have been difficult not to react to such an intoxicating scene as this. The bay in which the hotel nestled was surrounded by looming mountains. They blocked views to either side but not straight ahead. The scene stretched far into the distance under a boundless grey sky. Standing close behind her, he placed his hands gently on her hips. He couldn't stop the flow of blood outward and initially considered backing away, but why should he hide it? He wished they had the kind of relationship where he could simply melt into her right now without any awkwardness. The truth was that with every excuse, every physical avoidance, his paranoia was intensified. He had made incredible progress, but was unable to establish how he truly felt for her until the issue of penile penetration had been resolved. Then, with that out of the way, he could get on with the business of making a choice between her and Paula. That was of course if Paula hadn't ruled herself out of the running.

Standing so close, her body heat ran from his knees to his chest and she didn't seem to be showing any signs of discomfort. Perhaps he should make his move? His state was one of inner turmoil. Should he risk a rejection that could spoil the remainder of the evening? Or should he remain patient and wait for her signal to proceed?

Coconut badger! Coconut badger!

Just as he was about to corkscrew his tongue into her ear she stepped to the side and moved around him with a fluidity of movement akin to a net-bound basketball player.

'I need to unpack my bag and get ready for dinner.' Her tone seemed relaxed enough, but had she sensed the slightest of movements from behind and anticipated he was about to pounce? Perhaps she was simply nervous. In the car during periods of silence he toyed with the fantasy of getting the job done and out of the way before dinner. Perhaps the stiffness of a drink would help her.

'Fancy an aperitif?' He had heard the word once in a movie.

'Yeah whatever you're having.' He moved into the largest of the suite's rooms. It contained a long dining table, a scattering of sofas and a bar, not a mini bar, an actual proper bar. He stepped behind it with disbelief while admiring its optics and bar stools. Pouring large brandies into crystal glasses, he dropped thick ice cubes into each.

'How do they know what we've drank, to charge me?' As he spoke he walked into the wood-panelled bedroom where she unpacked the contents of her bag onto the wide four-poster bed.

'I would think it will be inclusive seeing as it's a suite.'

'Ah of course, that'll be right enough.' He felt annoyed at this mistake but quickly reconciled this with the belief it was an easy one to make. He was sure it hadn't necessarily exposed any shortcomings on his part.

'There you go, cheers.' He passed her the glass and they clinked them together in a toast.

'Cheers Tam.'

It was then that it happened. After drinking from the glass, she placed it down on the bedside cabinet continuing to unpack her bag. The cardboard box landing on the bed made no audible noise but inside Tam's head the impact could be described as deafening. Although she was saying something to him and he could see her lips moving he couldn't hear the words.

'Eh, what was that?' he asked.

Coconut badger! Coconut badger!

'I said why don't we get ready now if we've to be there for nine, that way we can have a look around and get a drink in the bar first.' He didn't even attempt to reply. Silently walking into the en-suite, locking the door he gripped the sink. It was a struggle to keep his weight vertical in its direction rather than horizontal. He had to get a foothold on the situation and formulate his thoughts. There was no way he could have disguised the visual impact on his face when the Tampax had landed on the bed, she must have seen it.

If it was her period then he totally understood it was simply bad timing. Was she meant to decline the invitation? Of course not. However, in view of the excuses to date it was at least a possibility that she in fact wasn't on her period and had orchestrated this in yet another manoeuvre to avoid penetration. His first reaction was to confront her and ask if she ever intended to actually have sex with him. If not, he simply wanted to know why, perhaps there was a perfectly logical explanation. That was what he wanted to say, to be direct and to the point. With his new-found skills he knew it to be within his capability. But his concern was how they could have that conversation and then find a way back. Regardless of how calmly he could deliver it he suspected it would still be a very risky strategy.

***

Despite the inconvenience of her menstruation the evening was going well. One of the regulars back at the pub had sold him a bag of charlie the previous night. Despite his preference being ecstasy he had accepted it, in view of his current financial status. In hindsight he was glad to have taken it. The convincing job he was doing at keeping a brave face on things was in no small part thanks to the alien substance in his bloodstream.

After being greeted warmly by the highly attentive maître d' they were shown toward their table. The restaurant was framed by a contemporary decor that managed not to be distasteful against the backdrop of a country house exterior. Tam walked behind Stella with pride. She looked breathtaking to him. Every inch the aristocrat, a full-length black and sequined couture evening dress cut back to reveal her thoracic curve surrounded by muscle curvature like sand dunes, and those incredible shoulders, so athletic and yet so feminine.

Pierre's table was situated in a far corner near the kitchen, on an elevated section of flooring. A heavily tanned couple were already sitting at one end and immediately Tam understood. This wasn't a table used by staff for their meals; this was in fact the most exclusive table available, the Chef's private dining table.

'Sir, Madam, I will notify Chef you have arrived.' The maître d' was a small man with shiny jet black hair and a pencil moustache. He stood in a permanent bow and didn't seem to establish eye contact with anyone other than his staff. He had an accent Tam couldn't place. The tanned couple smiled at them in the way unknown couples feel obligated to when they cross paths socially. The table was long enough that they could converse either privately or otherwise. Tam was reserving judgement on that option for the time being and the others seemed inclined to do likewise. All communication was non-verbal, friendly smiles bounced backward and forward like a game of mixed doubles. Tam thought they were a good-looking pair, everything about them oozed health and wealth.

Having just rattled a couple of lines in the gents, Tam was sublimely content with the world and everything in it. He allowed himself the luxury of savouring the collective jealousy from the busy restaurant below them. Not only was he sitting at the most exclusive table, his companion was à la carte. Stella slid her hand across the thick linen tablecloth and clasped her fingers around his.

What the fuck is she all about?

The time for analysis would have to wait, no way would he ruin his night by spending the next few hours trying to work out what this meant. Perhaps it was because the tanned couple were holding hands. Or perhaps she simply enjoyed the actual sport of romance, but wasn't overly keen on it becoming a game of contact.

The main kitchen door swung to and fro around a small army of expressionless and industrious waiting staff. Then a side door opened and the Chef approached their table. Pierre was, to put it bluntly, a fat greasy bastard and not at all what Tam was expecting of a revered Celebrity Chef. He spent time first with the tanned couple and then moved across to them explaining his menu, the concepts, and also his sources of inspiration. Tam didn't have a clue what he was on about and for once even Stella seemed out of her depth. Instead, Tam indulged himself in teasing Pierre about Scotland having once beaten France (world champions of the time) both in Glasgow and Paris. Pierre was obviously keen on football and launched into a lengthy explanation of the historical background of the 'Auld Alliance'. He also joked about fellow Frenchman Basil Boli (once employed by Glasgow Rangers) and his infamous head-butt on English hard man Stewart Pearce.

Tam sensed that the chap at the other end of the table was pissed at this extra attention. Stella also seemed impressed at his being able to hold his own with someone like Pierre. All thanks of course, to the international language of football.

Later, when the food arrived, Tam was blown away by its visual impact. It looked more like a work of art than food. Stella smiled back at him – she definitely seemed to be enjoying herself and at ease in his company. Could the Tampax issue be put to one side? It was the timing of it that concerned him, too obviously orchestrated in such a way that he should be in no doubt. It seemed that for reasons as yet to be revealed she wasn't into sex, or at least not with him. Or was it simply a preference to take her time with a new boyfriend, not wanting to rush things? But surely she could articulate that, put his mind at ease. Or was it in fact his place to bring it up? That could easily be placed in the awkward category of conversations, but if things were to carry on like this he knew he would have no choice.

As the evening had progressed, the tanned couple hadn't spoken to them so Tam had left it at that. But as the wine flowed their neighbours' volume levels had increased to the extent that heads were turning from below and Tam was becoming increasingly annoyed. Their evening had gradually degenerated into an argument – at one point the man listed a long inventory of expensive items, apparently a reminder of how grateful his partner should be for her position. Tam could scarcely believe his ears as the man went on to highlight how many younger and more attractive alternatives would gladly take her place. She was certainly getting a hard time and didn't seem to be having much fun.

'This place is amazing Tam, thanks again for bringing me.' Stella attempted to divert his attention as she could see he was getting more and more pissed off.

'It's my pleasure.' This time he slid his hand across the table and into hers, staring intently into her eyes, trying to understand what was going on between them. The maître d' arrived with a complimentary bottle of wine from Pierre's private collection. Having already polished off two from the wine list, this would be their third.

'I'm starting to feel a bit tipsy Tam.' They agreed it would be their last in the interest of avoiding paralysis by hangover in the morning. Tam had arranged some surprises in the form of clay pigeon shooting as well as the hire of a speedboat. Pursuits best to be undertaken with as clear a head as possible.

'Excuse me, I need to powder my nose.' Tam had never heard anyone utter this expresson before, but it suited the occasion. She pulled her hand away from his gently, wiped the corners of her mouth with a napkin and then glided through the lower level. He watched as men and women stared; his chest swelled. After all they weren't to know the difficulties he was having. For all they knew he could be throwing her about like an empty tracksuit.

'Have you any idea how much that ring cost me!'

At this, the tanned woman forced her chair back noisily and followed Stella's winding route through the tables below. Tam could see she was doing her best to hold her tears back from public consumption. The man was much older than Tam, probably late thirties, obviously thought he was a real ticket. Tam felt sorry for the woman, he didn't like the way she was being bullied. He was also annoyed that the ambience of Pierre's table was being impinged upon. The price tag on the table and its associated atmosphere was probably chicken-feed to this guy, but it was a small fortune to Tam. He knew exactly what would happen if Pat were sitting here. He also knew that Pat would be disappointed in him if he chose to do nothing. The old man would want him to explain to the stranger that his behaviour was unacceptable and that to continue would result in serious repercussions.

Coconut badger! Coconut badger!

Tam walked casually to the other end of the table, leaning forward into the man's ear.

'Any argument you've goet wae yer wuman will not be conducted at this fuckin table mate.' The man seemed shocked that someone would challenge him, and stammered something unintelligible, unable to properly despatch the words in his mouth. Tam felt an overwhelming desire to cause the man immediate and significant physical pain. He was also aware however that some of the staff and patrons seemed to have sensed what was going on.

'Wan mare fuckin word oot ay you mate an a swear tae god am gonnae take yer eye oot wae wan ay they spoons. Dae ye get me?' There was no response and although Tam was satisfied the man was fearful, he simply couldn't bring himself to walk away without a physical release of some kind. He was unaware of which had come first as he returned to his seat, the thought or the action. The man's stiff neck stared downward, a thick yellow splodge of phlegm dripping from the side of his face.

Stella returned from the ladies and Tam could see her condition had deteriorated. She had seemed fine going in the other direction, perhaps it was because she was on her feet for the first time in a few hours. Alcohol didn't seem to have any effect on him when he was on the charlie.

Taking a gulp from a newly poured glass of wine, she nodded toward the other end of the table. The man stood to leave without looking once at Tam.

'Must be away to top up his tan before bedtime,' Tam joked and she laughed heartily. It was as though everything he said tonight was either insightful or hilarious. This along with his chemically accelerated heart rate had generated a homeless sexual excitement of sorts. It would have been fine if he had something to work toward like intimacy with a beautiful woman in a five-star suite. It hadn't occured to him earlier but there were to be consequences of his taking charlie. The horn had now been initiated and although he didn't want or invite it, he knew he was stuck with it. It would be an unwanted distraction when they got back to the suite, but it was also messing with his ability to distinguish between reason and fantasy. One such example was the thought that although vaginal penetration was out of the question there may be something else on offer. While swimming in the image of saliva dripping from her chin, his mind did a quick orifice inventory before initiating an even more radical idea. Would she agree to anal? He couldn't actually be sure if he had ever done it. There was the drunken night with Paula when he thought he may have accidentally, but couldn't be sure. In truth it scared him somewhat. He worried about the associated intricacies and etiquette. Perhaps it was a procedure best reserved for those nestled in the comfort and trust that accompanied long-term relationships.

They were now the last guests and all the tables including their own had been cleared. The maître d' without actually looking directly at them had managed to diplomatically convey his wish that they leave so he could fuck off home. Tam concurred, with the realisation Stella was now completely shit-faced.

'What say we finish that bottle off in the suite eh?' Tam asked purely as an encouragement for her to move, in full knowledge she had reached her capacity. She seemed to be struggling to even raise her head to nod in agreement, but managed a wobble before the rubber of her neck released its grip, her chin falling back down onto her chest.

**

Back in the suite, Stella surprised Tam by staggering into the bedroom and rather than collapsing on the bed as expected, managing in autopilot to remove her dress and place it on a hanger. She then stepped from her black lacy thong and climbed under the covers wearing only her backless bra. Tam wanted her so bad he could feel his flesh being melted by the heat from his bones. The Tampax incident had of course been designed to illustrate that sex simply wouldn't have been on the cards even if she had been capable of it. Nonetheless the image of her without pants under the covers, had ensured he would remain wide awake and unbearably horny.

Tam understood that going to bed in such a condition would be a recipe for disaster and closed the bedroom door, deciding to try and ride out the storm. He filled several hours of insomnia with expensive brandy, cigars on the freezing cold balcony and a bout of restless channel surfing. Finally he managed to satisfy himself that the only twinge he felt was one of tiredness.

Opening the bedroom door, a faint light squeezing past the drawn curtains indicated a prelude to sunrise. He undressed, dropping his clothes where they would lie, and slid under the warm covers next to her nakedness. They were back to back but not touching and in a sincere effort to facilitate sleep he pushed his firmness down between his legs, tightened his eyelids and curled into a ball. She moved toward him slightly and they were arse cheek to cheek, her skin so warm and soft that he pulled away quickly. After several minutes though, he could stand the lack of physical contact no longer. Turning to face her, he moved into a cuddled spoon; she didn't flinch.

In this position, there was no getting away from the fact that the end of him was right on her panic button. He knew if the Tampax was a red herring and there were no blockages in the piping a couple of well placed thrusts would be all it would take, but he also knew that was out of the question, no matter how horny he was. What if she were to wake? He could say he was riding a horse in a dream perhaps, or having an epileptic fit, or even that in the dream he was having sex with her and hadn't realised he had somehow crossed the reality divide.

His condition was such that without ejaculation, he knew sleep would be outwith his reach. With each passing minute the early morning light struggled harder to find a way past the thick curtains. He considered leaving the bedroom once again but then quite suddenly and without warning, an image of Pat's sneering face was telling him what he had to do. Very carefully, so as not to wake her, he moved to his knees and pulled back the covers, exposing her lower back and buttocks. He gripped the headboard with his left hand and with the other slowly went to work on himself. After just a few minutes, being careful not to rock the bed, he picked up the pace. Soon after, in a sniper motion, he expertly delivered the entire package onto her upper arse cheek, so as not to drip and stain the sheet with any evidence. He allowed himself the extravagance of using his tip to rub the thick globules into the fleshyness of her perfect buttocks. Then he lay back, licking the spare from the back of his hand.

He was on the threshold of the sleep he so yearned for. Quite inexplicably, as though having no control and operating while under some kind of hypnosis, he stood from the bed. After some searching he eventually found the box, unopened, in the en-suite amongst her paraphernalia. Removing one from its packaging he returned to her fleshy spunk-smeared buttocks. In the same way the maître d' had used his little utensil to wipe their crumbs, he soaked up every last globule from her tablecloth. Then he meticulously replaced it back into the bastard box.

CHAPTER 12

Having arranged to meet Pat at his place around lunchtime, Tam left the Rannoch Moor, stepping onto a frost-covered pavement. A couple of days had passed since the hotel stay and Tam had called in sick yet again. Even accounting for the fact Shergar was shit scared of him he knew carrying on like this would cost him his job for sure. The truth was that after the hotel incident he felt a sense of shame at his behaviour, as well as being worried by it. It was as though a change was taking place in his temperament, one that he had little or no control over. In the distance he could see some commotion, a group of onlookers being held back by Police who had blocked the road on either side of a close.

His mind kept pulling him back to the decision he knew he would soon have to make. Either to continue with the pursuit of Stella or give it up and consider an attempt at resolving things with Paula. There was no doubt in his mind that he missed Paula. Since the visit to Loch Lomond, he couldn't stop thinking about her. He knew he would have had so much more fun if he had taken her instead. The more time he spent considering his situation the clearer it became. He didn't have the same emotional connection with Stella. It seemed to be more to do with hunting her down and achieving the conquest. There was also a part of him that wanted to prove that he could punch above his weight, compete with the likes of Campbell.

Tam could see as he approached the roadblock that he would be unable to pass. He considered whether to wait until the road was reopened or take a lengthy detour to Pat's that involved cutting across some waste ground. He decided to wait, and sent Pat a text to let him know.

Spending time at work was also becoming increasingly difficult for reasons that had nothing to do with Stella. He was struggling with the constant switching between that world and the one in which his mentor resided. In Pat's domain he was his own man and well respected – a fledgling reputation was being cultivated around him. To go from a life where anything seemed possible, to one where he spent his time on something as mundane as cold calling, was becoming more difficult with each passing day.

It certainly wasn't what he had been told to expect when he joined the firm. Others, like Stella, who had arrived around the same time, were being moved into different specialist areas. He had been stuck in the new business section and was beginning to resent this more and more. In view of this, he had been doing some calculations: the money from one more McGregor attack would mean he could resign from the firm.

'Whit's happenin?' Tam asked Jam Jar, one of the pub regulars standing among the spectators.

'Some Bushwaka took ees wife an wains hostage.' Jam Jar was of a heavy set with an acutely pock-marked face as a result of an extreme case of acne in his youth. Short cropped streaky blonde hair sat on a bulbous forehead. The name Jam Jar came from his teenage years when he was known to cover his testicles in the sticky preserve, encouraging stray dogs to remove it with their tongues. Even as an adult he was tracked most places by at least one mongrel. For this reason residents suspected he still indulged in the strange pastime.

'Any idea who it is?' Tam asked.

'Naw nae idea but it's a disgrace if ye ask me, shouldnae be pittin wumen an wains through this kind a shit.'

Tam could see the winter sun reflecting from a familiar bald head among the spectators on the other side of the roadblock.

'Polis don't seem tae huv a fuckin clue whit they're dayin here by the way.'

'How dae ye mean?' Tam asked.

'Well there's nae negotiator fur a start.' It was evident that Jam Jar's expertise on hostage situations was derived from his television set.

'Ur even somebidy oan wan a they megaphones. This lot urnae interested, they've no even sent somebidy up tae the door.' Tam nodded in agreement. All the Police seemed to be doing was observing the scene unfold like the rest of them.

The living-room window of a first-floor flat was opened. Tam recognised the man holding what looked like a machete. His name was Baz, he had been one of the Bushwakas sitting on Tommy Tattoo's sofa the night he was slashed by Pat. Baz shouted down onto the street.

'She widnae let me see ma wains! A jist waanted tae see ma wains that's aw!' After an uncomfortable delay a uniformed policeman with grey hair and a matching moustache stepped forward into no man's land at the entrance of the close. It would seem he was the only officer willing to take the initiative.

'Calm yirself doon son, moan doonstairs so we kin talk things through eh.'

'But whit aboot ma wains?' Baz's voice crackled with emotion.

'The quicker ye come doon the better it'll be fur ye son.' You didn't need to have a degree in social services to work out it would be a long time before this guy would be allowed to see his kids again. Every spectator knew it; the Police knew it; Baz himself must have known it. He was younger than Tam and wearing a white tracksuit top zipped to the chin. Tam thought he didn't even look old enough to have kids.

'A need tae see the lassie an the wains, tae make sure they're awright, kin ye bring them tae the windae fur me son.' The policeman removed his hat, wiping his brow with a sleeve. He knew that by being the only one to step up he was putting his neck on the line if things deteriorated.

'A wid never herm ma wains neether a wid.'

'Where's the lassie son?' Baz didn't answer but at the mention of her his face contorted with hatred.

'A said where's the lassie son?' The cop was trying to strike a balance between being insistent in that he needed an answer, but not aggravating things any further.

'Naw ma wains ur awright, but that fuckin slag's gettin it.' He turned away from the window, moving into the room out of sight where a woman could be heard screaming. The officers stared back at each other blankly. They were waiting for an armed response vehicle and none of them seemed willing to use their batons to confront a mad man with a machete. Apparently they were prepared to wait through the screams.

Pat's bald head broke the line of spectators, sprinting past the stationary Police into the mouth of the close. Tam didn't even have time to think. He and Pat were soon standing shoulder-to-shoulder, directing the soles of their shoes fast and hard under the Yale lock. The frame quickly submitted and the door snapped inward. The woman's screams met them as they raced up the hallway. In the living room, two young children, both girls, were sitting in a corner of the room playing with toy groceries and a cash register. It was as though they had simply blocked out everything that was going on around them. The young mother was curled up on the sofa, frantically emptying her lungs in staccato screams as the man towered over her. He turned, probably expecting to see Police.

'Whit you dayin here Pat?'

'Whit did a tell you cunts aboot takin liberties?'

'She widnae let me see ma wains, whit else could a dae?'

'Put the blade doon right noo, or you'll be sorry, a gurantee it.'

'Am no scared ay ye Pat, stye back ur al take er fuckin heed aff so a will, am tellin ye.'

Although the man tried to turn in such a way he could strike Pat with the long blade, it was too late. Pat had moved so quickly, he had surprise on his side, throwing his arms around Baz's upper body so that they both crashed to the floor. Pat had Baz's ear in his mouth, clamping his teeth shut. Tam could see Baz was still holding the machete so rushed forward grabbing his hand, but was unable to release his grip from the blood soaked-handle. With

Pat lying on the floor on one side of Baz, Tam moved to the space on his other side. He gripped the windowsill for balance, lifting his knee and with as much force as he could muster he drilled his heel into Baz's left eye socket. Crunch after crunch he pushed his foot downward until soon he lost himself. He had forgotten the objective had simply been to cause sufficient discomfort to release the grip on the machete. A hood had been dropped over his head, thrusting him into a lustful frenzy of violence. Pat had managed to sever the ear and spat it out onto the carpet. The old man wrestled Tam away from the mess, seconds before the room filled with guns.

***

Pat stood at his window, pouring generous measures of whisky into coffee mugs. The afternoon had turned to early evening as the upper section of an orange sun prepared to dip behind the darkening horizon. He and Tam had just returned from the local Police Station.

'There ye go son, get that doon ye. Thanks again fur backin me up, if it wisnae fur you ad a been oan ma tod. As per usual the Polis wur aboot as much use as a chocolate teapot.' Pat raised his mug in an appreciative toast.

'Och it wis nothin ataw neer it wis.' Tam felt a mixture of pride and confusion. He still wasn't sure exactly what had happened and why, it was as though he had blacked out. His behaviour was steadily deteriorating, as though a dark force in the shadows could no longer be resisted.

'It fuckin is somethin son, of aw they people ootside that close, you were the only wan thit followed me in. Ye helped save that poor wumin's life so ye did, ye should be proud ay yersel.' Pat opened his tobacco tin, removing two cigarette papers. Tam had noticed when he arrived a dog's face peering out from behind the sofa.

'A thought yer dug died?' Tam asked.

'It did, that's a new wan.' Pat sprinkled tobacco into both papers on the windowsill carefully as he spoke.

'Cheeky bastards, tryin tae charge us!'

'Dae ye think there'll be any comeback?' Tam asked; with Baz having lost an ear and also an eye in the attack, Tam had been told they may be looking at serious assault, possibly even attempted murder.

'The guy's gonnae chop ees mrs up intae wee pieces, we save ur life cos they're too feart tae dae anythin aboot it. An they waant tae charge us! Whit's that aw aboot?' Pat's reaction was a combination of both hilarity and incredulity.

'Naw son don't you worry yersell, a used ma phone call tae talk tae McGregor, he said he wid sort it fur us.' Within an hour of that conversation, both men had been released without charge. Adding to the persuasion could have been the group of indignant residents congregating outside the Station. There had almost been a riot on the Monkford when Police had marched Pat and Tam into a van, handcuffed. People couldn't make sense of how heroes could be treated in such a way. Then again not many of them got a proper look at the state of Baz as he was stretchered into the ambulance. The woman was in better condition and after stitches had been released to pick up her kids from social services.

Warmed by the whisky, both men stood in silence. Tam could feel Pat's eyes on him and without having to look, somehow sensed he was smiling widely. He suspected that from the second he was pulled away from the gaping eye socket, Pat had been bursting with pride. He had demonstrated the type of behaviour that was pleasing to the old man.

'By the way a meant tae ask ye, where did ye put that razor a geed ye?' Pat passed him a roll-up.

'Eh it's in the hoose.' The incident at work with Shergar had demonstrated to Tam that the mere sight of the thing could cause terror, but he didn't feel comfortable carrying it around with him.

'Huv ye thought aboot whit it wid be like tae use it oan somebody, in the flesh so tae speak?' Pat's smile was one of villainous irony.

'Don't think it's ma cup a tea tae be honest.' Tam had suspected this to be the case – Pat had wanted him to use it all along, why else would he have given it to him?

'A think ye could dae it.' On the one hand Tam was fearful at where this was going, but he also felt a pride of sorts. He wanted to have what it takes, he wanted to show his mentor, he wanted to impress. There was some more silence, and it was evident to Tam that Pat had something on his mind.

'So wid ye be up fur geein it a go then?'

'Geein whit a go?' Tam slurped the last of his whisky with a grimace and Pat refilled both mugs.

'A waant ye tae slash the next name we get fae McGregor.' Trepidation curled across Tam's face, and the old man took a long drag on his roll-up. Silence filled the room around them. Once again it occurred to Tam that whenever he was with Pat, he felt everything was possible, that he was capable of anything. He knew he didn't want to slash anyone but in some way felt obligated to take the suggestion seriously, after everything Pat had done for him. Besides, the targets were scum liberty takers who deserved it; it wasn't like he would be slashing someone innocent.

'Noo a don't waant ye tae be gettin yersel aw stressed oot thinkin that a wid throw ye intae the deep end, cos a widnae dae that tae ye son. Naw a wid train ye first, show ye the ropes.' Pat spoke in a matter-of-fact way, as though talking about a golf swing. The strangest thing occured to Tam just then, he was perfectly calm.

***

Tam had made the call. It was time to make the decision he had been putting off: he had no more time for Stella's games. He understood now that she had been nothing more than a distraction and that it had been his childhood sweetheart he wanted all along. Of course, he knew Paula would be completely within her rights to tell him where to go. He had taken her for granted far too long.

The afternoon light hung heavy below low clouds, newly opened and releasing a vertical rain. Tam and Paula had arranged to meet at the busy supermarket cafe on the outskirts of the scheme. He arrived first, finding a vacant table and clearing away some plates. Looking out onto the car park, he watched shoppers rushing to and from their cars for shelter from the onslaught.

'Ye been waitin long?' she asked.

'Naw jist five minutes.' The cafe was long and narrow, running along the front of the building with an entrance at either end. She must have come in the one behind as he hadn't seen her approach.

'A goet ye wan ay they flavoured teas ye like.'

'Thanks.' She smiled with an apprehension he couldn't quite read. 'Ye been busy wae yer work?' she asked, removing her burgundy beret with matching scarf and gloves.

'Am actually thinkin aboot wrappin it tae be honest.'

'A thought ye said ye liked it?'

'A did tae start wae but it's always the same thing day in day oot, constant cold callin, dayin ma nut right in so it is. They telt me at the start that a wid be able tae move intae another section efter a while, turns oot they were talkin a lot a shite basically.' He scanned her face carefully. Those piercing eyes grey in the dull light, she was beautiful there was no doubting it, why had it taken him so long to make this decision?

'How dae ye know they're lyin tae ye?' She blew softly on the rim of her teacup.

'It's aw the ex Uni wans that huv been gettin moved oan ye see, a don't think ma face fits. Besides av been dayin a wee bit a work wae Pat so a might jist concentrate oan that, the monies better anywye.'

'Whit oor Pat, fae the Monkford?'

'Aye that's right.' Tam's tone was a defensive one.

'Jist be careful, ma Da always said he's no right in the heed that yin.'

'Yer Da's right, but ees heart's in the right place wance ye get tae know em.' Pupils from the high school they had both attended descended in swarms for their lunch. He found it strange to see that same uniform again. Boys showing off and girls in their short skirts, fleshy upper legs turned purple by the biting cold. He realised he should get on with it; it was time to deliver his well-rehearsed speech.

'A couldnae wait furever Tam ye know that daint ye.' She looked out onto the wet landscape as she spoke, not meeting his eye.

'Wait furever fur whit, whit ye oan aboot?'

'Well we've been pals fur a long time, an then when we goet aulder an we started sleepin the gether, a thought we would still be friends but somethin chynged efter that.'

'How dae ye mean?'

'Well, efter we started sleepin the gether a thought we wid become...'

'A couple?' Tam smiled at her awkwardness as well as the realisation that she might be about to save him the trouble of delivering his speech.

'Aye that's right, a couple.' Those angelic eyes seemed on the verge of tears and her face held a defiance that worried him. 'And whit's so bad aboot that?'

She must have misinterpreted his smile, which hadn't been mocking in nature. He attempted to appease. 'Naw am no sayin there's anything wrang wae that, far from it...'

'So why hus it never happened then? Why huv ye only ever used me fur sex?'

He decided he would try his best to explain. 'Well tae be honest a always thought you wur awright wae things the wye they wur. We huv a good laugh, we enjoy wan anothers' company, we

141

obviously fancy each other.' He was lying of course; he had always known she was never okay with sex outside the reassuring walls of a relationship. Her never having said anything until now had simply allowed him to continue unchecked; of course, he couldn't tell her that. This thing with Stella had shown him that he now wanted the full package with Paula. Frequent texts, monitoring the other's movements, developing relationships with her family and friends, agreements of exclusivity, he wanted the works.

'Aw a ever did wis love ye Tam, an a thought you felt somethin fur me anaw.' Whichever barrier had been holding back the tears now disintegrated, like the rain outside filling the cracked tarmac. He pulled a napkin from the dispenser, reaching across to wipe at the moistness seeping down her cheeks. She pulled back sharply. She had been wounded badly by his behaviour, he could see that now, this was without her even having the full picture. If she knew about Stella god only knows what her reaction would be. He had always known he was taking the piss but in those perfect eyes he could now see that she was broken and needed to be fixed.

'Huv ye been seein somebody else?' She asked the question while folding the napkin into a triangle and dabbing at her lower eyelids in an attempt to avoid make-up run. He wanted desperately to be honest but knew that was too high-risk a strategy.

'Naw, there's no been naebody else.' What could he do? If she knew what had been going on he would have blown it for sure. He began to quickly formulate in his mind how he would word his effective U-turn. He did want the same thing. He would tell her that and also explain how sorry he was for all the hurt he had caused. But before he could speak the wind of their conversation seemed to change direction, as did her body language.

'Well av been asked oot by somebidy else and av agreed, as a said tae ye a couldnae wait furever.' Her back straighter now, in a swift motion she lifted the cup to her face finishing the tea, a movement that indicated as far she was concerned the meeting was concluded.

'Who?' Fire spread across his chest as jealous rage fanned the flames of his male pride, despite knowing he had no right.

'A don't see how that's any uv your business neer a dae, you hid enough chances did ye no?' She stood from the table, looking out onto the car park. The rain had eased during their conversation but the low ceiling of cloud cast a dim light across the scene. His initial reactions were confusions and muddles. He wanted to find out who it was so he could put his new-found skills to work. He also wanted to convince her she shouldn't go out with anyone other than him. It was important that he didn't seem to be begging or desperate though. In addition, he understood she would be completely justified to cut him loose and felt genuine sorrow for how he had treated her.

'A um really sorry fur messin ye aboot Paula.' She took a couple of steps away and then hesitated, turned and leaned forward to kiss him goodbye on the cheek. Turning his face to meet her at the last moment with his lips, he reached up with both hands holding her head tight. He pressed his lips hard against hers feeling only bone and lip balm in a defiantly closed mouth, then she was gone.

CHAPTER 13

As arranged, Tam had walked up to the Hill in order to meet Pat in the quiet Quadrant area. The now-deserted flats had also been earmarked for demolition. Walking out the back of one of the closes brought Tam into a large enclosed triangular space the shape of a baseball field. Every close had its own slabbed backyard and bin shed, each of which was fenced off from the other. In the middle section was a spongy floored playground of swings, climbing frames and see-saws. It was an eerie space even in daylight, but at night it took on a new and sinister dimension.

Tam waited on a bench next to the playground as the scene around him bathed in a bright moonlight. His thoughts were of Paula. Or more specifically, he was experiencing an intense anger at how much of a fool he had been. She was there for the taking all this time and as soon as he decided to claim her she was gone, snapped up by someone else.

'Awright ma man how ye dayin?' Tam turned, startled by Pat's voice as he hadn't heard him approach across the playground.

'Ye gave me a fright there.'

'Sorry a didnae mean tae.' Tam stood from the bench, stepping onto the spongy floor. Pat carried a white plastic bag which Tam suspected must be booze of some description, probably whisky. The premise of the meet was to get Tam ready for his first slashing but the accompanying refreshments weren't a surprise. The old man placed the plastic bag on top of a ladder at the back of a metal-framed space shuttle. He began to bounce slightly on the soft surface beneath him.

'Fuckin weird walkin oan this stuff is it no?'

'Aye it's so the wains don't gee therselves a sore heed intit,' Tam replied.

Pat grinned. 'Talkin aboot people gettin sore heeds did ye

bring yer razor?' Tam removed it from his trouser pocket and held it out in the palm of his right hand.

'Naw you hing oan tae that yin, that wis a present.' Pat was holding the other of the matching pair. Tam hadn't noticed its removal.

'Right so let's start oaf wae the actual openin ay the thing. Hus tae be done wae the wan hawn, ye cannae be usin baith hawns, that's fur baw bag amateurs.' Pat demonstrated a light grip-and-swivel manoeuvre that split the blade from the handle. Tam could light a zippo one handed and was able to use the same technique: as a result he mastered the movement fairly quickly.

Pat removed his tobacco tin from a pocket before walking to the space rocket, taking an item from the plastic bag. In the moonlight, Tam couldn't make out what it was. Pat used both hands to position the object at eye level, just below the tail of the shuttle at the top of the ladder.

'Right ye are then, come oor here an huv a gander at this bad boay.' Tam moved closer; as the outline came into view he had to do a double take and catch his breath.

'Whit the fuck is that!' As Tam spoke, Pat patted the object with his right hand. It made a slapping sound.

'It's a pig's heed whit did ye think it wis?' In the moonlight as he had approached, for a split second Tam had thought it was a human head.

'Whit ur ye dayin way a pig's heed?'

Pat reached out, gripping the top rung of the ladder for support as he doubled over himself in laughter. 'It's fur ye tae practice oan ya dafty, whit did ye think a wis gonnae dae, stick an apple in its mooth and roast it?' Pat managed to compose himself and straightened his posture in preparation.

'Originally a wis gonnae use a waater melon ur somethin, but a saw the bold yin here in a butcher's windae and a thought tae maself, that'll dae the joab much better. Disnae get any mare realistic than that son.' Pat positioned himself in front of their overgrown guinea pig, motioning Tam to come closer.

'Right, enough cerry oan this is serious business, so efter yuv split the blade fae the hawnle ye grip the back rim ay the blade like so.' Pat waited for Tam to copy.

'Like that?'

'Aye that's it, jist like yer hawdin a pencil.'

'Then ye push the tip ay the blade intae the tap a where ye waant the openin tae start fae. Ye waant tae be gawn doon the wye, noo up ur sidewise.' Pat pushed the tip of his blade into the upper area of the pig's face on the left side.

'It's important ye make yer move quick, cannae be wastin time, straight efter yuv shoved in the tip ye need tae go fur it.' Pat looked at Tam to ensure he was following and then back at the pig. In a flash he made a twisting movement with his wrist. The slice ran in a long angular line down the entire side of the head beyond the jaw.

'Right, your turn.' Tam moved forward hesitantly.

'It's awright son this yins no gonnae cause ye any problems a widnae think, c'moan.' Pat smiled reassuringly and Tam proceeded to replicate his movement on the other side of the head. Pushing the tip into the hard flesh at the upper section and then quickly twisting his wrist while pulling down trying to make as long a line as possible. The blade had moved so effortlessly, Tam was unsure if he had in fact done it properly. A knife would have been a rowing boat in a swamp compared to the apparent ease with which the razor had slid through the hard flesh.

'That's a dillion son, look it the line.' Both men leaned in, studying the wound Tam had inflicted, each visualising it on an actual target.

'An the bold yin here's probably been in and oot the freezer a few times so the skin's gonnae be tough oor the flesh. No like somebidy's coupon, aw soft an waarm. Naw son yur blade'll cut a face so easy ye wulnae believe it neer ye will.' Tam stared at the length and depth of the line he had just created. Based on what he had witnessed with Pat's previous attacks he could imagine the extent of the damage that would have been inflicted on a human face. He was still unsure if he would be capable, no matter the crimes they were guilty of. A memory came to Tam of a scene from a western he had once watched. An ageing gunslinger and his young apprentice shooting at cans in a dusty yard. The younger man rushing forward excitedly to check the number of hits. The older cowboy watching, a face overcast by nostalgia.

***

The night air was bitterly cold but it was dry thankfully as Tam and Pat stood among the unsuspecting revellers on Sauchiehall Street, searching the oncoming traffic for McGregor's car. The second target had been identified as Spud McPherson of the Springtown Tongs. He was to be attacked in the city centre rather than on his home turf. That decision had been made by McGregor and Pat didn't seem best pleased.

'A don't see how we huv tae dae this yin in the toon, whit's that aw aboot?' Pat spat the words into the freezing air; McGregor being ten minutes late also seemed to have aggravated his mood.

'So how come we're no dayin it oor in Springtoon then?' Tam's nausea was ramping up in severity and his words were delivered between bursts of shivering that had little to do with the cold.

Coconut Badger! Coconut Badger!

'McGregor said he wisnae happy cos a done Blondie in front ay the locals. Said he waanted them done discreet fae noo oan. A mean he's the wan thit said he waanted tae make a statement dinte? A wid a thought dayin them oan their ayn schemes wid be better.' Tam could sense a deterioration in relations between Pat and McGregor. It made him uncomfortable as he could see the DCI was not a man to get on the wrong side of. Then again, neither was Pat. Like walking a tightrope Tam would have to try and somehow strike a balance, facilitating good relations between them.

'Maybe it makes it mare difficult fur him tae make sure we don't get lifted if there ur witnesses.' Pat stared at him and Tam immediately averted his eyes; he couldn't return that stare.

'Jist remember son, am the wan runnin this show no that fat bastard.'

'A know that Pat, am jist sayin.'

'Well don't, an remember not a word tae McGregor aboot you dayin this wan. That wid jist gee the big sweety wife somethin else tae moan aboot.' For the briefest of moments, Tam considered deliberately letting slip in front of the DCI.

McGregor double-parked directly in front of them on the busy street, making no effort to find a parking space. He sat there with his hazards on as a queue of traffic formed behind him unable to pass. A few vehicles blasted their horns but were completely ignored. As Tam stepped toward the back door he could see the shaking fist of the driver directly behind, who had removed his seat belt. The stranger seemed to be considering embarking on some road rage. Tam knew the man's evening was likely to take a serious turn for the worse if the sole of his shoe touched the tarmac.

'Whit ye dayin keepin is hingin aboot fur? It's fuckin baltic.' Pat made no effort to disguise his annoyance. The tension between the two was making Tam almost as nervous as his responsibilities for the evening. He couldn't even bring himself to consider the ramifications of the two men falling out.

'Aye awright keep yer hair oan, a goet held up wae somethin back at the Station dinta.' Tam was unclear on whether that had been a deliberate pun directed at Pat's baldness. Either way he could see slight vibrating and twitching in the muscles at the back of Pat's neck. He was pretending to ignore the DCI, looking out of the window instead. They spent the next ten minutes or so travelling directionless within the city centre one-way system. McGregor gave them some background on the recent details of Spud McPherson's liberty taking. They pulled in across the street from a busy sports bar, engine running, headlights off. It was the kind of establishment that was busy seven nights a week. As with the first job, the thick brown envelope containing payment was passed back to Tam. Then the DCI opened a folder with a head shot of Spud.

Pat continued to stare out of the window and McGregor shook his head in frustration, handing the folder to Tam. He surmised that the younger man must be doing the spotting again. According to the DCI's intelligence, Spud was on the stag night of his soon-to-be brother-in-law. The stag was a decent sort so McGregor didn't expect any other Tongs to be in attendance. It was a similar story to the other low-life scum. Like the Monkford Bushwakas and the Clarendon Monks, the Springtown Tongs were described by McGregor as a constant scourge of local residents. He also reported that since the Blondie McAvoy attack there had been a marked reduction in gang activity on the Clarendon. It would seem his plan was working, not city wide perhaps but one scheme at a time. Tam wondered how many schemes and gangs there actually were in the city. After some quick mental arithmetic, he calculated that he could end up a very wealthy young man. Provided he could prove his worth, of course.

'Right then, ur yees ready?' McGregor twisted to face Tam as Pat was still facing out the window.

'Aye, we ur.' Tam replied, the adrenal dump that had subsided during their conversation returned. Its output seemed to increase, accompanied by a tight chest and a numbness around the throat.

Coconut Badger! Coconut Badger!

Pat opened his door, speaking to McGregor through the back of his head.

'Don't bother waitin fur is oan this yin, me an the boay ur goan fur a few bevies efter it's done.' As they crossed the street approaching the unsuspecting door staff, Tam could feel McGregor's eyes following them. Fortunately the door policy of this particular establishment wasn't ageist. Their only concern was generating as much turnover as possible. Provided you could walk and had money to spend you were welcome. T a m was despatched to the bar as Pat looked for a suitable vantage point. He had no cash other than what was inside the brown envelope. Realising this, he had to open it discreetly and extract a note without removing the package from his jacket.

When he found the old man again, he was standing in a corner on a raised level that overlooked most of the bar below. Tam passed him a pint and also a half. Pat left a foam moustache on his top lip and as Tam raised his own pint to his mouth he was aware of a slight tremor working its way from his elbow to wrist, so he used the other hand also in order to steady the glass. Pat looked immediately at the second hand being used, somehow aware of its significance.

'You awright?'

'Aye, wee bit nervous but am awright.' Pat continued to look at Tam's hand each time he raised his glass, as though monitoring any tremor.

'So describe tae me specifically how yer feelin.'

'The usual Pat, feel like am gonnae be sick.'

'And huv ye been dayin whit a telt ye tae?'

'Aye a huv, a jist keep repeatin the memory tae maself and focussin oan it as soon as a feel any sickness.' Tam used both hands to place his pint on the ledge.

'Well it's been workin up tae noo so there's nae reason why it shouldnae work fur ye the night. It gets easier every time, soon enough you'll no even need the memory, sooner than ye think. That sickness'll get less an less until eventually it'll jist stoap aw the gether.' Tam was struck by the fatherly tone of Pat's voice, managing to strike a balance between tenderness and authority.

Coconut Badger! Coconut Badger!

Not only did he repeat the words inside his head this time, in view of the test ahead he attempted to go a stage further. He tried to replicate the words using his father's actual voice. Pitch perfect placement of the screaming, just as the bedroom wall took the last thrusting thud from the parental headboard.

'Jist remember whit a great joab ye did oan that pig's heed son eh. Nae difference here neer there is, if anythin this yin's gonnae open up a lot easier, much softer than the pig. It'll be like the difference between a ripe peach and an auld leather handbag so it will.' Pat took a few steps away, resuming the siphoning of his pint. He seemed to be giving Tam the space to get himself in the zone as it were. In the continued interests of maximum efficiency, Tam instructed his memory to bridge the divide between audio and visual. After the last headboard thrust he despatched his mind's eye, allowing it to levitate over the adjoining wall. He was now looking down on their post-coital moisture of an embrace.

'That's him oor there.' Tam nodded discreetly in the direction of a group at a table on the other side of the bar. There were roughly ten of them, on the shots, obviously well gone.

'Whit wan issy?' Pat had to ask, having not looked at the surveillance shot while in the car.

'The fat wan stawnin up, see em, oor there.' Tam couldn't point for obvious reasons and Pat's eyesight wasn't the greatest.

'A cannae see em, disnae matter anywye it's you thit needs tae see em no me, is he pished?'

'Aye, a think so.'

'Good, that'll make it even easier fur ye so it will.' For Tam, this comment inadvertently compounded the feelings of pressure. If he were to be unsuccessful with such an easy target that would make it even more of an embarrassment. Spud McPherson didn't look much older than Tam, early to mid twenties. His almost freakishly large head was ably supported by a rotund torso. He had short cropped brown hair with a small fringe gelled to his forehead. His face had a dark shade to it, due to being covered in a high number of freckles. The remaining features were standard issue with the exception of his mouth, which was very wide and seemed to be suffering from an uncomfortable protrusion of teeth.

'So am gonnae wait fur em tae go intae the bog right?' On the one hand Tam was dreading it, but on the other he knew the sooner he could get it done and out of the way the better he would feel. When he wasn't repeating his mantra he was reminding himself the guy was scum and deserved everything he had coming.

'Aye that's right, nae point drawin attention tae urselves in here, there'll be cameras fur sure. Mare privacy the better, It'll be easier fur ye that wye.' Again more references to how easy this should be, he made it all sound so simple. With reassurances ringing in his ears, Tam readied himself.

'Right that's him makin a move, al see ye when a come back oot Pat.' Spud staggered toward the gents and Tam manouvered his way through the groups of drinkers, trying to time his arrival so that he would be close behind the target. On entering the gents, Tam could see things had been complicated by Spud going into a cubicle. Had he stood at a urinal this would have afforded maximum access to the side of his moon-like face. Tam also realised that Pat had entered behind him. That hadn't been discussed; he had anticipated he would be on his own. Was this because of the hand tremor? Didn't Pat have confidence in him? Rather than reassure, it had the opposite effect. How could he hope to perform to satisfaction with the old man watching every move?

Pat leaned forward over a sink, studying his fleshy face in the mirror. He ran a tap, placing his wrists under the water while watching events unfold carefully. Tam looked from the only closed cubicle door over to a couple of guys pissing at the urinals. Standing statue-like in a male toilet will always draw attention. So despite not feeling the need, Tam moved to a vacant urinal at the far end, flopping himself hopelessly into the fresh air. After some small talk between the two strangers and a couple of shakes, they were gone.

Pat moved to the door so as to stop anyone from entering and Tam stood ready next to the cubicle. His razor was extended, ready and waiting to open up a real target. One who hadn't spent the last few days in a freezer. He looked over at Pat and raised his foot as if to say silently should I kick the door in. Pat shook his head, indicating he should wait for Spud to come out voluntarily.

'Ye need tae come back in ten minutes ur use the ladies, wuv goet a burst pipe.' Pat barked the words from the doorway while obstructing the path and view of the person trying to enter. It seemed to do the trick and they were left alone again.

'Hey you in the cubicle, am the manager, this place is gonnae flood in a minute ye need tae get oot ay there, am gonnae huv tae shut it fur a bit.' Pat obviously wanted to hurry things along.

'Whit! kin ye no jist let me finish fur fuck sake?'

'Naw a cannae, an if yer no oot in ten seconds you an yer pals ur gettin lobbed oot, c'moan am no messin aboot.' Pat nodded at Tam to ready himself.

'Kin a use the flush?'

'Naw ye cannae, jist fuckin hurry up.' There followed the noise of a belt buckle and some mumbled complaints before the door opened and out stepped the larger-than-life target. Looking straight ahead, he saw Pat but hadn't seen Tam to his left who had the perfect vantage point. The side of his face was right there. Tam tried to lift his arm. The neural impulses were despatched but for some reason nothing happened. The nausea was gone; he was in the eye of the storm, relaxed, calm. Coconut Badger had worked yet again, so he couldn't blame that. But something operating outwith his control was stopping him. He wanted to please Pat desperately, to repay him for everything he had done, but something didn't feel right. No matter what Spud was guilty of, would this make Tam just as bad? Take him down to that level? How would Lina feel if she found out? He knew she would be disgusted, as would his parents, and Paula. In the split seconds he was trying to overcome these uninvited thoughts, Spud turned, looking directly at him. First Spud looked at Tam's face and then down at the razor. The scene was being played back to Tam in slow motion, but he could see Spud was pretty agile for a big bloke. His body mass spun and he pulled his arm backward into a clenched fist.

Tam hadn't even been aware of Pat making any movement, but before Spud had the chance to pull the trigger and despatch his fist the old man had pushed him back into the cubicle. Spud managed to steady himself, gripping on the empty loo roll canister. Quickly he shifted his weight, preparing to spring back out of the cubicle. Pat was too quick for him though and had launched himself in order to put maximum velocity behind the downward gravity pull of his body weight. He extended his arm toward Spud's face. It wasn't until a split second before impact that Tam realised Pat's razor must have been ready for action all along, just in case.

The only noise Tam heard was the thump of Pat's feet landing on the floor and echoing around their porcelain chamber. Spud fell backward into the cubicle and the left side of his face fell through his fingers like sand. Regaining his balance, Pat threw the razor quickly into his other hand and went to work on the other side with equal devastation. Tam had never seen him do both sides and he seemed to be in more of a rage than was usual. Perhaps his anger at Tam was being projected onto Spud in the form of geometric symmetry.

Spud hadn't made a noise. Sitting on the piss-drenched cubicle floor he seemed to be confused somehow, in shock perhaps. Both chubby hands reached up to his head, which was completely saturated in a thick jam-like substance. Stumpy fingers were pushed into gaps where once there had been face. Pat then aimed a few well-placed heel thrusts around the wounds to open them further. Turning, he took Tam's arm, indicating it was time to leave.

***

There had been no celebratory drinks after the attack as Pat had promised, and Tam was consumed by a need to apologise for his failure. He suggested that perhaps it would be for the best if Pat took care of the razor side with him assisting from the sidelines in future. Pat surprised Tam by claiming he wasn't angry. He said he blamed himself, for not having prepared his protégé adequately.

The taxi driver had been as confused as Tam when Pat asked to be taken to the tower block on The Hill, and Pat snapped at him, saying he was fully aware it was uninhabited. So in the late evening winter chill, both men were left standing at the base of the redundant tower block. It climbed high into the sky above them as they each stared at the cab, waiting for it to dissapear. As soon as the red glow of the tail lamps were out of sight, Pat turned to Tam.

'Right ye are then son, nae point dwellin oan whit happened, a bit mare practice fur ye. Follow me, an watch yer step it's dark in here.' Pat used his key to unlock the perimeter fence and Tam followed behind.

'A don't see how pigs' heeds ur gonnae make any difference Pat. Av already tried it kin we no jist call it a day, a don't think am cut oot for aw this slashin stuff tae be honest.'

It felt to Tam as if an important crossroads was being traversed. Pat's world wasn't for him, with its extreme violence, risks, never-ending uncertainty. A big part of him was yearning for a return to his old world with its safety, security and Paula.

'Nae mare pigs' heeds fur you fae noo oan son, that wis a fuckin stupid idea in the first place.' Each landing on the way up the stairwell had a horizontal slant of frosted glass, offering them just enough moonlight to proceed.

'Whit you need tae be practisin oan is the real thing.' Pat stopped and looked back at Tam with a wide and sinister smile.

'Kin we no jist leave it till the morra? We kin huv a proper chat then so we kin.' Tam wasn't hopeful as he spoke the words.

'Naw we cannae jist leave it till the morra. It's important ye don't sleep oan it trust me. Wance yuv done it that's it oot

155

the road, then it'll be nae big deal fae noo oan a promise ye.'
Pat continued to climb the stairs and Tam followed. He didn't want to do it, but didn't know how to refuse the old man. As they continued to climb, it occured to him for the first time how unusual a location this was for a target.

'Ur ye sayin that wan ay McGregor's names is in here then?'

'Eh, aye that's right but this wan's different so he is, McGregor delivered this wan eeself.'

'How dae ye mean he delivered em?' Tam was confused.

'Like a say, some scumbag fae a gang somewhere. Rether than takin us tae him he delivered this wan. So he's tied up waitin fur us tae arrive an dae the business. He's no gonnae come bouncing oot some cubicle, naw this wan's gonnae be nice an easy fur yer furst time. Nae bother ataw, shoulda probably done this wan first wae hindsight.'

'Whit's ees name?' Tam asked.

'Eh, whit dae ye mean?'

'A mean, whit's the guy's name?'

'Och a cannae remember, whit dis it matter tae us anywye?' Tam wasn't sure what it was, but he knew something wasn't right. Pat led him from the stairwell and after leaning against the wall briefly to catch his breath, moved down to the last door at the end of the narrow landing. Tam noticed as he passed each of the flats that most tenants had left their nameplates behind. At the door Pat unlocked the padlock and turned to face him, speaking in a whisper.

'Listen tae me carefully son, McGregor disnae waant this yin tae know anything aboot where he's been held ur whose dunnit ur anythin, so when were in here dayin the business, nae talkin.'

'Pat, a really don't waant tae dae it neer a dae.'

'Ye'll be fine son trust me.'

'Naw am no sayin a cannae dae it. Am sayin a don't waant tae dae it.' For the first time and in a moment of clarity, Tam knew the difference between the two. He just needed to make the old man understand.

'This guy is pure scum, jist like the rest ay them so he is, disnae deserve any mercy son.' Pat evidently wasn't hearing what he was trying to tell him and pushed him hurriedly into the darkness of the hallway. The layout was familiar to Tam with the long straight hall, two bedrooms to the left, kitchen and bathroom to the right and living room at the far end. The front room windows were the only ones boarded so the moon cast a light in through the two bedrooms to their left. It covered the hall floor in front of them, helping Tam with the placing of his steps. When they reached the living room, Pat picked up a torch that had been propped in the corner and as he flicked it on Tam heard a whimper from the centre of the room.

The man had his back to them and was tied around the chest and ankles to a kitchen chair weighted down by bits of concrete. His wrists were bound and he was gagged and blindfolded. As Tam approached the man and his whimpering increased, Pat put his finger to his lips reminding Tam not to speak. He indicated to his reluctant student in a downward slashing motion that he wanted him to get on with it quickly, immediately in fact.

Tam removed his razor, holding it out for Pat to take from him but the old man shook his head in a firm refusal. Tam didn't want to do it but simply couldn't escape from the sense that he owed Pat so much for everything he had done. The man had obviously heard their movements and his whimpering increased.

He's pure scum, why should I care anyway...

The man's condition was confusing to Tam. He looked to have been here for some time but Pat said McGregor had only recently delivered him. He tried to put these thoughts out of his mind, instead focussing on the skin just in front of the ear. He visualised his preferred entry and how far downward he could extend the slice. To the chin perhaps, or even the trickier manoeuvre of extending beyond and over the throat. But why would Pat lie to him? McGregor hadn't dropped the guy off recently, that was obvious so why would Pat say that he had? If he had in fact delivered him previously McGregor would have mentioned it at some point. Something wasn't right. Pat began thrashing his hand about in a hurry the fuck up motion and Tam moved closer still to the whimpering target. He looked from the facial skin, to the razor, to Pat. Just then his downside peripheral vision offered him an unexpectedly familiar sight. Pig skin Palermo loafers.

***

Tam managed to sprint down the stairs into the moonlit street without falling. Such was his state of shock he felt almost unable to stand and had to steady himself against a lampost. Soon after he heard the padlock on the perimeter fence being locked and Pat's footsteps retracing his own.

'Whit's the problem son?' There followed a silence as Tam tried to untangle all of the different thoughts racing through his mind.

'You've been hawdin Campbell here aw this time?' Pat's face was a portrait of bemusement as if completely shocked at Tam's confusion.

'A don't understawn, a thought ye wid be happy a goet some revenge fur ye. That guy took a liberty wae you did he no?'

'But ye jist tried tae trick me intae slashin em.'

'Awright fair enough, maybe that wis a bit sneaky, but efter whit he did tae you he deserves it dis he no?'

'Dae ye no think it's a bit over the top Pat? The guys we've been targetin ur guilty uv serious liberty takin, aw Campbell did wis gee me a doin.' Tam had forgotten it was Pat he was speaking to.

'Hing oan a wee minute, you an Lina asked me fur ma help. It the time the wye a seen it a hid two joabs. First wis tae help you wae yer confidence and second wis tae deliver some retribution. Av told ye before son, somebidy wrangs me or mine an there's always gonnae be a reckonin, somethin hud tae be done.'

'Did ye slash em up there efter a left?'

'Naw a didnae, a thought a could maybe come doon an talk some sense intae ye, you're the wan that he geed the doin tae no me.' Pat spoke without a hint of remorse. If anything it seemed to Tam he was proud of all the effort he had gone to and expected gratitude.

'A jist don't see how we kin target people guilty uv takin serious liberties and then become hypocrites by takin liberties urselves.'

'Am no huvin that, that's way oot a line.' Pat's tone was almost hurt, as though winded by Tam's lack of appreciation or understanding.

'So when did ye pick em up?' Tam asked.

'The Monday mornin efter he attacked ye when you took the time aff. A found oot where ye worked, goet alayn ay a van an bundled em in the back, nae bother neer it wis.' Pat removed a roll-up, his lighter producing a steady flame in the cold evening air.

'How did ye know who he wis?' Tam asked. Pat looked into him with an impatient pause, as though considering whether or not he would continue answering these impertinent questions.

'Lina telt me ees name, a knew where yer work wis, the rest wis easy.'

'So whit huv ye been dayin wae em aw this time?' Pat paused again, as though increasingly annoyed at being expected to justify himself.

'Well ma original plan wis jist tae gee em a fright, fuck em up a wee bit, nothin too heavy.' Pat seemed uncomfortable as though he had done something else, something he wasn't keen on discussing.

'And, whit else did ye dae tae em?' Tam sensed the old man was holding back.

'That week when ye went back tae yer work ye told me things were goan well wae the Stella bird. An ye wur stawnin up fur yersel wae yer boss anaw. A suppose a jist thought fae whit ye hud telt me there might a been somethin between Campbell and the burd. So a decided tae hawd oan tae em fur longer. A didnae waant him messin things up between you an her.' There was no doubting he was way out of line but still Tam couldn't help feel a sense of appreciation. His friend really was prepared to do anything to help him.

'Listen Pat a dae totally appreciate everythin yuv done fur me. A dae honestly, but this means that even if a managed tae get things oan track wae Stella, it widnae uv been be fair an square. A couldnae be dayin wae that, never knowin if she wis wae me jist cos he wisnae aboot. Naw a wid need tae know she wis wae me because she waanted tae be.' Tam knew his priority now had to be the safe passage out of the Monkford for Campbell. Although lies, he felt this spin on things might appeal to Pat's sense of sport. Pat slowly nodded his head as he looked up at the tower block above them. It looked like he was beginning to grasp Tam's logic.

'Aye a kin see yer point there right enough.'

'So naebody else knows it wis you that snatched him?' Tam knew Pat wasn't stupid and that Campbell wouldn't have a clue where he had been taken or by who. This would be a Police matter soon enough though and not something covered by McGregor's immunity. Tam knew he himself would be heavily implicated and wanted all the facts.

'Naw naebody else knows anythin aboot it.'

'An yuv no hurt him physically?'

'Whit is it wae you an aw these fuckin questions? Yer startin tae get right oan ma tits so ye ur.'

'Am jist sayin Pat, a need tae know where we stawn that's aw.'

'Well a hid tae slap em aboot a few times, efter he started makin a nuisance uv eeself.' Tam was worried that if he told Pat he was no longer interested in Stella, Campbell's fate would become an even more perilous one. He decided he should continue with the premise that he wanted success with Stella while Campbell had his liberty, thus ensuring he had won the spoils fair and square.

'Let's jist let him go eh Pat? If Stella chooses him well am better aff knowin wan wye ur the other. Besides it's no right, the guys that McGregor gees us ur pure scum an deserve everythin they get but Campbell disnae deserve aw this. You've said it yersell, innocent people who urnae part ay the gang scene shouldnae get touched.' Tam had rarely up to this point even answered his mentor back, let alone given him a lecture. He knew within a heartbeat he had crossed a line, as Pat lunged at him grabbing fistfuls of jacket and shirt.

'Exactly who dae ye think yer talkin tae?'

'Take it easy Pat am jist sayin that's aw.'

'Yer jist sayin aye! Who dae ye think ye ur tae be tellin me whit a should and shouldnae be dayin? You're the wan that asked me fur help, dae ye no remember that?' Pat's face had quite suddenly been covered in a hood of rage.

'A know that, an av already telt ye how grateful a um, am sorry, a didnae mean tae upset ye.' Tam's weight was half supported by Pat's iron-like fists on his chest.

'You think am a dafty! You an McGregor baith think am soft in the heed, daint yees?' A large residue of white foam was building around each corner of the old man's mouth as he spoke.

'Naw Pat a don't think that ataw, honest a don't, an a dae appreciate everythin yuv done fur me.' Tam tried to hide the reality of his thoughts behind the filter of his eyes. Of course he knew Pat to be completely insane. Even more so than any of the low level scum on McGregor's hit list.

'Well that's awright then intit, cos am nae dafty mark ma words.' The hood seemed to be lifted as quickly as it had appeared, and he slowly released his grip on the younger man.

'Listen am sorry aboot that. Ye know whit am like, a get a wee bit touchy sometimes.' Tam tried to smooth out his shirt and jacket, turning his face away while doing his best not to cry. Coming so close to Pat's dark side had scared him to the core and despite his best efforts he couldn't stop the tears.

'Whit ye greetin fur? A said a wis sorry dinta.' Tam attempted to keep his face turned away; he didn't want anyone, least of all Pat, to bear witness to his upset.

'Am no greetin, av goet something in ma eye that's aw.'

CHAPTER 14

On the night of the robbery, he could remember gripping the banister tightly, soaked in piss. Staring with intensity at the payphone downstairs, as though he could dial the Police purely by the power of thought. The payphone was a large wall-mounted type and although he couldn't reach the receiver from the floor, he knew he could by standing on the second step. He wanted desperately to find the courage to make that call, but was struggling. The voices were coming from a section of the Lounge that was out of view from the base of the stairs. There was a decent chance of not being seen if he could whisper their location into the handset. But there was still that possibility he couldn't help but focus on, that one of the voices would see him and pounce. What would they do to him? After all he was only a child. They could hurt him, he was sure that bad men were more than capable of killing children who tried to call the Police. There was also a chance they would come upstairs in any case and he would be discovered. But if they were simply after the takings there was no need as the safe was downstairs.

But what of his father? He was the man of the house, surely it was his job to protect them. Why should Tam put himself in danger? He was only a child. The head of the family was in charge of everything, including its protection. He strained to listen, but couldn't hear his father, all he could hear were the desolate screams from his mother. No, he wouldn't act: perhaps Tam's attempt to use the payphone would scupper plans his father already had in place.

***

Tam waited for a lift going down. It had been a difficult day, one he was glad to put behind him. In view of his recent attendance he had been issued with a final written warning. Just prior to the disciplinary meeting Shergar had been unexpectedly called away from the office, so a partner had stepped in.

Stella made no reference to their hotel stay – it was as though it had never happened. Like everyone else in the firm her focus was the news that Campbell was home, after having suffered some kind of breakdown.

'So what do you think has happened to him then?' Stella asked Tam the question over his shoulder, they both looked up at the illuminating floor numbers.

'I heard he had taken himself away on a holiday somewhere.' Tam was doing his best to act casual.

'Yeah that's what I heard, but I did think it a bit strange at the time that he didn't mention to anyone he was going away. We saw him on the Friday in Dalry's, do you remember?' Tam thought of that night in the realisation so much had happened since; it was as though he had become a distant memory of himself.

'Maybe he just fancied getting away, a last minute thing perhaps,' he replied. 'Is he coming back to work do you know?' Tam asked, hopeful the response would be negative.

'I've no idea but I hope so, it's such a shame for the poor guy.'

Tam found himself coming full circle on recent events. The only difference now was that the old pangs of paranoia were gone. He cared nothing of her concern toward Campbell. Asking Pat for the opportunity to win Stella's affections fair and square had been purely to help secure Campbell's safe passage. The irony wasn't wasted on him.

He had been unable to stop thinking of Paula and he was sure it wasn't simply jealousy at her having met someone. It was more than that. Besides, he had decided he wanted to be with her before she told him he had competition. Could she forgive him? Just one more chance. The only fight he was interested in from this day forth was the one for Paula. Of course, he would have to delay telling Pat as it might look suspicious and then Campbell's position could become perilous again.

They passed the smiling concierge into the cold marble reception and stepped into the darkness of a late winter afternoon. She paused, as though something was on her mind. Tam's line of thought, however, was interrupted by the sight of McGregor across the street, leaning on his car.

'I'll give you a call later Stella, I've got to see this guy about one of Pat's security contracts.' He turned and she was looking straight into him. It seemed whenever his interest waivered she somehow knew and turned on the voltage. She surprised him by leaning forward and kissing him on the mouth, before melting into the passers-by.

'Ye mind walkin wae me fur a wee bit son?' McGregor's hands were pushed deep into the pockets of his crombie.

'Aye sure, nae bother.' Tam tried to stay relaxed but knew something wasn't right. The low cloud had released a light drizzle and the detective removed a golf umbrella emblazoned in whisky branding from the boot of his car. Tam considered how pissed off Pat would be if he knew they were meeting behind his back.

'So how long ye worked in there son?' McGregor nodded back toward the bank as they walked under the umbrella.

'No sure exactly, fur a while.' They turned right from West Nile Street onto the climbing slope of St Vincent Street, stretching up into the horizon. Tam was of course fully aware they were moving through the formalities of small talk prior to the meat and bones of the matter.

'Ye like workin there?' Mutant butterflies gnawed at his intestines.

Coconut Badger! Coconut Badger!

'Aye it's awright.'

'It's good tae see a boay fae somewhere like the Monkford dayin so well fur eeself so it is.' They walked alongside the slow-moving vehicles of rush-hour traffic. An awkward silence indicated to Tam the detective was just about ready to get to the point.

'A think we might huv a wee problem son.' McGregor lowered the umbrella and then shook it, stepping backward into the deep shadow of a redundant doorway.

'Pat shouldnae huv snatched that boay withoot talkin tae me furst.' He shook his head solemnly, as though trying to convey the severity of the problem. Tam was unsure whether to even attempt a denial. His understanding was that no one including McGregor knew anything of the abduction. In the interests of self-preservation, he decided honesty was the best policy. Besides, they were supposed to be on the same side, kind of.

'A didnae know anythin aboot it, and when a did find oot it wis me that persuaded em tae let em go,' Tam replied anxiously, deciding not to elaborate on Pat's efforts to have him slash Campbell.

'Well if he hud goet me involved in the furst place a could've helped. But noo it's been reported an some young DS is investigatin. Apparently there's CCTV fae reception showin some bald guy hingin aboot the day the boay claims tae huv been abducted.' McGregor removed cigarettes from his pocket, lighting one.

'If a don't get ma hawns oan that CCTV, you an yer pal ur fur the high jump.' He offered the pack to Tam as an afterthought; he declined.

'But a didnae know anythin aboot it! Whit's it goet tae dae wae me?' Tam's tone conveyed an acute panic in the knowledge he and Pat's futures could be very much intertwined.

'Disnae matter, you an him ur a team, the Procurator Fiscal wulnae be arsed aboot who knew this ur that. Yees'll baith get loaked up in the big hoose.' McGregor turned to face him, touching his elbow gently.

'At least the guy disnae know who snatched him ur where he wis held, that's somethin. A kin try tae help yees but a need you tae help me anaw.' The detective's voice was softer than Tam had ever heard it, almost caring.

'Whit kin a dae?' Tam asked, in the knowledge it was very unlikely he could influence Pat's behaviour. If the old man wanted to do something he doubted anyone could stop him, even McGregor.

'A need ye tae keep an eye oan Pat fur me, am worried aboot em. A don't know if it's some kinda delayed reaction tae losin his Mrs ur whit, but he's no playin things cool. A cannae huv aw this madness, a need things tae be quiet, discreet, ye understawn whit am sayin?' The detective leaned forward as though trying to read Tam's expression carefully.

'Aye a dae.' Although he had a sense of betraying Pat, he also felt he had no choice but to cooperate. They had a shared interest and that was to try to ensure Pat's behaviour didn't spiral any further out of control.

'Awright then young yin, yuv goet ma mobile number so if there's any mare madness a waant ye tae phone me straight away. You're a bright boay, at least if av goet you keepin me up tae date a kin relax a wee bit.' McGregor continued to study Tam's face in a way that made him feel his thoughts weren't his own.

'An am gonnae huv tae see if a kin get ma hawns oan that CCTV, before that DS makes a link back tae oor mutual friend.' As the detective stepped from the doorway, he opened the umbrella. From the loud spluttering on its surface it was evident the spray had become a downpour while they sheltered. Tam also stepped under the umbrella but McGregor moved back; he would return to his car alone, leaving Tam exposed to the elements. As the detective turned, he spoke one last time as though to underline the severity of Tam's predicament.

'Don't let me doon son ye hear me? Otherwise there could be serious consequences.' McGregor raised his eyebrows and Tam nodded affirmatively. Then the old man disappeared among those scurrying to avoid the vertical onslaught. An image of Barlinnie's Victorian chimney steeples came to Tam. He had never been to prison but suspected that it would take a lot more than Coconut Badger to survive in that environment. He had no intention of finding out though and knew he must do whatever was required to avoid it.

Scanning the street, he established his exact location to determine the nearest bus stop. Salmon's old Hat Rack building with its squashed facade of glass and iron loomed over him. He turned casually in the knowledge he would be drenched regardless of pace. First he walked east and then south into the artery of Union Street, pumping its traffic out over the fast-flowing Clyde and beyond.

His head rested on the condensated interior of the bus window, periodically bumping against the glass. He weighed up the two options open to him. Cooperate with McGregor and risk the wrath of Pat. Tell his mentor about the meet and potentially aggravate the already strained relations between the two men. He braced himself in preperation to navigate waters that he knew to be well outwith his comfort zone.

**

It felt appropriate to finish things completely with Stella before resuming his pursuit of Paula. The more time he had to think about both women, the more he understood it had been Paula all along.

The heavy rain had stopped during his journey and as soon as he stepped from the bus he was met by a rusty vapour. He stared downward at the tip of each shoe as he walked in the last of the afternoon light. How would he break the news to Stella? She had certainly been cock teasing him and he was curious as to why. She must have had her reasons though and he genuinely didn't harbour any ill feeling. It was never meant to happen and part of him was glad they hadn't had sex as surely that would have complicated things further.

'You look freezing, in you come.' She took his coat as he rubbed his raw and bloodless hands together. He sensed discomfort but was unsure if it was his own projected onto her. She leaned forward, he hesitated between cheek and lips, making contact awkwardly on her jaw line.

'Why didn't you get a taxi?' Her tone was motherly.

'Tried to but couldn't find one anywhere,' he lied. He still had plenty of McGregor's money but thought it possible he might be asked to return it when he told Pat he wanted out, so he was trying not to spend any more. Despite not being asked to, he removed his shoes and socked feet took him silently across the dark wood floor to the living room.

'Tam can you come into the kitchen first there's something I need to tell you.' She definitely sounded uncomfortable – his senses had been right, it wasn't just him.

'This sounds ominous.' His previous apprehension relating to dumping her shifted into a suspicion that he was in fact the one about to get the elbow. He knew he should be glad as it would save him the grief but nonetheless it still felt a bit unpleasant. She stared into the open fridge and he moved to the breakfast bar, leaning back with folded arms, waiting.

'Can I get you a drink of something?'

'Whatever you're having is fine.' From the interior fridge light he could see her expression was austere. She closed the door gently holding a bag of filter coffee, which she kept chilled for reasons unknown to him. Standing with her back to him and staring down at the silent kettle, she flicked the switch.

'Stella it's fine, whatever it is.' Tam tried to convey in his voice that he knew she was going to dump him and that he also knew it was for the best.

'Promise me you won't be angry.' He hated it when people said that, how could he promise without knowing what she was about to say? An outlandish notion popped into his head. Perhaps she was about to tell him that her physical avoidance of him had been because she was a post-operative transexual. The therapy was incomplete; she needed more time.

'What is it Stella, just tell me.' He stared at the back of her

169

head.

'Campell's asked if I can help him for a bit, get back on his feet.' As soon as the last word left her mouth, she turned to face him. Most of his thoughts since entering the kitchen had related to the process of dumping or being dumped, this wasn't what he expected at all.

'I don't follow, why would he ask you to help him?'

'Well we went to the same school, he was a bit older, but I've known him for a long time and our fathers are friendly through the tennis club.' Tam had always known their families knew each other but not to what extent.

'What's the matter with him, why does he need your help? I thought he just went on holiday.' Self-preservation kicked in. From what McGregor had told him he now knew it was in his own best interests to ensure Pat wasn't implicated. It would do no harm to find out if there were anything incriminating.

'Promise you won't say anything to anyone.'

'Of course.'

'Well it depends which version you believe. Campbell's father reckons he's been off on a jolly somewhere and had some kind of substance induced breakdown. Campbell on the other hand...'

'What?' He was impatient for her to continue.

'Well, he reckons he was abducted.'

'Abducted, what by fucking aliens or something?' Tam tried to play it cool, reacting with a forced amazement.

'Well, the Police are investigating his claims. He reckons he was kidnapped and then pumped full of drugs against his will. Says he has no idea who he was snatched by or why though. You can see why his dad is sceptical, it's a bit far-fetched to say the least.' The kettle gurgled to a boil and she reached up to a cupboard, removing cups and saucers.

'Are the Police taking him seriously?' Tam attempted to ensure his dialogue was riddled with disbelief. Pat had failed to mention anything about drugs, Tam thought that even by Pat's standards that was pretty nasty. He began to feel a sense of guilt;

170

none of this would have happened to Campbell if Tam hadn't accepted Pat's help in the first place.

'It would seem they are taking him more seriously than his father. He called him a junkie liar and threw him out of the house. He had nowhere else to go Tam, what could I do?' He counted the cups and saucers. There were three.

'What you mean he's here?' There was no need to manufacture any disbelief into that statement.

'Keep your voice down, he'll hear you.' She nodded in the direction of the living room. Tam hadn't spoken to Campbell since the night he had taken a one-sided beating in Stella's name. Since developing his new-found skills, Tam had daydreamed often of this encounter. Campbell had come off second best in every imagined circumstance. For life to offer up this scenario today was another example of irony in the extreme. Now he had decided he was finished with Stella, things had taken on a different texture. She simply wasn't his priority any more. His focus was on Paula, putting an end to his involvement with the McGregor attacks, as well as general prison avoidance. He would have no chance of a normal life with Paula from behind bars. There was also the fact that Lina was obviously struggling with the running of the bar and needed his help. He could do nothing for either Paula or Lina from the Big House.

'It's not how it looks Tam, I've set him up in the spare room.' She seemed to be searching his face for some indicators of how he was taking the news. It was devoid of emotion, his brain unable to focus on anything other than his mantra.

Coconut Badger! Coconut Badger!

His stomach churned in on itself. He knew he would soon come face to face with a man who had witnessed his one-time cowardice. Stella moved forward, reaching her arms around the back of his neck into a hug, her soft face nuzzled under his ear.

'Thanks for being so understanding Tam.' She seemed to be taking his silence as some kind of acceptance. He felt the warmth of her lips and breath on his neck. In a stirring he had

171

little control over, blood was pumped between them. He knew she must have felt it and he wished it hadn't happened, but that part of his anatomy simply operated independently of him.

He opened the living-room door silently. Campbell was standing at the bay window, scratching his arm and looking down into the street. Tam had been asked to make the house guest at ease while Stella prepared the coffee. A mixture of emotions bubbled to the surface. He wanted to attack him right now, to avenge for himself the unprovoked attack he had been a victim of. But there was also guilt. Tam knew Campbell had been put through far more than he deserved. His punishment at the hands of Pat had certainly been disproportionate to his crime. Tam moved forward, his socks silent on the thick carpet. He stood behind Campbell, for a few moments watching what he watched; and then Campbell turned suddenly.

'Jesus Tam, you gave me a fright there.' She must have told Campbell at least something of their relationship. The scare faded and left a face with no trace of surprise at Tam's being there. He seemed to read from Tam's expression that their last meeting was still very much on his mind. Campbell glanced toward the door, speaking in a lowered tone.

'Listen Tam, I'm really sorry about what happened that night. I was way out of line, had a few too many, no excuse I know but just want you to know that I am sorry.' Tam was shocked by everything. His hair, skin, physique, even his voice seemed to belong to someone else. He was less than a shadow of his former self. Pat had well and truly fucked him up.

'How much smack did he put intae ye fur fuck sake?'

'How did you know about the drugs?' As soon as Tam said it, he panicked momentarily but then remembered Stella had told him in the kitchen.

'Stella told me.' Campbell turned back to the darkness of the street, his face covered in confusion and fear.

'It's as if I wasn't even there Tam. Like I've just woken up from a nightmare and I'm not that sure it even happened to me in real life. The man who held me, he was like, well he was like the devil.' He turned to face Tam, his face raw with tears.

'He said it was antibotics, but I knew it wasn't. After a few times it got so I ended up needing it, my headaches and stomach cramps got worse until he came back with more. Then after he gave it to me everything would be fine again. A couple of times I even felt good, despite being in hell, I felt good, can you believe that?' Campbell continued to scratch his arm. The skin was covered in a slight moisture, like a sheen; it would soon become a cold sweat.

'Any idea where he took you?'

'None, I had a hood or blindfold on most of the time.'

'I just can't understand it Tam. Why would someone go to all that effort and not even want anything from me? It doesn't make sense, why not ask for a ransom, or kill me? It was like death wasn't good enough.' Campbell stared into him and it occurred to Tam that he may think, or be asked by the police, if there was anyone he had recently had an argument with. Perhaps a connection would be made. Although he suspected Campbell was the type who had stepped on quite a few toes, if the investigating DS identified the bald man in the footage as being from The Monkford, Tam would be heavily implicated. No one would believe Pat had been operating without his knowledge.

Campbell's goosebumps ramped up the length of his body, vibrating in steady waves. He began to sob noisily and collapsed into a small bundle of rags on the floor.

'It's awright yer safe noo.' Tam knelt, placing a hand on his shoulder. The muscle he had once been so jealous of seemed to have been washed away like dirt. Pat had placed the bullet in the chamber and the odds of his survival (like everyone else on the poison) had crashed through the floor. He may not have selected the garment himself but nonetheless Campbell was now shrouded in a cloak Tam had seen often. The uniform of the junkie with its meek and inevitable wretchedness. He was fucked.

CHAPTER 15

Tam perched his arse cheeks on the thin bench inside the bus stop across the street from Paula's salon. Last night he had considered going straight to her house from Stella's. But on reflection, in view of there being as yet unidentified competition, a degree of strategy would be required.

She had worked here since leaving school and often spoke of how much she enjoyed it. Her dream was some day to have her own chain like her boss, who she had often said was an inspiration to her. Landshaws was an area halfway between the Monkford, its neighbouring schemes and the city centre. It had mostly everything you could get in town only on a much smaller scale. The winter air resting on his face was mild and still, as the lunchtime scene around him bustled with shoppers and groups of schoolchildren.

He watched her work the scissors and could even make out some of the facial expressions that were so familiar to him. He was satisfied though that the busy street between them gave him sufficient cover. In the shiny blue bag with its thin rope handles he had a gift. This wasn't just any gift though. He hoped it would communicate everything he wanted to say but was incapable of articulating.

During their childhood, at some point no one including Paula could quite remember, she had developed a fascination with bubble wrap. Friends, family, neighbours, any of them who came across a piece would save it for her. The cupboard at the end of her hall had been jam-packed with the stuff for years. Everywhere she went a piece would accompany her and people would often hear popping noises before establishing visual contact. Prior to their first sexual encounters they had been close friends and Tam had been vigorous in his pursuit of bubble wrap for her collection. This was as they made the journey together through adolescence, unaware of the shadow looming ahead. Tam began the inevitable badgering relating to issues of penetration. Eventually after much resistance and with a high degree of trepidation, she opened herself for him. It had been under both the cover of night and a local sycamore's thick branches, on a blanket she brought with her. They used to swing from the sycamore's thick branches as children. From that night on as the rate at which Tam's sexual demands increased, conversely his efforts relating to all things bubble wrap diminished. At some point, they stopped altogether.

He had managed to convince the reluctant jewellers' assistant to give him a large gift bag, even though the inexpensive earrings were in such a small box. He needed the largest bag they had so he could wrap them inside the sheets of bubble wrap. He felt that words would somehow spoil the impact of the gift and its significance, so waited for her to leave the shop. But as lunch crept into mid-afternoon, it occurred to him that she might not be taking a break today. He nodded back at a confused bus driver who recognised him from his previous journey, having lapped his entire route. Tam's arse cheeks were numbed but still they perched on the uncomfortable metal bench.

Fortunately as the flow of customers into the salon began to flag, she removed a small mirror from her bag, touching her make-up. Then she pushed her arms into her coat and left the shop laughing with a colleague. They disappeared out of sight. Tam asked the giggling girl at the counter to make sure and pass the bag to Paula on her return.

***

He had received a text from Stella, asking to meet in a park near her flat. Sitting next to a boating pond on a bench with blistered green paint, he watched a man and boy control a motorised boat in the rancid water. A folded newspaper sat at his side; he was too anxious to read. Instead, he considered how he could deliver the news. With the Campbell business at her flat he hadn't said anything that night. He knew it was cowardly, but simply hadn't made contact since, he had been avoiding her.

There were several winding paths leading down through the manicured lawns to the pond. Other than the man and boy operating the boat the only other person he could see was walking with a lead and an unseen dog. And then he saw Stella approach and although from distance her expression couldn't be read, her body looked stiffer than the mildness of the afternoon warranted. With each step toward him her face began to focus into his eyes. It was gradually revealed to him that they felt the same way.

'How are you Tam?' She managed a perfunctory smile while he considered the pantomime of small talk in situations such as these.

'I'm fine, how's the patient doing?' He moved the newspaper from the bench to his lap.

'He's not doing too good actually.' She didn't mirror his relaxed posture as she sat, her spine bolt upright she perched on the edge of the bench.

'Why, what's wrong with him?' He knew of course, it would be cold turkey.

'Before we talk about that, can we clear the air?' She was staring at the motorised boat as she spoke.

'Yes of course, what is it?' His decision to pursue Paula was further enforced with the realisation he wasn't even arsed. In fact he was glad he wouldn't need to do it, suspecting he would have fluffed it in any case.

'Can we just go back to being friends Tam? Everything has happened so fast, one minute we were good pals and the next we were...' Her voice tailed off and he wondered if it was because like him she didn't even know what they had been.

'We were what?' he asked.

'I don't know, in a relationship I suppose.' As the conversation progressed she seemed to be relaxing slightly and leaned at least some of her weight backward on the bench.

'Right then Stella, cards on the table, there is something that's been bugging me.'

'Go on.'

'You must have known for ages that I fancied you. Then things developed from us being just friends, but time after time there were always excuses to avoid having sex. Have you got any idea how that made me feel? If you didn't fancy me, well you shouldn't have agreed to go out with me in the first place. Some people might call that cock teasing.'

'I'm not a cock tease.' Her tone was part pained and part hesitant, as though unsure if she could tell him.

'Well what was it all about then?'

'YOU SCARED ME TAM!' She raised her voice, standing from the bench and walking toward the pond where she stopped with her back to him.

'What are you on about, I scared you?' After a pause during which she seemed to be gathering her nerve, she turned to face him.

'I mean exactly that, you scared me Tam. You changed, you used to be such a nice guy, considerate and gentle, really laid back, I liked that. That was the Tam I fancied, but just as we started to develop things further you became the complete opposite. Much harder and forceful, it freaked me out but I couldn't get my head round it. I thought it was me or something, I was confused with the whole thing couldn't make any sense of it.' Tam relaxed his weight back on to the bench and couldn't help allowing some ironic laughter to escape.

'What's so funny?' She smiled, hoping this meant that he hadn't taken it badly.

'I thought that was what you wanted. I thought that was what all women wanted, assertiveness, a man who takes control.'

'Well obviously not all of us.' Again the irony, it had been the pre-Coconut Badger version of him she had liked all along. The one who was too scared to even ask her out on a date. She leaned back on the bench, her knee pressed slightly against his thigh and he shifted a fraction to keep some fresh air between them.

'Can we be friends again?' she asked.

He felt a great sense of relief. No need to try and explain the Paula situation for which he was grateful. In all likelihood he would have probably made things much worse. Now that they moved away from the discussion of their brief relationship, it was like a weight had been removed from both their shoulders. She stood from the bench.

'Shall we walk for a bit?' she asked. Moving slowly beside the boating pond, she slipped her arm inside his.

'I've decided to leave the firm,' he said.

'Why, I thought you liked it.'

'Lina is struggling with the pub, the brewery have said they might take it off her.'

'I'm sorry to hear that.' He stared at the small boat, which seemed to be stuck on some branches as the father took the control from the boy in an attempt to release it. He considered how his priorities had changed. From the bank and Stella, to Lina and Paula.

'Just think about it, don't walk away from your career without giving it plenty of thought.' The late afternoon light began to fade and their steps took them away from the pond, approaching a gate they both knew represented their parting point.

'Listen Tam, I've got a big favour to ask you.' They stopped just inside the gate under a dense network of leaveless branches.

'Sure, what is it?' If someone had told him before this meeting that by the end of it they would both be so relaxed about parting as friends, he simply wouldn't have believed it.

'You're the only person I can think of who may be able to help.'

'Help with what?'

'He's climbing the walls in my place Tam, in a real bad way. If I give you the money could you get him some, while he gets himself back on his feet.' He couldn't believe what he was hearing.

'Are you taking the piss?' He removed his arm from hers, stepping back. His initial annoyance was nothing to do with Campbell.

'So because I'm from the Monkford I'll definitely be able to score you some smack, is that what you're saying?' Stella looked over his shoulder, he turned. The boy held the boat in both arms, waiting for his father who walked behind talking into a mobile. Tam moved away from inside the gate out onto the pavement where the boy couldn't hear, still he lowered his voice to be safe.

'That's out of order Stella, we're not all junkies for fuck sake.' The father walked past them still talking into the mobile; the boy followed a few steps behind staring back at Tam.

'That's not what I'm saying at all, it's nothing to do with where you're from it's just that you're a good friend who I know I can trust, you also just happen to be the most streetwise person I know.' She had managed to somehow manipulate the situation in such a way that he felt pride at being described as streetwise. Although in truth he wasn't sure either of them knew exactly what the term meant.

In addition to feeling further pity for the unfortunate Campbell, he also knew this development would help Pat. Strathclyde Police had a policy when it came to junkies: everything they said was either regarded as a blatant lie, or better still completely ignored.

***

Tam decided to keep walking past his bus stop and make the journey from the park back to the Monkford on foot. He often found it easier to clear his head when he walked. The afternoon although having lost most of its light had lost none of its mildness. He considered his lack of concern at being dumped by Stella as further evidence of his depth of feeling for Paula,

179

although in truth none was needed. He walked alongside the dual carriageway that stretched toward the Monkford in the distance. The noise of vehicles thundering past was soothing and his pace wasn't fast. He lost himself in thoughts of both women.

The facts were these. When Paula had told him she had met someone he had been upset and saddened. Yet today after leaving Stella he felt nothing more than a mild disappointment at never having sex with her. The majority of his efforts previously had been invested in the pursuit of the impala he judged most desirable. Part of that was simply because that was the only one that was running away. An impala like Paula who doesn't run, can't be chased. Conversely when something or someone makes itself more elusive, its intrinsic value is propelled beyond that of things already owned or controlled. In addition to this, Stella with her middle-class pedigree wouldn't be considered an option, in the eyes of some, for a scheme boy like him. This factor combined with the chase meant that Paula's position was always likely to be a precarious one.

In truth he had probably always been more physically attracted to Paula. Yet her being from the same background, her lack of self-confidence, her making no attempt to offer a chase, these were all factors that combined had resulted in the decline of her value to him. Basic supply and demand theory. Now it was clear to him though and he quickened his step.

***

Lina stood over the sink like an aged statue. She had been peeling spuds for their evening meal but had stopped. Motionless, she stared out of the kitchen window. Tam approached and could see his reflection in the darkened pane of glass.

'Jesus, ye geed me a fright there.'

'Sorry, didnae mean tae.' He opened the fridge door, removing a can of juice and deciding it best to get straight to the point.

'So whit dae ye know aboot this guy Paula's seein then?' He

sat at the kitchen table behind her, pouring into a tall glass. She paused, on the edge of a thoughtful silence. Tam knew it would be out of concern for her friend who she didn't want to see being hurt any more than she had already.

'Listen see before ye answer that question Lina, me an Stella are done. A wis kiddin maself oan tae be honest, she wis never right fur me. It wis always Paula that a waanted but sometimes ye jist dont see the thing that's right in front ay yer face dae ye.'

'That's whit av been tryin tae tell ye aw this time son.' She dropped the peeler into the basin with the half scraped spuds and dried her hands on a dishcloth. Leaning back on the edge of the sink her demeanour took on what he perceived as a totally justified air of cynicism.

'A know she's yer pal Lina an yer right tae be protectin er. Av been an idiot, whit else kin a say av messed er aboot somethin rotten.' He covered his face in sincere regret, hoping she would see that he was genuine. Moving slowly from the sink she sat across from him and reached out, holding his hands in a motherly way. She looked almost wasted to him. He knew her fourteen-hour days were an attempt to keep the brewery at bay. For the first time he could see the physical impact this life was having on her and he was grateful for everything she had done.

'There is no other guy Tam, never hus been.' He was still pondering her wearied look as the words travelled to him. Even after processing them he didn't quite understand what she meant.

'Am no wae ye, how dae ye mean there is nae other guy?' His eyebrows arched in a confused squint.

'She jist said it tae make ye think ye hud some competition, dae ye no get it?' He could tell from her smile of satisfaction that she must have had a hand in the change of strategy.

'Whit wid she dae that fur?' Tam felt a stabbing pain in his chest accompanied by a warm forehead; he was annoyed.

'Maybe she thought ye took er fur granted ur somethin. Ye said it yersel, sometimes people don't appreciate whit they've goet, until they think they might lose it.'

Lina returned to the spuds in the sink. There followed a long silence during which she seemed to be conveying to him that the moral highground wasn't his to take. He knew she was right, especially in view of what had been going on between himself and Stella. If she had known, it would be Paula who could claim any right to feelings of hurt or annoyance.

With no competition, the way ahead was clear for him to do the right thing. She would have received the gift on her return to work and he was hopeful she was now waiting for him. Just one more errand and they could be together. Tam and Lina framed the silence with smiles of contented conspiracy, each knowing exactly what would happen next.

**

The old man had been on the toilet when Tam rattled his letter box. Pat opened the door, crouching over holding his trousers around his knees.

'Make yerself at hame son, am jist gonnae wipe ma arse.' Pat hobbled back into the toilet and a pair of desperate eyes darted toward Tam from the living room. They sailed straight past him and down the close.

'Shit! Pat yer dug's jist bolted.' The old man left the flushing toilet holding a crossword page.

'Fuck it, plenty mare were that came fae son.' They moved down the hall into the living room, where Pat flicked the lid of his tobacco tin next to the open window. Tam sat on the low sofa, a dog bark rising incessantly from the street.

'Cheeky fuckin bastard.' Pat picked up an empty whisky bottle and threw it out the open window at the dog. After the smashing of glass, the barking stopped.

'Whit's up wae ye son, ye seem a wee bit tense?' Pat handed him the obligatory triple whisky in a Glasgow Celtic mug.

'Here get this doon ye, it'll sort ye right oot.'

'Naw yer awright Pat al pass if it's aw the same.' As part of his renewed commitment to Paula and Lina, his excessive drinking would now be curtailed.

'Ye'll whit? Stoap bein a fuckin girl's blouse an get it doon ye.' Refusing a drink from some Glaswegians could be described as a faux pas, but with Pat it was regarded as inflammatory, the old man was insistent.

'So huv ye heard anythin fae McGregor?' Pat didn't look at him while asking the question. He lined up more empty whisky bottles on his windowsill in preparation, watching the street below. Tam considered lying but in the context of his decision to terminate their partnership didn't see the point.

'Aye apparently there's some CCTV fae the day ye picked Campbell up.' Tam studied the side of Pat's face in order to guage how pissed off he was at there having been a meet he wasn't at.

'A heard that, he telt me he's tryin tae get he's hawns oan it.' Tam was relieved he had decided not to lie as it was evident the old man knew about the meeting.

'Av goet a bad feelin he's gonnae stitch us up so he is. Aw he needs tae dae is no bother ees arse way that CCTV an were fucked.' Tam winced after gulping on the whisky, still trying to formulate in his mind how best to break the news.

'That's you anaw by the way, ye undersdawn that daint ye? He'll no be leavin any loose ends. It'll be the fuckin big hoose fur the baith ay us.' Tam remained silent but Pat turned from the window, staring into him in such a way it was obvious he expected a response.

'So whit ye gonnae dae?'

'Dae ye no mean, whit ur we gonnae dae?' Pat continued the stare, raising his eyebrows questioningly. Tam tried to despatch the words doing a spin cycle in his mouth but was unable to, so reverted to his mantra.

Coconut Badger! Coconut Badger!

Pat flicked his fag doubt onto the street and closed the window.

Sitting in his armchair, he removed a fresh crossword page from the magazine rack by its side.

'There's actually somethin a wis waantin tae talk tae ye aboot Pat.' Tam wiped the moistness of his palms on the knees of his jeans.

'Oh aye, whit's that then?' Pat continued to study the crossword page, not looking up once. Tam lifted the mug to his face, emptying the last of the burning liquid to ready himself.

Coconut Badger! Coconut Badger!

'This isnae fur me Pat. A really dae appreciate aw yer help an that but things huv chynged, ma circumstances huv chynged.' Tam was aware that for the first time he was using the strategy on the old man himself. Once again it seemed to work, and he found himself passing into that familiar calm landscape. Pat's face lifted from the crossword page, a quizzical look as though confused.

'Whit dae ye mean, circumstances?' He lowered the magazine onto his lap.

'A waant tae make a go a things wae Paula and a waant tae help Lina wae gettin the pub back oan track. It's gettin tae be too much fur er.' Now that he had articulated his reasons, they seemed plausible. The old man had been in love with Betsy after all, he must understand. He was also very fond of Lina, so surely he would be happy at his efforts in helping her keep the pub opened, Tam was hopeful.

'Aye fair enough son, but that shouldnae huv any impact oan oor business arrangemets. Nae reason why ye cannae cerry oan behind the scenes withoot sayin anything tae Lina ur Paula, oor wee secret. Ye know there's good money in it, surely wae the money ye kin help Lina an Paula even mare?'

Pat was right about the money being attractive and there was no doubt it would help them. But Tam had seen enough to know he simply didn't want that life. He had been scared by the speed with which his behaviour had deteriorated. What was so wrong with the old Tam anyway? Stella had fancied that version after all. What of Paula? What if he continued to change and, like Stella, she decided it was the old him that she loved? Other than the undoubted buzz he got from the reverence shown toward his 'reputation', he couldn't think of one reason why he would want to be like Pat. He could certainly think of several reasons why he didn't. It had to be stopped. If he continued down this road he might end up unable to switch direction. It was a very real possibility that he would become like Pat. Could psychosis be contagious, he wondered?

'Yer right Pat the money wid be handy but a jist cannae risk it. Yuv said it yerself McGregor's no tae be trusted and he jist flicks he's fingers an were baith fucked. Am nae use tae them if am inside. Naw a waant tae jist keep maself oot ay bother if it's aw the same. As a said a really dae appreciate everythin yuv done fur me, a really mean that.' Tam did mean it; he may have been petrified of Pat but there was a fondness also. He knew he was unlikely to meet anyone like him ever again. Pat stared back at him with a face that could have held pride or just as easily scorn. Tam felt it was important to hold that stare.

Coconut Badger! Coconut Badger!

He somehow managed it and Pat was indeed the first to look away. The old man removed a bookie's pen from behind his ear, staring at the black and white squares on his lap and licking the nib optimistically.

'Awright then but there's somethin ye need tae dae fur me before ye swan oaf tae play yer happy families.' Tam could guage by the tone that he had wounded Pat and he was sorry for that.

'Al dae anythin ye waant.' He would much rather have made the break a clean and immediate one but suddenly and surprisingly he felt a deep sense of sorrow for what he was doing. Tam knew that while Pat was undoubtedly a psychopath, that didn't detract from the fact that he was a lonely old man who missed his wife and had nothing to do with his time but drink.

'A waant ye tae take me tae that burd's hoose were that guy's dayin ees convalesin.'

Now, Tam was genuinely sorry that Campbell had been put through so much. He had been curious as to exactly what Pat had been thinking of in force-feeding him heroin, but also knew better than to question the old man or make reference to the fact. Tam hadn't told Pat that Campbell was staying with Stella but he obviously knew. This was a concern as it meant Pat had decided Campbell was a loose end that needed to be tidied up. Tam also knew that Pat would be perfectly capable of finding Stella's flat without his help.

'Whit ye waant tae see him fur, that's the last place ye waant tae be seen. If you make contact then there's a chance he kin ID ye tae the Polis.' Tam moved to the window, feeling the need to be on his feet. He knew he had to try and orchestrate things in such a way that Campbell would not be put through any more trauma: enough was enough.

'A jist waant tae huv a wee word wae the boay make sure he's no gonnae dae anythin daft like grass me up.'

'But he disnae even know who yer ur, he cannae grass somebidy up if he disnae know them.' When Tam had secured Campbell's safe release, Pat had known nothing of any CCTV evidence. Things had now taken a dramatic turn for the worse as far as Campbell's safety was concerned. Tam suspected it was a very real possibility that Pat planned to do serious harm to Campbell and that Stella could also be in danger. Pat returned the crossword page to the magazine rack and stood, joining Tam at the window. Opening his tobacco tin he passed him a pre-rolled, putting a hand on his elbow to stop Tam's pacing.

'Whit dae you care aboot eether ay them fur anywye? If it's Paula ye waant then ye shouldnae care whit happens tae Stella should ye? As for Campbell, ye seem tae keep forgettin whit he done tae ye so ye dae.' Pat was right, Campbell wasn't his friend but he had suffered more than enough already. Stella on the other hand had always been his friend, or at least before the issue of penetration had complicated things.

'A know, am no arsed aboot eether ay them.' Tam felt it important that Pat believed that.

'It's jist thit a think there's a better wye fur ye tae hawnle things that's aw.' Pat looked back at him with indifference and Tam suspected he would have his work cut out to change his mind, but he had to try.

'As things stawn neether Stella or Campbell know who ye ur, right?'

'Aye we know that, but that disnae matter, am oan the CCTV fae the mornin he goet snatched fae the bank.' Pat's tone hovered between impatience and irratibility; Tam suspected he only had a small window of opportunity.

'Fair enough, but me an you ur pals. A could tell the Polis that you came tae the office that mornin tae see me aboot something, that gees ye a reason tae be there.' Pat seemed to be considering that possibility for the first time.

'Aye a know, but still, better safe than sorry is it no?' Tam studied the old man's fleshy face in the room's dim light. He could tell Pat wasn't convinced and in that instant, somehow it was revealed to him what he had to do.

'Aye but yuv no heard ma idea.' He was aware of the grievous implications of what he was about to suggest, but if the alternative was a visit from Pat, surely it was in Campbell's best interests.

'Oh aye, whit's that then?'

'Al make sure Campbell gets back oan the smack and styes oan it. Polis wulnae be interested in anythin he's goet tae say when ees oot ees nut.' He was stabbed by guilt as he spoke the words. His initial refusal in the park may have stopped Stella from sourcing it. There was a chance she would have given up. Campbell could have attempted to get the poison out of his system. Putting him back on the heroin was likely to be a death sentence. He didn't deserve any of this and for that Tam was genuinely sorry. As things stood it was simply the lesser of two evils.

Tam paused again, trying to read the wordless page that was

Pat's face. The yellow stained teeth opened into a smile akin to a Monkford sunrise.

'You're fuckin good son, a taught ye well dinta?' Pat reached forward, enthusiastically crunching on his hair.

'But how ye gonnae get em oan it, if he disnae waant it?'

What Tam wanted to say was: 'you mean without tying him to a kitchen chair?'

What he actually said was:

'Let me worry aboot that, al sort it.' He wasn't quite sure why he hadn't told Pat that Stella had already approached him for supplies. Partly he wanted him to think that getting Campbell on heroin would require skill or at least some work on his part, for which he would take credit. The question he would soon ask himself was whether he was trying to save Campbell from danger or whether he was more interested in using Campbell's predicament to facilitate an easier exit strategy for himself.

CHAPTER 16

Despite a sense of urgency to be at Paula's side, it had been decided by Pat that whatever Tam had in mind in terms of reacquainting Campbell with the smack should be executed immediately. It wasn't ideal but Tam knew it was vital he keep the old man as placid as possible.

During the time Tam spent chatting with Stella and Campbell in her kitchen, he was consumed by such guilt that he felt discomfort holding either's eye. Had he refused to source the goods he knew they might have tried elsewhere, but he also knew they might have simply given up. He had to find a way to reconcile this with the reality of what a visit from Pat would mean. To this end, Tam spent the minimum amount of time he deemed to be polite and then made his excuses. In his wake he left an apprehensive Stella, a cold turkey Campbell, and the largest bag of Monkford brown he had ever seen.

It had been snowing lightly when he arrived but stepping from Stella's close to the pavement, he could see the snow had become much heavier and visibility was low. In anticipation of traffic delays he continued past the bus stop, deciding instead to make the journey to Paula's by foot. Each of his steps crunched loudly beneath him – an undisturbed blanket stretching into the distance, waiting for his mark. The dark grey sky of earlier had been painted over by a violent shade of violet. Tam thought it to be like walking into a postcard, the experience almost hallucinatory as the sky gently released trillions of soft snowflakes.

His heart rate increased, not with his pace, but with thoughts of what he would soon say to Paula. If she wasn't home he would wait, even if it meant becoming a human snowman.

Beside him, traffic moved in single file with slow-turning wheels seeking out the tracks of those in front. There were screams of laughter from up ahead, he could see a group of children firing snowballs at passing vehicles from a slope. He knew walking past he would be a likely target and considered crossing to the opposite pavement. His heart was so full of love though that he felt it would be in the spirit of the moment to offer himself up, even sharing in their infectious laughter. A car left the now well-defined tracks, making two fresh lines and stopping near his last footsteps. The window opened, a man's voice.

'Polis, get in the back.' Tam's heart palpitated. Recently his life had consisted of activities riddled with incidents associated with serious jail time. Had it not been for McGregor and his guarantee of immunity, making a run for it would have been a serious consideration. He quickly calculated that it would be for the best to comply and as soon as possible request to speak with the DCI. The car was unmarked and he sat behind two stiff-necked men of silence. He had no idea where he was being taken or why and simply stared from the warmth at the passing white landscape. His most urgent hope was that the ageing detective would be true to his word. The journey was long, and this was only partly due to traffic chaos. For some reason they weren't interested in taking him to one of the many local Stations they had passed. The longevity of route had given him time to reflect. Both the Tommy Tattoo attack and also Campbell's kidnapping had been conducted outwith McGregor's protection. His anxiety was compounded with this realisation, his stomach churning in on itself, bubbling uncomfortably.

Coconut Badger! Coconut Badger!

The car pulled up to a large iron gate at the side of an anonymous building. They waited several seconds before it slowly opened in front of them. Then he was driven down several corkscrew levels into a bunker-like space deep below street level. Stepping from the car, Tam was relieved when the calmness came to him. Anxiety would in no way assist with this situation; it was vital he keep his cool.

They moved through several keypad-controlled doors and down a long straight corridor before Tam was eventually left in what he took to be an interview room. He sat silently in a scene he had watched on countless TV and film dramas.

He hadn't been waiting long when the door opened and a man in jeans and a white T-shirt entered, sitting across from him. He was probably early thirties and, in stark contrast to McGregor, definitely one of a new breed. His clean-shaven square jaw sat on a hard and well-defined torso.

'So Tam, any idea why you're here?' He spoke into an open folder of papers as Tam tried to cling to McGregor's guarantees for confidence. Coconut Badger had worked well when used in instances of sudden adrenal dumps. However this environment and situation was different as the dumps were coming in waves. He felt like he was passing through the calm back out into the storm and knew he was out of his depth.

'No I'm sorry I don't.' He felt embarrassed by his small boy tone, imagining Pat in a room nearby sounding much more masculine.

'Fair enough. So the way you want to play this, is basically to start things off by pretending that you don't know why you are here, is that the case?' He looked up from the folder for the first time.

'Eh I'm not sure, I don't know what you mean exactly.' Tam's mind scattered, racing in different directions. He simply wasn't sure how much this guy knew or if in fact he worked with McGregor on their covert operation. If that was the case surely Tam had nothing to worry about. He decided his only hope was to speak with McGregor. Hopefully that would clear things up in a way that would be mutually satisfactory.

'I need to talk to DCI McGregor from your headquarters.' His tone had risen a notch slightly on the masculinity scale but still there was a quiver he couldn't shift.

'Is that right... You need to speak with DCI McGregor?' He smiled, looking over Tam's shoulder at a large mirror. Tam turned also, realising that fictional depictions of interview rooms must be accurate. He wondered who could be behind that mirror – possibly McGregor he thought, or rather, hoped. The policeman's demeanour changed quite suddenly.

'Listen Tam there's no point us dancing round each other here, this could go on all night, let's just cut to the chase yeah. I know everything about pretty much everything and right now you don't know anything about pretty much anything, so in the interests of saving each other a lot of stress I'm going to give you the bottom line straight off the bat.' Tam's calmness was now a thing in the distance as all of the sensations from old rushed at him. Pins and needles attacked his scalp and a hot flush rose from his shoulders. He clung to the hope that the discussion would centre on a McGregor slashing with its associated immunity. The alternative was making him increasingly horrified with each passing second. Could it be that he had been lifted for either the Tommy Tattoo attack or the Campbell kidnapping? If that were the case, immunity was unlikely to be an option.

'There's no easy way to say this Tam, so I'll just get straight to the point.' Tam stared back at him, trying unsuccessfully to look relaxed.

'I'm afraid to have to tell you that DCI McGregor is as bent as a two pound note.' The words had certainly travelled beyond Tam's inner ear but the process of actually absorbing their meaning had been stalled somehow. Part of him refused to accept the sheer scope of their implications. His abdominal thrusts were so severe it was as though invisible arms were squeezing his midriff. In the last second, he managed to avoid the table and projectiled downward and over his lower legs and shoes. One of his companions from the car journey entered with a box of tissues and then left.

'I can totally understand that reaction Tam. In fact, if I were you I would probably be feeling exactly the same way.' Wiping himself ineffectually with the hankies, the only thing Tam could focus on was the audible vibration of the fluorescent strip above them. His world seemed to be caving in on itself.

'We know everything Tam. The supposedly covert work he

asked you and Pat to do. I've got to tell you I actually sympathise with you, McGregor is quite a piece of work and a young guy like yourself never really stood a chance.' Tam stared back with a vacant wonder at what this all meant.

'I'm with internal investigations. You can call me Frank and right now I'm afraid to tell you I'm the only thing standing between you and a very long stretch.' The slightest glimmer of hope seemed to present itself with those words. Tam sensed Frank had some kind of proposition or deal to offer.

'Blondie McAvoy and Spud McPherson weren't targeted as a result of their gang activities or liberty taking, despite the bullshit you were fed about these being vigilante attacks. Don't get me wrong, they're no angels, but they were targeted because they had crossed McGregor in some way. The scheming old fox has been selling franchises to criminals in Glasgow for years. Technically I've got enough to lock you and Pat up, but the alternative would be my preference. You testify, Pat and McGregor go away and I'll help you set up a new life for you and your girlfriend, Paula right?' Her name tugged at Tam's heart, and he raised his eyes sadly to meet Frank's.

'As I said, it's my business to know everything.' He hadn't mentioned Tommy Tattoo or Campbell's kidnapping. Tam took that to mean that those were a couple of things he didn't know about, although he suspected it didn't really matter that much in any case.

'I can help you with McGregor, but not Pat.' Tam felt bound by the scheme code never to grass, although he certainly didn't feel that was applicable to bent coppers who had stitched him up.

'No can do. I need them both. Pat links McGregor to the attacks.' Frank sighed, as if knowing exactly how difficult it would be for someone from Tam's background to grass on anyone, especially the likes of Pat.

'I can't do it.' Tam's voice quivered with the realisation that his liberty was slipping through his fingers like sand. After a long silence, Frank left the room and all Tam had for company was the stench of vomit, his hopeless thoughts and the fluorescent vibration. An acute sense of anger rose up inside him, one directed at himself for being so naive, for agreeing to go along with Pat in the first place. Why hadn't he just refused? He had wanted so much to rid himself of his cowardice and at the time Pat seemed to be his only chance.

Frank returned with another folder, a thicker one. He sat and began to drum the fingers of his right hand thoughtfully on the surface of the desk.

'Alright then Tam. As I said earlier I make it my job to know everything and I'm going to tell you some things that initially you will probably refuse to believe; all I ask is that you keep an open mind, besides which, I can prove everything.'

Tam was confused and looked at the contents of the folder as it fell open. He spotted some upside down pictures of Pat looking much younger which grabbed his attention. He straightened himself, listening intently as Frank went on to explain how Pat and McGregor had been doing business together for many years.

'The Tommy Tattoo attack was carried out by Pat as retribution for the young boy that died, TV John's son. We know that wasn't initiated by McGregor. It would have been approved by him though, no way Pat could carry out that attack without McGregor's agreement.' So it would seem Frank did know about the first attack after all.

'One thing I don't get Tam is why a young guy like you with no previous all of a sudden started spending so much time with someone like Pat?' Tam weighed up the disadvantages of being anything other than straight against the embarrassment of the truth.

'Lina asked him if he would help me with a problem.'

'Lina, you live with her at the Rannoch Moor?'

'Aye that's right.'

'What kind of problem?'

'Toughen me up a bit.'

Frank's face opened into an ironic smile. 'Is that not a bit like asking the Pope to take someones first communion?' Tam didn't answer.

'So did it work then, did he turn you into a hard man like him?' Again Tam didn't answer.

'You seem like a nice enough young guy, this is a chance for you to get your life back on track. Forget about any loyalty you think you have to Pat, the guy's a nutter – save yourself.' Another burst of heavy silence before Frank resumed.

'After the Tommy Tattoo attack McGregor had some names he wanted sorted out. When Pat told him he would be taking you along for the ride McGregor wasn't happy, but Pat was insistent. So McGregor created a cover story, to hide from you that they had worked together previously. McGregor suggested he approach Pat as though meeting for the first time, with a request to covertly replicate the Tommy Tattoo attack.'

Tam stared at the surveillance shots laid out in front of him. Pat looked so much younger, but his essence had remained the same. That expression still framed a menacing chill, regardless of the ageing process.

'The interesting thing is that McGregor was pissed off big time by Pat snatching your colleague.' Now Tam realised there were no more secrets: Frank was holding a royal flush, he knew everything.

'That was extremely unprofessional in his opinion. What he was even more pissed at was the fact it had been done without his clearance. Had he asked for McGregor's approval it could have been carried out in such a way there would have been no evidence, like the CCTV from the reception area. He was extremely agitated because he knew it could eventually lead to Pat and that could cause McGregor serious problems.' Tam remained silent, experiencing an increasing resignation to his fate.

'Of course the irony is that the detective investigating the

Campbell case, whether it be workload or incompetence I don't know, hasn't as yet made the connection between the DVD on her desk and Pat. It would compromise our investigation of McGregor to bring it to her attention. So as things stand, it remains undiscovered. It would be interesting to see what McGregor's next move is if she makes the link though. Something tells me self preservation would be his priority.'

There was no doubting the evidence being presented to Tam was convincing. But still he felt a loyalty to Pat. So what if he had worked with McGregor for years. The only reason he had lied to Tam was because the detective had insisted on a cover story to keep their history secret. That wasn't all that unreasonable. It was the old man's fondness of him and his wanting him to tag along that had been the reason the cover story had been created in the first place.

'I'm sorry, as I said I'll help you with McGregor, but not Pat.'

Frank blew out his cheeks in a long, frustrated sigh.

'I'll tell you something else you don't know about our friend Pat shall I?' Frank slid a photocopy of a faded charge sheet from the folder and turned it to face him. Tam stared at it but didn't understand its significance.

'This charge sheet is almost twenty years old and the names on it were Monkford men who worked exclusively for Pat.' Tam shook his head.

'No, he went straight after he married Betsy.'

'That's what he liked everyone to believe. He actually continued his association with the Gorbals gangs behind the scenes, all very discreet. Used those contacts to provide muscle for hire. Oh and by the way, don't buy all that I loved my Betsy bollocks. We've got several reports stretching back over the years. The beloved Betsy had a habit of bumping into furniture it would seem. He's done a great job on you hasn't he, they both have.' Tam was dumbstruck that Pat could have possibly harmed Betsy in any way.

'Did you really think everyone was terrified of him purely because of his younger days in a Gorbals gang?' Frank leaned over the table, pointing at a list of three names on the faded charge sheet that Tam didn't recognise.

'These guys didn't steal a bag of crisps without getting approval from Pat.'

'Alright if you say so, but I don't see...'

'This is the charge sheet from the night your parents' pub was robbed.' Tam considered Frank's expression, which seemed to be looking back at him almost apologetically.

'They were arrested a couple of days later but released due to lack of evidence. Look at that name there, the arresting officer.' Frank placed the tip of his finger next to a name at the bottom of the sheet.

'McGregor?' Tam spoke the word without even having to read the faded print.

'That's right, McGregor concluded there was insufficient evidence to pass a report to the Fiscals office, so they walked. Bottom line, Pat either organised, or at the very least approved, the robbery. As he would have, and still does, approve anything that happens on the Monkford. You think just any sixty-year-old lunatic could slash a Bushwaka in his own flat without there being any comeback? After the robbery, it was up to McGregor to make sure he was involved in the investigation. Pat has operated under a licence for all these years, he and McGregor looked after each others' interests.'

Slowly the impact of exactly what Frank was saying came to him. Tam had recently been confused by experiencing both fear and love for the same person simultaneously. Now that he knew Pat was behind the robbery, the fear would remain but the love would be lost forever. He knew it would be swallowed hungrily by hatred. Frank stood and slid the sheets and photographs back inside the folder.

'I know it's a lot to take in Tam. I'll give you some time to think it over and then I'll make contact. Needless to say any mention of this to either Pat or McGregor and you're fucked. Please believe me when I tell you, right now I'm the only friend you've got.'

CHAPTER 17

The early morning sky was a muted silver and heavy with clouds. The previous night had been spent in a sleepless but fairly comfortable cell and Tam had just been dropped off at the exact spot from where he had been picked up.

Looking down at the pavement, he could see the snow had turned into a brown slushed mess. He walked slowly up the steep footpath from the dual carriageway to the Monkford while considering his next move. Reaching the top of the stairs he stopped in order to catch his breath, his now over-rehearsed speech would have to wait. Paula would have left for work. In fact he realised that speech was now useless and its lines would have to be rewritten to reflect his change in circumstances. He picked his pace up when passing Pat's; he didn't look up at the window and was hopeful he could avoid contact, at least until later. The old man didn't normally make an appearance at the Rannoch Moor until early evening.

If Paula refused to join him on a witness relocation package he knew that would be the end for them. There was no way he could stay here if he co-operated. Turning the corner toward the pub, he could see a Police car sitting directly outside.

Entering the back door he heard a noise that gripped his chest vice-like. It split him in two, pushing a brutal nausea below and a wild dizziness above. Lina's voice rose into a howl of anguish that filled the entire building. It was coming from the Public Bar and he rushed in quickly. She lay lifeless like a ragdoll on the floor as the cleaner and a WPC tried to pull her unsuccessfully onto a small stool next to a table.

'Lina, whit's happened?' Tam knelt down low in front of her. Her eyeliner had made a thick black line down each cheek, giving her the sinister look of a grief-stricken clown. He looked at the others who immediately averted their eyes from him.

'Is your name Tam?' He followed the voice behind to a table where he hadn't noticed another WPC sitting.

'Aye, will somebidy tell me whit's happened for fucks sake?' A sickness rose up within him with such ferocity he had to concentrate on every breath.

'You should have this.' She handed him an opened white envelope with his name on it and then left with the other WPC. He sat on the seat where she had been sitting – it was still warm. His hands began to shake.

Tam

I know you never promised me anything but I did totally believe you loved me like I did you. I tried not to put you under any pressure but I always thought that by saving myself only for you, well I thought you would like it and think I was special, me never having been with anyone else but you. I thought you might have the occasional one-night stand and although that did hurt me I could live with it. I even made up the whole story about there being someone else to try and scare you, trying to make you think you had competition, but there was no one, ever.

What I couldn't live with though was being a pathetic joke and people laughing about me behind my back. Now I know you were actually in a relationship with someone while leading me on. Making me think there might be a chance for us, even sending me a gift that you knew would mean so much. You were always very careful with your words of course, you never made any promises to me but then again you never gave me any closure by telling me the truth. I suppose you will say the reason you didn't tell me the truth is because you didn't want to hurt me. I don't believe that. I think you are a coward Tam, simple as that, nothing to do with not wanting to hurt me, just not having the balls to tell me to my face. I know you will want to know who told me about her and why but I don't see that as being important. All that matters to me, is that I've had enough.

Paula

After he finished reading, he stared at her name for a while before looking at Lina who had now been lifted onto the stool. She stared straight ahead into space and her sodden expressionless face offered him nothing.

Outside on the pavement, tears quite suddenly spilled onto his face as he walked toward the Police car, the window lowered.

'Dae er Maw an Da know?' As he asked the question he wiped his cheek with a sleeve and then put the envelope in his pocket.

'Yes they're at the mortuary, do you want us to take you?'

'Naw, dae they know aboot the letter?'

'No, nobody has seen it apart from CID.'

'How did she dae it?' The WPC hesitated.

'Please, I'll find out soon enough anywye.'

'She hung herself from the big tree on the edge of the scheme, she was found early this morning.' After the mandatory are you sure you will be okays, the car circled the bus terminus and then accelerated out of sight.

***

Tam was sure Lina would blame him, as she should. Besides this, he didn't want to be anywhere near the Rannoch Moor, with its patrons offering undeserved condolences. He walked the quiet streets of the Monkford without direction as the clouds rinsed away the earlier slush with a soft but steady downpour. Finally and despite having done his best to avoid it, his legs had taken him with a feeling of inevitability he was too weak to fight.

The Lord Darnley tree as it was known to locals stood alone in an ungraceful position. Its once rural setting had been encroached on by many years of urban progress. A colossal sycamore, its name derived from a tenuous link to Mary Queen of Scots. She supposedly sat beneath its branches with her lover Lord Darnley, possibly even touched the impressive girth as she attended to his needs. The legend might have been sketchy but the Council had deemed it sufficient to erect not only a square perimeter fence for the tree's protection, but also to commission a plaque.

Henry Stewart Lord Darnley and Mary Queen of Scots sat under this great Sycamore tree when she nursed him back to health after an illness.

Already some effortless but well meaning petrol-station bouquets were propped up against the railing. A line of blue-and-white plastic Police tape zigzagged through the front section of the fence. Along with the plastic wrappers it fluttered in the growing wind. Tam gripped hard on the rusty railing, staring up into the familiar branches. Memories of childhood rope swings, climbing dares and sexual encounters merged into one. Unlike the rest of them Paula had never fallen, a good climber, a bit of a tomboy infact. They had been inseparable for so long. He could touch her desk in class simply by stretching out a ruler. Their whole lives they had lived only streets away from one another and he had probably spent more time with her than anyone else.

The rain grew heavier as the relentless charge of passing vehicles thundered across the busy intersection behind him. It was loud in his ears as the body beneath him began to feel limp, sliding down the railing and onto the waiting mud and grass. His hands gripped the metal tightly as he opened his lungs and although the screams couldn't be heard above the wind and traffic, he gave them everything he had to give.

***

Just as his legs had carried him on autopilot earlier, they now decided he should be taken to Pat's. He had no idea why, perhaps he simply wasn't ready to face Lina. Or was it that he had to see Pat's face one last time? He had of course hoped he would be with Paula tonight. He would have explained how foolish he had been, tried to sell her on the idea of a new life away from the Monkford. Of course she may have rejected him, he would never know now. Her cadaver in a darkened fridge was a struggle to comprehend. Lina would blame him he was sure of it; he blamed himself.

'There ye go son, take that.' Pat handed him a well-used towel to dry himself with, taking his sodden jacket by the fingertips. Tam didn't much feel like speaking, especially not to Pat.

'Terrible business. Fuckin shame fur that wee lassie so it is.' Pat twisted the dial on the electric fire to maximum, then placing two coffee mugs on the windowsill filled them high with whisky.

'Any idea why she did it son?' Tam didn't answer and during the silence it appeared Pat decided a change of subject would be for the best.

'Listen a know it's a bad time fur ye but the reality is that we've goet oor ayn problems anywye. McGregor's still no been able tae get ees hawns oan that CCTV.' Pat gulped greedily on the whisky.

'Av goet a bad feelin aboot aw this so a huv, an ma bad feelins ur normally bang oan, somethins no right am tellin ye son, a kin feel it in ma bones.' Tam stared into the orange glow from the electric bars, saying nothing. He briefly fantasised over images of strangling the old man or slashing him, but those soon faded. What had happened to Paula made everything else seem trivial: the robbery, the lies, everything.

'Av goet a bad feelin aboot McGregor. A mean he wis tellin me how the CCTV widnae be a problem tae get ees hawns oan tae start aff wae. But noo he's sayin he's strugglin. As a said son av goet a bad feelin. Efter aw these years a think the ungrateful bastard's gonnae try tae stitch me up.' Pat up ended his mug and then looked at Tam's.

'If yer no gonnae drink that al huv it eh?' Pat took the untouched whisky from Tam and opened his tobacco tin. Tam's mind replayed the words.

Efter aw these years.

If he had doubted Frank, there was further evidence that McGregor and Pat's alliance hadn't started with these recent attacks. Tam wasn't only quiet because of the numbness of the day's events but also from the underlying fear he was delaying facing up to. Paula's suicide, whilst traumatic, still hadn't changed his precarious life circumstances. He and Pat would be locked up if he didn't co-operate. If he did co-operate it would be McGregor and Pat for the Big House, with him being forced into hiding. In truth the thought of getting away right now wasn't all that unpleasant to him, away from the Monkford and its memories. Surely now he was left with no other option but to start a new life for himself. He had no intention of going to prison. He also knew that becoming an informer would make staying within a hundred miles of the place impossible. The life expectancy of a grass on the Monkford could be counted using the longer arm on a clock face.

'Av been dayin some thinkin son. A know ye took Campbell that bag a smack but even so, if McGregor disnae get ees hawns oan that CCTV we still might end up fucked. A think am gonnae huv tae huv a word wae the boay efter aw. Jist tae be oan the safe side, make sure he knows the score, understawns that he cannae be talkin tae the Polis.' Pat looked out onto the quiet street below as he spoke.

'Ye'll need tae take me tae that Stella's hoose efter aw son, so a kin huv a word wae the boay.'

***

As soon as Pat had asked Tam to take him to Stella's, Tam knew he had no choice but to help Frank. It was bad enough that Campbell had been kidnapped and force-fed on heroin because of him. He simply couldn't stand aside and have anything else happen to the poor guy. The hatred he felt for Pat after finding out about the robbery seemed to have been interrupted somehow by Paula's death. With both Campbell and Stella now in danger though, something had to be done. His priority now was to help get Pat off the streets and into custody.

As he waited for Frank in the supermarket café, he stared at the nearby table. An elderly woman looked back at him nervously, but he couldn't avert his eyes. She was sitting in the same chair as Paula had the last time they spoke. The tannoy announced another special offer, the nearby checkouts beeped the passing bar codes, his mind was pulled back to that day. He lifted the warm coffee mug, blowing on its frothy surface.

As dusk approached, he looked out onto the fading light of the busy car park. Frank sat down across from him.

'Made your mind up then?' Tam wondered if plain clothes officers wore their own casualwear or if it was special issue; he stood out a mile.

'Aye, but there's a condition.'

'What's that then?' Frank's eyebrows lifted into a don't push your luck arch.

'Stella an Campbell ur in danger. Pat's worried that McGregor's gonnae stitch him up oor the CCTV evidence. He waants me tae take em tae Stella's, so he can huv a chat wae Campbell. Although a think it's likely tae be mare than a chat he's efter.'

'Why did Pat snatch him in the first place?' Frank opened a can of diet-juice, pouring into a tall thin glass containing two small ice cubes. Tam hesitated but realised he needed to tell Frank everything in order to ensure the detective could help.

'This aw started because Campbell gave me a doin', that wis the reason Lina asked Pat to help me in the furst place. A didnae know Cambell hudnae made it intae work because a phoned in a sicky. Even efter a went back tae work a didnae huv a clue. Didnae find oot until much later, as soon as a did a managed tae persuade Pat tae let em go.' Tam wanted Frank to be clear that he had nothing to do with Campbell's abduction or what was done to him while he was being held.

'So what's this condition then?' Frank's tone satisfied Tam

that he believed he hadn't been involved.

'Campbell's been through enough. Pat wis way outta line, there wis nae need for aw that. As fur Stella, she's guilty uv nothin mare than bein ma friend. So a will agree tae testify, but you need tae get Pat aff the streets straight away, a mean like immediately, before he gets the chance tae hurt Campbell ur Stella.'

'How do you know he hasn't got to them already?'

'Well, he agreed tae leave it till efter Paula's funeral. A told him a wid help him dae whitever he waants tae Campbell but that it wid huve tae wait until a goet the funeral oot the wye, so ma heed wis right.'

The old woman's husband sat across from her and she smiled. Tam stared hard at her face – they had probably been married for a very long time. Life was being cruel, almost goading him by sitting them at that particular table. His eyes stung and he looked at Frank in an attempt to distract the tears.

'Am no sure if he bought it right enough, ye jist cannae tell wae him neer ye kin. He agreed at the time but am worried he might chynge ees mind.' Frank nodded his head, he seemed to be considering the condition.

'I understand your wanting Pat lifted quickly but it's not as easy as that. I need more time to prep my case against McGregor and Pat for the Procurator Fiscal's office and I can't lift either of them until I get a green light. I honestly can't tell you when that will be, it could take a while.'

'Ye mean yuv goet nae idea?' Tam was gripped by panic.

'Tell you what, I can't tell them much obviously but I'll explain that they may be in danger from the man who kidnapped Campbell and they need to lie low for a bit. I'll take them to a safe house so he can't get to them.' A weight was lifted from Tam's shoulders.

'Kin ye dae it straight away? A couldnae live wae maself if anythin happened tae eether ay them as well as Paula.'

'Alright but I've got a condition of my own.' Frank shook the

206

ice at the bottom of his now empty glass and Tam's relief faded into anxiety.

'I need you to set up a meet between McGregor and Pat.' Tam swallowed a sharp intake of breath.

'That'll be tricky, a never arrange any meets, that's always done by wan ay them.'

'Well, you're going to have to arrange this one and you're also going to have to get them talking as much as possible about the attacks McGregor paid for.'

'Why dae a need tae get them talkin?' He was confused.

'Because you'll be wired up.' Frank's tone was matter-of-fact.

'No way, you're kiddin me on right? Av agreed tae testify, al never be able tae go hame efter that, is that no enough fur ye?' Tam pleaded.

'It's not as bad as you think, tiny wee transmitter, no chance it'll be spotted. Not like the old days with a chunky box taped under your shirt, technology has moved on.' Tam's coffee was cold; he drank it anyway.

'You know, you're up to your eyeballs in shit here. You were with Pat on every attack so you're an accessory at the very least. I've got bosses like the next guy and your get out of jail card is based on the contribution you make to the case. As things stand all you've agreed is to give us your testimony. Any decent brief will say that's just you trying to save your skin and that it's simply your word against theirs. The more you help me the more I can help you: your testimony on its own might not be enough to secure convictions.' Despite being opposed to the idea, Tam knew he wasn't in any position to negotiate.

He also knew that explaining to Pat and McGregor why he had orchestrated any meet behind their backs would be challenge enough. The prospect of then having to steer their conversations in a specific direction was decidedly overwhelming. The fact remained that if he wanted to stay out of jail and also keep Stella and Campbell safe, he had no option but to try.

CHAPTER 18

On his arrival back at the Rannoch Moor, Tam considered trying to avoid Lina but decided it was best to get the encounter over with. At the bar, staff informed him she was resting. Climbing the stairs with a sense of dread, he prepared himself for the worst. She was sitting at the kitchen table, her back to him. A barely audible voice from a radio and wisps of smoke rising from an ashtray. He leaned against the doorframe as dusk slid into darkness beyond the window and her reflection stared back at him. He didn't know what to say, where to start; fortunately she spoke first.

'A know it's no your fault son.' He sat across from her at the table, looking out at the darkening sky.

'Well it cannae be anybody else's fault.' He lit a cigarette from her pack.

'Ma reaction wis doon tae shock that's aw, it wisnae anythin tae dae wae blamin you. Me an the lassie were awfy close ye know that.' He looked at her face, the extent of the makeup run indicated she had been crying for some time.

'So ye honestly don't blame me fur whit happened?' he asked, and she looked directly into him.

'It's no your fault. She didnae know ye hud decided tae put things right. But eether wye, whether ye did ur ye didnae waant tae be wae her ye cannae be held responsible fur whit she done.' Tam relaxed his shoulders, arms falling to either side of the chair. He knew she didn't know about the note, or that someone had told Paula about him and Stella. He considered being honest, but decided against it in the interests of ensuring her condition didn't deteriorate any further.

'A jist cannae help thinkin if a hud made ma mind up sooner that a didnae waant tae be wae Stella, well that none ay this wid a happened.' A heaviness rolled across his eyelids, tears were close.

'That might be so, but whit she didnae get is that a couple ur two separate people. Ye cannae be sayin that if the other person in the relationship eether disnae waant ye or waants tae leave ye thit yer gonnae top yersel. She should've been happy enough in erself tae live her ayn life regardless uv who she wis wae.' He realised she was right. Although he suspected the guilt would travel with him forever there was no disputing the fact that Paula's relationship with herself had obviously not been a great one. Lina reached over the table, pulling him closer as she spoke.

'She wisnae happy in erself and there wis nothin you ur me ur anybody else coulda done aboot it. Noo we jist need tae focus oan gettin the funeral oot the road and then try an get oan wae ur lives, is that no aw we kin dae?' The kitchen flooded in his eyes and gripping her wrist, he kissed the perfumed skin. His tears were a cocktail of loss for Paula, who he knew he had badly treated, combined with Lina talking about getting on with their lives. That simply wasn't going to be possible. He realised it might be rash but decided to sound her out.

'You ever fancied throwin the towel in oan this place?' The promptness of her response surprised him.

'How dae ye mean?' Her darkened eyes narrowed, as though scanning his face for subtext.

'Take it easy, a wis jist wonderin that's aw.' Lighting a cigarette, she stared hard at him.

'Am very fond ay yer Maw an Da ye know that daint ye?' He nodded.

'Aye of course, a know ye ur.' She passed him the cigarette, lighting another for herself.

'Well av actually been tryin tae find the right time tae talk tae ye aboot things.' Her face once more crumpled with pain, and she began to sob quite suddenly.

'Am sorry Tam but a jist cannae keep goan oan like this.' It was Tam's turn to console.

'Hey c'moan you, whit's the matter, c'mere it's awright.' He held her tight to him; she was trembling.

'It's the brewery son. They're no happy wae the takins, that's why av been dayin aw these double shifts, a can barely afford tae pye the staff. Am done in so a um, even wae you helpin a don't know if we'll be able to turn things roon in time.' Tam looked at her sodden face, to which he knew the relentless workload must have added at least ten years.

'How did ye no mention it before noo?' he asked.

'You've hud enough oan yer plate as it is without me makin things worse fur ye. A promised yer Maw an Da a wid look efter ye dinta?' He shook her gently in an affectionate reprimand.

'Aye a know that. An ye huv looked efter me so ye huv, yuv done a brulliant joab.'

'Well if the brewery put somebody else in here, ur decide tae jist shut the place doon, you're oot oan yer ear like me, that's hardly lookin efter ye is it?' He wanted so much to tell her about the witness relocation. He suspected she would be reluctant initially and that the idea of him grassing was bound to be upsetting to her. But he was sure that when she discovered Pat was behind the robbery she would agree he had done the right thing.

'Who else huv ye telt?' Tam asked.

'A told Pau...' She lifted her hand to her mouth, having momentarily forgotten her dead friend with the distractions of her own problems.

'Anybody else apart fae her?'

'Naw naebody else.'

'A cannae say too much the noo Lina but a might be able tae come up wae a solution that could get us fixed up somewhere wae a new pub.' She looked back at him doubtfully.

'Am serious. Av goet a mate whose Da works fur another brewery.' Slowly her expression lifted into one of guarded optimism.

'An ye reckon he could maybe get us another place, maybe

somewhere decent?'

'Well it's no a definite, but he did say he might be able tae sort somethin. A jist didnae say anythin cos a wisnae sure how ye felt.' Her enthusiasm was like the sun appearing from behind a cloud-filled sky. He knew she needed hope, something positive to focus on, and he watched as her demeanour slowly transformed before his eyes. Although Frank's initial offer had been to relocate himself and Paula, now she was gone the offer could surely be adjusted to include Lina. What did Frank care who it was as long as he got what he wanted? There was of course the chance that Lina might not want to make the move under a cloak of secrecy. Although from what she had just told him about the financial prognosis for the Rannoch Moor, well she had said it herself, they could soon be homeless. As for encouraging her to consider there might be a new pub for her to run, well he had no clue if Frank would be willing or even able to make that happen. That was pure wing and a prayer stuff.

***

Tam had thought long and hard about the best location for the meet. Dalry's seemed somehow appropriate, to come full circle and attempt to put an end to things in the place where everything had started. Most of his previous visits had been after work and he was struck by how different the place looked at lunchtime. It seemed like a completely different bar.

He was first to arrive and selected a table upstairs on the unoccupied mezzanine with a view of the entrance. The bay windows seemed to be washing the interior in a bright winter sun. Tam's gaze stopped on the window he had been sandwiched against by Campbell; he couldn't help but dwell on how much had transpired since. McGregor was next to arrive. He spotted Tam waving from above, and squeezed his bulk up the narrow stairs.

'Where's yer baldy pal?' He slid the crombie from his wide

shoulders, hanging it on a nearby coat stand.

'He's no arrived yet.' Tam handed him a lunch menu.

'So whit's this aw aboot then? How come he couldnae jist phone me eeself?' McGregor was of course under the mistaken impression that Pat had asked Tam to set up the meet.

'He waants tae talk aboot this CCTV cerry oan.' Despite being the only diners on the mezzanine, Tam slid his chair closer.

'He's freakin oot aboot it, waants me tae take him tae Stella's place so he kin huv a word wae Campbell.' Tam knew that discussing Pat with McGregor was undoubtedly a betrayal. Whilst highly risky, in view of the fact they would both hopefully be arrested very soon it seemed to be a punt worth taking. Besides, it was the only reason he had been able to come up with that sounded even vaguely plausible. Tam hoped that McGregor wouldn't want Pat going after Campbell. He had already intimated that he was concerned about the old man's deteriorating behaviour.

'So whit surprises hus he goet lined up fur the poor bastard this time?' McGregor asked.

'Your guess is as good as mine, but a reckon whitever it is could make things a whole lot worse than they already ur.' Tam heard the stairs squeak and turned to see a waitress approach.

'What can I get you gentleman?' As was standard for Dalry's, she was young and very attractive. Blonde hair pulled back and a striking face with the skin and lips of a Bisque doll.

'Eh can we just have some drinks, we're waiting for someone.'

Tam thought it best to wait for Pat who was now ten minutes late. His anxiety intensified. Could he somehow know about Frank's deal?

'Of course, what drinks would you like?'

'Fuck that, am starvin, am no waitin fur the wee tadger.' Tam could see she was startled by McGregor's language and manner.

'Al huv the steak and ale pie, a pint ay lager and a large malt.'

He leered over her delicate frame in a way that obviously made her uncomfortable and handed her the menu.

'And you sir.' Her piercing eyes stabbed at Tam; they hovered between light blue and grey, just like Paula's.

'I'll have the same thanks.' He didn't feel like drinking but certainly didn't want to arouse any suspicion. The front door banged closed with the same thud he had heard the night Campbell raced out to confront him. He looked down at the black suit, white collar, and bald head surveying the scene. Tam managed to attract his attention and Pat walked through the bar area with his usual swagger, greeting confused patrons and bar staff as though he knew them.

'Sorry boays, wee bit a business tae attend tae, yees know how it is.' He sat across the table, smiling as Tam worried himself further about the exact nature of his wee bit of business. Hopefully Frank had got to Campbell and Stella in time.

'Yoos ordered?'

'Aye posh pie, pint an a hawf,' McGregor replied. Rather than walking downstairs to the bar or waiting for his order to be taken, Pat leaned over the balcony, shouting at no one in particular.

'Al huv the same as ma two pals ur huvin!' Even McGregor shook his head.

'Right, so whit's aw this aboot then?' As Pat spoke Tam knew this was going to require some skill as well as a high degree of luck. With both men under the mistaken impression that the other had requested the meet, Tam decided he must seize the initiative and try to navigate proceedings through the tricky waters.

'Kin the three uv us get ur heeds roon this CCTV business then?' As Tam spoke, he could feel the tickle of a quiver under his words. He was conscious how far outside his comfort zone he was operating as Pat and McGregor looked at each other, mirroring the same confusion.

'Whit dae ye mean?' Pat's tone was terse.

'The evidence, the CCTV.' Tam squeezed the words out of his throat as though it were a tube of toothpaste. Now that he heard his own reasons for the meet verbalised, he feared the worst. There was a pause as McGregor and Pat seemed to be talking to each other through their eyes; McGregor spoke first.

'It's no your fuckin place tae be settin up meetins.' He leaned over and gripped Tam's forearm, vice-like.

'Dae ye understawn whit am sayin tae ye?' Tam thought his arm might actually snap.

'Aya! that's fuckin sore.'

'Awright take it easy for fuck sake.' Pat spoke and McGregor finally released his grip.

'Al deal wae the boay masel.' Tam was too terrified to look, instead he stared at his polished silver cutlery. He could feel Pat's eyes on him all the same.

'The boay hus goet a point but, whit is the fuckin score wae that CCTV, did ye get yer hawns oan it?' Pat asked the question and McGregor looked over each shoulder. He knew no one was there of course, it was as though he wanted to discourage the discussion of the matter in public. Tam could only hope that the rapidly deteriorating relations between the two men would cloud their judgement and loosen their tongues in equal measure.

'If ye hid spoke tae me in the furst place none ay this wid a happened wid it? A could've arranged things tae be done right.'

'Aye awright awright but a didnae did a, so whit's the score?' Pat spoke through clamped teeth, as though ready to launch himself across the table. McGregor was about to reply when the squeak of the stairs signalled the arrival of the waitress.

'There we are gents, three steak and ale pies with three pints of lager, and three malts. Anything else I can get you?'

'Naw sweetheart yer awright, if we need anythin else we'll gee ye a shout eh.' Pat knew of course that shouting from the balcony was completely inappropriate, but he flashed back at her the ironic grin of a helpless sociopath. She flustered a polite smile and returned down the narrow squeaking stairs. McGregor burst his pie's pastry with a fork and a waft of heat escaped upward as he spoke.

'Kin ye no jist leave it tae me like a telt ye tae? A um workin oan it but you'll need tae be a bit mare patient.'

'Av been a lot a things in ma time big yin, but patient isnae wan ay them. As soon as that lassie's funeral's oot the road, me an Tam ur gonnae huv a word wae the boay. Am no in the business ay takin chances.' Pat stared at Tam and his face seemed to take on an even more sinister appearance than was usual; he was actually enjoying himself.

'That's right intit son?'

'Aye that's right.' Tam knew it was paranoia, but he felt as though Pat were reading the details of his treachery from his face.

'Well if a kin get ma hawns oan it then yees'll no need tae huv a word wae the boay wull yees.' Gravy escaped from McGregor's mouth as he spoke, dribbling down his wide chin. Pat either had an alcoholic's appetite or had decided his pie was too warm; instead, he attended to his drinks.

'Whit funeral ye oan aboot?' McGregor had quickly finished the body of the pie and now scraped at the pastry from the walls of the bowl.

'Paula, young lassie fae the Monkford,' Pat answered him after a pause; Tam was unable to.

'Aye a a heard aboot that, is she the wan that hung erself?' McGregor didn't lift his head from the bowl as he spoke.

'Dae yees mind if we talk aboot somethin else.' Tam didn't want to discuss Paula.

'Him an the lassie were close.' Pat showed unusual sensitivity in steering the detective away from the topic.

'Oh right, sorry aboot that, didnae know.'

With McGregor's bowl now cleaned, Tam offered his own dish in the interests of keeping the meeting and its dialogue flowing.

'Here ye waant mine?'

'Hus a rockin horse goet a widen dick? Ye don't need tae ask

215

me twice son, lovely pie that.' McGregor swapped plates as Tam attempted to formulate in his mind how he could keep them talking, without drawing any more attention to himself than he already had.

'Gonnae go doonstairs and order another round a drinks son?'

Pat asking him to go downstairs may have been innocent enough, but then again it could have been an attempt to get rid of him so they could discuss something in private. He didn't want to miss one word of dialogue just in case. So he took up temporary membership of the sociopath society, leaning over the balcony and shouting: 'Kin ye bring up another three pints a lager an three double malts when ye get a minute!' Every face, staff and customer alike, stared up at the mezzanine in bemusement.

'That's ma boay eh!' Pat might have been angry about his setting up the meet but nonetheless this was pleasing behaviour to him. Tam decided to ride the crest of this wave and push his luck. He addressed McGregor directly.

'So hus things improved oan the schemes where we slashed they guys fur ye?' Tam gulped on his lager, trying to act casual.

'Whit ye oan aboot?' McGregor looked first at Pat then stared hard at Tam who immediately realised he shouldn't have forced the issue so soon or even at all.

'Ye know something, a don't understawn whit your fuckin problem is ya wee cunt?' Tam looked at Pat for backup, but he simply stared into space as though distancing himself. Possibly as a punishment for having set the unauthorised meet up in the first place.

Coconut Badger! Coconut Badger!

'Whit dae ye mean? Av no goet a problem, we're supposed tae be oan the same side ur we no?' Tam was glad when the calmness slid an arm around his shoulder.

'Whit ye oan aboot same side? Only reason you're involved is cos yer pal here insisted. If ye ask me yuv goet a brass neck takin the money fur dayin hee haw.'

Tam knew this was a fair comment. As his anxiety made the transition into calmness, he also saw an opportunity to ruffle the detective's feathers.

'How come Pat asked me tae slash the last wan then?' McGregor almost choked.

'He whit?' The detective was unhappy and stared hard at Pat who was equally unhappy, staring hard at Tam while speaking to McGregor.

'Al handle things whitever wye a see fit, if a waant the boay tae slash somebody then that's ma business.' McGregor looked to have lost his appetite, picking up the malt. As was standard, soon after it touched his oesophagus he began to shudder into a violent wheezing fit and gripped the table edge to steady himself. Tam knew this may be his only chance to get Frank what he wanted.

'So huv things improved then? It's a valid question is it no?' McGregor regained his composure and looked back at him silently, as though considering Tam's actions carefully.

'Whit is it wae you? Settin up this fuckin meetin by lyin tae me and him sayin the other wan waanted it. An then ye turn up talkin aw this shite. Ye think am a fuckin dafty son is that it?' McGregor stood, wiping the gravy from his chin with the back of his hand, his huge menacing face bearing down on Tam.

'You wearin a fuckin wire ya wee cunt?'

'Whit ye oan aboot?'

Coconut Badger! Coconut Badger!

'Cos if ye ur, am gonnae snap yer neck before the cavalry arrives.' Tam hadn't even discussed with Frank what would happen if he were compromised. Just in time he was able to slide into his post adrenal calmness. He considered Frank's reassurance that the transmitter under his shirt collar wasn't standard Police issue, that it was more advanced than anything McGregor would be familiar with. Tam held McGregor's stare as the detective spoke.

'Mind if a search the boay, tae satisfy masel?' Pat had shown no interest in getting involved up to this point.

'Tae be honest a dae actually, yer oot a line as far as am concerned, the boay's wae me an that should be the end ay it.' But Tam knew that to leave this meet without the trust of either man wouldn't help his cause any. He decided to take a gamble.

'Naw it's nae bother Pat a don't mind, av goet nothin tae hide.' McGregor looked again at Pat, who gave the slightest nod to indicate he was okay with it.

'Awright then, put yer hawns up against the waw.' As Tam leaned against the wall such was his relaxed manner he went as far as to laugh at the detective's clichéd instruction and McGregor began his search. All Tam could do now was wait to see if his gamble would pay off.

'It's awright darlin wur jist playin a wee drinkin game.' None of them had heard the squeaking staircase. Their waitress was now standing just a few feet away with their order and had obviously overheard. As Pat spoke, she placed the tray nervously on the next table. As she was about to turn away Pat stood, stepping behind, trapping her between him and the table edge.

'You jist stawn there sweetheart an al show ye how we play this wee game ay oors.' She tried to wriggle free but he gripped her shoulders hard. Thankfully for Tam this was a distraction for McGregor, who had now turned from the wall. The young girl's body trembled nervously.

'See aw we dae is this, we check the kinda places where somebidy could be wearin a wire.' As he spoke, he leaned his groin into her buttocks and then slid his arms around her sides to her front. He hooked his thumbs under her bra wire, lifting it over her soft flesh, twisting her nipples before cupping his hands over her. He nuzzled his face behind her ear.

'So a kin tell thit yur no wearin any wire under yer bra, apart fae the wan that's supposed tae be there that is.' He took a deep breath of the scent around the back of her neck.

'Noo the question is sweetheart, where else could a be lookin, whit other kinda places could you be hidin a wire?'

'Pat, take it easy fur fuck sake whit ye dayin?' Tam didn't like to question him as he knew from experience that was hazardous, but he simply couldn't stand aside and let him terrorise the young girl. McGregor's search fortunately for Tam hadn't included the lifting of his shirt collar, and he tapped his shoulder indicating he was satisfied.

'She's no scared ur ye, were jist hivin a wee cerry oan ur we no?' McGregor seemed to be weighing up his options before reaching for his crombie and hurriedly sliding his arms into it.

'See Pat this is exactly whit av telt ye aboot. It's the kinda thing that's bad fur me, a cannae be aroon when yer dayin things like this.'

Tam was unsure what Pat hoped to achieve by such a display. Perhaps he simply wanted Tam and or McGregor to be reminded that he was a psychopath. The detective scanned the deserted mezzanine for cameras and then made for the stairs.

'Right well thanks fur lunch boays al be seein yees later.' Within a few seconds his heavy footsteps could be heard quickly moving through the bar below. As the front door closed, Pat stepped back from the terrified waitress, sitting casually in his chair as if nothing of note had happened.

'Well yer no wearin a wire darlin so you get to order any drink ye waant fae the bar, that's the rules, jist add it tae the bill.' Tam was still standing from the search and now looked sadly at the teary face of the waitress. Shaking, she twisted and lowered her bra back into position.

Pat was as much of an enigma to him now as he had ever been. There was one thing however that Tam did know: the sooner Frank could get him off the streets, the better. Tam only hoped that the dialogue from today's meeting would help accelerate the process.

CHAPTER 19

The day Tam had been dreading finally arrived and he stood with Lina outside the crematorium. Some mourners had gone in to take their seats, others were gathered in a scattering of small groups under little clouds of cigarette smoke.

'It's freezin, a think it could snow again so a dae.' After Lina spoke, they both stared up at the ash sky. Tam could see smoke from the chimney being despatched in discreet wafts.

'Aye ye could be right, it's cauld enough.' The late morning breeze did have a sharpness to it, although his shivering was more down to the anxiety of the occasion than the cold.

'Ye sure yer gonnae be awright?' Lina touched his elbow softly as she spoke.

'Aye al be fine, whit aboot you?' She nodded unconvincingly and he pulled her close. The small crematorium was almost hidden in the centre of an old cemetery overrun by weeds, unkempt trees and dilapidated headstones. Their taxi had brought them down a poorly maintained dirt track, the only access road. It was riddled with wide rain- filled potholes that their driver had avoided more for the sake of his suspension than the comfort of his passengers. Tam thought of the hearse that would soon follow and couldn't prevent an image of her being thrown against the interior of her coffin.

'Good turn oot eh?' Lina nodded toward the groups of people, their numbers steadily swelling around the entrance.

'Aye, there's nae chance we're aw gonnae fit in there.' As he spoke it was somehow understood between them that neither would enter the building and that the lack of seats would give them the excuse needed. As those around them began shifting position, they found themselves being swept along until they were standing involuntarily just a few yards from the entrance. Tam tried to lose himself in the crowd by stepping back and sideways but was blocked and unable to hide. He heard the tyres on the gravel nearby and his only thought was to avoid seeing her. Being so tightly packed, any attempt to flee would have been obvious so he gripped Lina's arm, staring at his newly polished shoes. He continued to focus downward, chin clamped tight on to his chest. As the crunching of the gravel stopped, he found himself looking at a shining chrome wheel of the hearse. It occurred to him he would have been better to enter the chapel earlier, sitting in a distant corner. He hadn't intended getting this close to her, she was literally feet away. He refused to allow the back of his neck to straighten, as two stretched cars pulled in behind and her parents and family stepped out. There followed crying, gravel footsteps, words of condolences but still he stared downward, not once looking up at her.

'A don't know Archie, a think he might be a wee bit too upset.' He could hear Lina's voice talking to Paula's dad.

'It wid mean an awfy lot tae me an the wife so it wid.' There was silence and then a soft tug on his arm. He had no choice but to finally raise his face to meet that of her father, Archie. He couldn't avoid it any longer, his peripheral vision took in the coffin and floral displays he had been avoiding.

'Am no up tae it Tam, could you take ma place son? You an her were pals fur years.' He had always liked Archie, a small round man with silver swept-back hair, followed as was usual by an odour of brylcreem. He didn't want to do it, but knew to refuse would only add to the man's upset. If only Archie had read the letter, Tam was sure he wouldn't be asking him. Lina squeezed his elbow supportively as he stepped out from the crowd. He moved to the back of the now open hearse with five men he didn't look at.

'You're number wan.' He didn't know it then but it was Archie's younger brother who had just handed him the small card with numbered positions around a coffin. Number one had been destined for her father, the closest family member. The others were undertakers and she was expertly slid from her carriage up onto their shoulders. Tam's ear now pressed against the cold wood, inches from her head. He slid his arm under her, gripping the uncle's shoulder tightly. He considered using Coconut Badger to steady himself, but under the circumstances it didn't feel appropriate. It could be argued that the strategy had contributed to her death. He attempted to control his nausea instead by taking short sharp breaths as they shuffled into the chapel.

'Yer awright son yer dayin well.' The uncle must have heard his frantic breathing. When they stepped up onto the small platform behind the open curtain, they gently lowered her down on to the plinth with its shining rollers, her feet pointing toward the hatch. Before stepping back, Tam leaned forward, tenderly kissing the wood over her face.

'I'm so sorry Paula.'

As her uncle took his seat in the front row Tam paused, hesitated, everyone seemed to be looking through him, as though they knew. He had no seat so followed the undertakers down the aisle, walking from the chapel out into the grey morning light. Lina was ready and had to take his weight as he stepped out and onto the gravel.

'Yer awright son, c'mere av goet ye.' After a mostly silent embrace that lasted a long time, Lina suggested they go back to the bar. That way they could help her staff get the buffet ready. TV John and his wife offered them a lift back and they agreed.

***

Having spent so many nights with her over the years in the Rannoch Moor, he would rather have been anywhere but there. Wherever his eyes rested, a memory stabbed him. His absence would have seemed inappropriate though, so he had no choice but to stay.

The Lounge was the venue for most Monkford funerals. Along with weddings, birthdays, christenings, most of the scheme's family gatherings and functions were held there. Funerals were normally late morning or early afternoon affairs. It was one of the few occassions when wives allowed their husbands to start on the drink early without the worry of being reprimanded. Tam brought some drinks over to their table and sat with TV John and his wife Rina. Rina was a well presented rotund lady with a face that was always sombre, had been even before her son was murdered. He decided he would stay for the minimum amount of time and then make his excuses.

His priority was to make contact with Frank. He had no idea what the hold-up was but still Pat hadn't been arrested. He would also ask if a new pub could be found for himself and Lina, somewhere as far away as possible. In addition, he hadn't seen Stella or Campbell in some time and wanted to check they had made it to the safe house OK. Lina fussed over the buffet, which had been spread across four tables next to the bar. Gradually the mourners returned by the car-load, and soon the Lounge was busy.

'A jist waanted tae say thanks fur helpin tae cerry ma wee lassie earlier.' As Paula's mum Jean spoke, Tam was struck by how unlike her husband and daughter she was, long and thin. He wasn't sure if her strange textured copper hair was a wig or just heavily sprayed.

'It wis nae bother ataw, honestly.'

'A know you an her were good pals. Infact me an er da hud always hoped you an her might uv ended up the gether, a know she really liked ye.' She smiled through a mask of tears.

'A know, a liked her anaw.' His voice quivered.

'It's awright son don't you go upsettin yerself, It's no your fault. She wis jist in a bad place that's aw.' She wiped at his moist cheekbone with her thumb.

'You an Pat huv been very kind tae ma wee lassie, don't think me an Archie will forget it.' Tam's brain stalled in a reaction to Pat's name being mentioned.

'Eh how dae ye mean, whit did Pat dae fur er?' He cast his

223

mind back but could think of nothing.

'He came tae the hoose tae talk tae er the night before it happened, said he wis thinkin aboot investin money in somethin and maybe she could reopen the salon next tae the bookies.' Archie had seen her tears and approached, putting an arm around her.

'Thanks again fur earlier Tam, really appreciate it.'

'Nae bother Archie.' None of them knew about the letter. His feelings of guilt though, were now consumed by curiosity. Why would Pat be speaking to Paula and not mention it to him? His mind was in a jumble, but he attempted to cast it backward. That was the night he told Pat he planned to terminate their partnership. To make a go of things with Paula. Pat had then insisted he take the heroin to Stella's place for Campbell immediately before going to see Paula. Then he had been taken in by Frank for questioning and held overnight. So while all that was going on, Pat had visited Paula?

He watched Pat moving among those at the edge of the buffet, managing to somehow crack jokes without crossing any lines of bad taste. This was standard behaviour, for Monkford wakes tended not to be sombre affairs.

'So how ye bearin up son?' Pat handed him a whisky.

'There's a real drink fur ye.' Tam said nothing, looking over at Paula's mother. He considered just leaving it, did it really matter? Hopefully he would be off the streets soon enough in any case. But there was something inside him rising up, he had to know.

'Jean said ye went tae see Paula the night before she died.' He did his best to extract everything but casualness from the words as he spoke.

'Aye, so whit if a did?' Pat stared straight through him in a look Tam had become familiar with. It meant he was approaching the line it was best to avoid crossing.

'So whit did ye speak tae er aboot?' Pat's eyes scanned every inch of his face as though it were a newspaper.

'No bein funny son but al talk tae whoever the fuck a waant

tae, an it's nae concern ay yours ur anybody elses.' Pat offered up a tobacco- stained smile. Since the meet with McGregor something had changed between them. There had been a shift of some sort and the fondness he had felt projected onto himself by the older man seemed to be evaporating. Tam wondered again if he could possibly somehow know about his deal with Frank. The fear of the man wouldn't release its grip. He wanted to force the issue, demand answers, but simply felt too weak, even with Coconut Badger. So he decided to use a different, more subtle approach.

'Naw don't take it like that, a don't mean anythin by it Pat. A ended up chyngin ma mind aboot Paula anywye, wisnae right fur me, neether wis Stella. Am better aff bein single, too young tae be settlin doon, should be enjoyin maself at ma age.' Again Pat seemed to be reading subliminal print on his face, but his previously frosty attitude was cautiously lifted.

'That's good son, see ye cannae let burds complicate things fur ye. You gettin the gether wae some burd isnae a problem in itself. It's when ye start turnin yer back oan yer pals, that's jist no the done thing, cannae huv that.' Pat pointed over to one of his preferred tables and Tam followed.

'Ye don't mind dae yees boays?' Two men rose in silence, departing the scene.

'Haw big yin, gonnae get me a couple a large whiskys, an wan fur yerself anaw.' Pat passed a cashline twenty to a man at the next table. Tam didn't know him and wasn't even sure if Pat did; he was compliant in any case.

'See a wisnae totally honest wae ye aboot ma Betsy son.' The old man paused as though searching for the right words and Tam remembered Frank's claims of domestic violence.

'Efter we goet merried a tried tae go straight an dae the whole nine tae five thing but it jist wisnae fur me. A knew she widnae stawn fur anythin dodgy so a jist went aboot ma business discreetly.' No confession then about having hit the woman he supposedly worshiped. Tam was confused and anxious, the

225

timing of this revelation was a concern to him. Why now? Did he know he had been speaking to Frank and wanted to put his own spin on things?

The stranger returned with the drinks, placing them carefully on the table along with his change.

'See a discovered at a very young age that ye kin make a lot a money scarin cunts. You've seen that fur yerself wae the money McGregor's been throwin it us.' The old man continued to stare at him.

'Me an Betsy were never able tae huv weans, efter we started workin the gither you became like a son tae me. Part ay me thought ye might be able tae take oor in the future, like wae a family business.' Pat nodded, indicating he should respond.

'A don't know whit tae say.' This was a shock. First the frosty response when asked about Paula, then a disclosure about his past, and finally a vote of confidence. Was he being softened up for the kill?

'Don't get me wraang, am plannin oan bein aroon fur a long time tae come. But av already taught ye alot uv stuff, mare tae learn, but a um fond ay ye, ye know that daint ye?' Pat put a hand on Tam's knee. He felt a guilt of sorts at his betrayal of the man, but quickly reminded himself of the robbery. Then something occured to him. What if the men hadn't had his approval after all? Frank was only able to prove who did it and that McGregor had reported insufficient evidence to convict. He hadn't technically demonstrated that Pat had in any way endorsed the attack. Pat took a throaty gulp of his whisky. Tam briefly considered asking him outright. Pat after all had opened up to him about his past. After a few moments' consideration, and despite the fact that he now had two questions he desperately wanted to discover the answer to, Tam decided it would be best to ease off and give the old man some space rather than arouse suspicion. He knew if he were to have any chance of getting out of this he had to stay within the perimeter of Pat's trust. Moving to the bar, he spoke with Lina who asked about his friend with the brewery connections. He made her promise again not to tell anyone and said he would hopefully find out within a few days. He chatted to some familiar faces, all offering him undeserved sympathy, none of them knowing about the letter.

The scene gradually, inevitably, descended into an alcohol instigated party atmosphere. Nothing to do with Paula, just another excuse for Monkford blooterdom. Tam had deliberately been going easy in an attempt to keep a clear head. He could see Pat being bought round after round as was usual. He was in high spirits and going through an improvised ensemble of his favourite Deano renditions. The crowd around Pat seemed transfixed by his display. It sickened Tam that these people had just a few hours ago been appropriately long faced, obviously for the benefit of Paula's parents, who had now left thankfully.

Pat was singing another of his favourite Martin songs. The lyrics of this one were Italian; Tam suspected he wouldn't have a clue what they meant. The sight of Pat standing there, using a bottle of beer as a mic, while the people around him swayed from side to side, made Tam nauseous. It seemed like everyone had all forgotten why they were there.

Tam considered going upstairs to try and make contact with Frank, but something was stopping him. He knew Pat could be arrested any minute and after that he might never know the truth. This might be his last chance, so he stood at the bar, watching, waiting. Eventually Pat slumped back on a seat and Tam made his move quickly, before the entourage got the encore they were desperate for.

'That wis brilliant so it wis Pat, yuv certainly goet auld Deano doon tae a tea hint ye.'

'Ye think so son, very kind ay ye tae say that, the guy wis a fuckin legend in ma book.' Pat had the nodding head syndrome and was obviously struggling to keep his focus on any one object for more than a few seconds. Tam supped his pint casually. He couldn't ask him outright of course but thought if he could just steer the conversation, in his current condition he might slip up.

227

'Aye she wis a nice lassie right enough, how aboot a wee toast tae Paula, Pat?' Tam lifted his pint.

'Yer right son, she wis a nice lassie.' Pat tried to stand but struggled, so Tam grabbed an elbow helping him to his feet.

'Quiet doon yoos lot, a waant tae make a toast.' Pat's words were slurred, but sufficient to bring the Lounge to a gradual hush.

'As yees aw know it wisnae that long ago we wur in here sayin cheerio tae ma Betsy, but the day it's that beautiful wee lassie Paula we're here tae pye ur respects tae. Av known er since she was a tiny wee thing an Archie an Jean did a great joab bringin er up so they did. She wis born oan the Monkford an she died oan the Monkford. A know we've hud a few problems in the past but am very proud ay this scheme uv oors so a um. An a hope when ma numbers up yees'll gee me as good a send aff, an a waant yees aw in here blastin Deano oot that jukebox oor there. Charge yer glasses, tae Paula!' After some muffled laughter at Pat's Deano reference and also pointing to the wrong wall when mentioning the jukebox, the Rannoch Moor joined in unison.

'Tae Paula!'

Tam guided him back down into his seat as the rubberness of his neck now completely relaxed and his chin rested on the top button of his shirt, saliva drooling from the corner of his mouth. He looked to be completely out of it and Tam resigned himself to the fact he was too far gone to get any information from. In silence he considered his next move but was startled when without warning Pat's neck pushed his face up like a jack-in-the-box.

'A did it fur yur ayn good son, fur yer ayn good so it wis.' Pat was looking back at him but his eyes focussed somewhere above Tam's head.

'Ye did whit fur me ayn good?' He was met with a wobbling face and Tam shook him lightly by the shoulders to keep him from sliding back into his stupor.

'Whit is it that ye did fur me?'

228

'A offered the lassie a deal.'

'Whit kinda deal?'

'She wid get tae open a salon, but in return she wid need tae tell you she wisnae interested.'

'Why did ye dae that?'

'A thought if she knocked ye back then ye wid come back tae me.' The old man looked back at him with a wounded grimace. Tam knew he had been unhappy at his dissolving of the partnership but he hadn't realised just how much it had upset him.

'So whit did she say?'

'She wisnae huvin it, babblin oan aboot bubble wrap ur somethin, so a hid tae try something else.'

'Whit dae ye mean try something else Pat, whit dae ye mean?'

'A telt er thit ye wur in love wae that Stella burd.'

Silence.

From the moment he had read Paula's note, part of him had suspected it. Now here it was, proof in the form of a confession. Pat had made up lies about Stella in order to scupper his plans with Paula. Tam stared hard at a pint tumbler, thoughts of pushing and twisting it into the fleshy face till he could hear the grind of glass on bone. He would never have an easier opportunity than this. The monster was paralysed by booze, helpless – he could have done it in that instant without even using Coconut Badger. Somehow though, all of the time spent with Pat seemed to underline what he should have known all along: they were not the same.

'Am sorry Tam, a didnae mean fur this tae happen.' The drunken slabberings rung in his ears as he departed the Lounge. The early evening salmon sky was doing its best not to yield to the uninvited clouds. The streets around him were bathed in a fuchsia syrup and he walked slowly, knowing he would end up there but trying to delay it for as long as possible. Soon enough, he couldn't put it off any longer and as the last tear of pink wept from a darkening sky he arrived at their lone sycamore.

Climbing the fence, he lost his balance and fell down onto his side; the earth was soft and wet as he crawled toward the huge trunk. Sitting with his back to the sycamore, he looked out at the passing traffic thundering in both directions. They had sat here so many times as children. Talking about all the things they would do when they were grown ups. A gentle breeze reached down from the branches stroking his face, and soon he drifted into a deep sleep.

***

On the edge of the dream place, he knew that the night of the robbery was being offered up to him in its entirety. The initial noises jolting him from the innocent slumber of a child. The tentative steps down the hall before squeaking floorboards forced him to crawl on hands and knees. Arriving at the top of the stairs breathless and light-headed. Sliding arms through the banister, which he gripped so tightly his chest was left bruised. The pyjamas slowly covered in the warm piss and rancid shit. The inner turmoil over not having the courage to descend the stairs to use the payphone. The seed of hatred planted for a father who wouldn't or couldn't protect his family. But what of the shame he felt for his mother. She had done nothing wrong and yet after that night he had never held her eye in the same way.

Finally it came to him. He had gone downstairs after all. Standing on the bottom step from where he knew he could reach the receiver. But he had hesitated; he wanted to know exactly where the bad men were standing. To make sure they were far enough away. Slowly he stepped barefoot across the cold linoleum. Heart like a drum in his ears, he gripped the doorframe before cautiously leaning the top of his head out, just enough to see.

His father on his knees sobbing, a bad man standing over him holding what looked like a knife. Mother lying on a table. Her legs pushed apart by a man whose jeans were at his knees. She was fighting, trying to scratch, punch, kick, but a third man held her arms. He was laughing, they were all laughing. His father sobbing, doing nothing other than averting his eyes, trying not to watch. Tam knew the man was hurting his mother. Woven into their laughter there was dialogue but none of that came back to him now. All that is except one word that the man leaning over his mother repeated.

Buckaroo! Buckaroo!

***

He had no idea how long he had slept for. But his face had a numbness he would normally associate with a deep sleep. It wasn't uncomfortable to be sitting out, as the night air was mild. The council had installed lights around the famous old tree, illuminating the scene upwards of the lowest branch but not the trunk, so he was content he couldn't be seen.

Looking up into the myriad of leafless branches, he stared at the the thickest and lowest. The one he knew she would have used. It was that one they had swung from as children. She would have known that branch was as symbolic as her bubble-wrapped earrings. He could only rest his eyes on it for a few seconds before having to look away. He slid a hand into his pocket and removed the razor Pat had given him. So now he knew everything. This man he had become so fond of. He was responsible for Paula's death as well as the robbery during which his mother was raped. He extended the blade; the lights from above glimmered back at him.

Gradually the noise of traffic came to him and he stood, managing to climb the fence without falling this time. Approaching the busy dual carriageway he turned, looking back at their lone sycamore. A sense of peace washed over him, unlike anything he had ever felt. Somehow in death she was reaching out to him; he was sure it had been her who had brought him here to this place of dreams. He smiled.

***

Tam had been waiting for the right moment to speak to Lina. She was in the kitchen on a rare break. The door was never closed so when he entered and shut it behind, she turned from the sink.

'This looks ominous.' She spooned coffee into a cafetière.

'Av been givin things a lot a thought Lina.'

'Whit is it son?' He suspected her inital thought would be that he was about to tell her he was leaving. It had been a conversation she must have considered over the years, and especially now, with the trouble the pub was having.

'Turns oot that pal a mine cannae help wae the other boozer efter aw.' Her face dropped.

'It's awright son, al undersdawn if you waant tae find somewhere else tae stye.' She dropped dejectedly into a chair.

'Am no goan anywhere Lina, a belang here wae you.'

'That's awfy sweet ay ye son but you've goet yer ayn life tae live, a understawn that, av always known that.'

'This place is ma life Lina. It's took me a while tae see it but a know whit it is a need tae dae noo. A waant us tae huv a right good go at convincin the brewery tae gee us another chance. Al gee a hundered percent so a will, we cannae gee up oan the place withoot a fight.'

'An dae ye think we've actually goet a chance?' she asked.

'Aye a dae, if baith uv us ur workin at it a think we huv goet a fightin chance. It's taken me a long time tae realise whit's really important tae me. But a know noo, makin sure your awright, an helpin ye get this place back oan track. It's whit ma Maw an Da wid waant me tae dae, they widnae waant us tae lose the place.' He sat next to her at the table, taking her hands in his.

'You waant a coffee?' she asked.

'Aye thanks, this is ma home, am no goan anywhere.' She passed him the steaming mug, her fingertips gripping the rim as

232

she listened intently.

'A wis born here Lina. A waant tae make it work, a waant us baith tae make it work. Nae mare runnin away like ma Maw an Da done. Am no runnin anywhere.'

'Ye cannae blame them fur that, the robbery must a been traumatic fur them baith.' He was unsure if she knew about the rape but understood that some things were best left alone.

'A know that, don't get me wrang am no bein critical ay them. They did whit they felt wis fur the best, that's fair enough. But we aw agreed at the time that a wid stye behind, so a could make ma ayn life.'

'Aye yer right enough, we did.'

'Well it's clear tae me noo what a need tae dae, whit a waant tae dae. Tae help you get this place back oan track, makin money again.'

'Whit if it's too late?' she asked.

'At least we'll uv geed it oor best shot.'

'Ye waant a biscuit wi that?' It was the first time he had seen her smile in days.

'Huv ye goet any tea cakes?' She handed him the same old battered biscuit tin his mother had used when he was a child.

'Ur ye sure it's whit ye waant Tam?'

'Av never been surer aboot anythin else in ma life. Nae mare runnin.' She pulled him into an embrace, forgetting about the biscuit tin between them. The metal pressed painfully into his chest; he didn't care if it left a bruise

.

CHAPTER 20

Tam was being shown the ropes by Lina and it was an experience he found to be quite surreal. After having spent so many years around the bar, this was the first time he had started an actual shift. The evening was going well and the regulars were all pleased he had made a commitment to their local. Although Lina hadn't told anyone, some had sensed there was a danger of closure.

Tam had decided he would not be forced into hiding. There would be no deal with Frank. His only objective now was to find some sort of resoloution. He knew this would mean having to make a stand.

'Yer a good boay Tam, helpin Lina oot.' Archie had shuffled despondently into the bar for the first time since his daughter's wake. Tam had decided Lina wasn't the only one he would be looking after from now on.

'Seemed like the right thing tae dae Archie. By the way a wis meanin tae ask ye, how aboot ye bring yer good lady here the morra night an al cook yees yer dinner, wan ay ma world famous lasagnes?' Archie's face lifted just enough to show Tam he appreciated the gesture.

'Very kind uv ye son, she'll like that thanks.' His hand crossed the bar with payment for his pint. Tam pushed it back gently.

'Oan the house.' The old man smiled for the first time in a while.

As the evening passed, Lina made several positive comments about his performance. This made Tam proud in a way he had never known and he concentrated on trying to learn everything there was to know. Hopefully in the short term he could get himself to a level where she could take some time off. Maybe even go and visit his parents in the sun; she deserved a break. When the place was on an even keel he himself would make that journey. He knew that his relationship with them both needed some attention.

Kneeling in front of a fridge as he replenished the bottled beers, Lina popped her head through the doorway.

'Somebidy in the Lounge waants a word.' His heart began to race; this would be the first time he had seen him since the drunken confession. As he passed Lina in the hallway however, he noticed a look of apprehension that indicated whoever it was, it wasn't Pat.

The Lounge was much quieter than the Bar. A scattering of patrons dotted around the tables and a female was leaning with her back to the bar. Looking through the hallway at Lina, he could see she was staring back still with the same look. His confusion suddenly evaporated when he turned back to the quiet Lounge, everything became clear.

'Hi Tam, long time no see.'

'Stella, whit the fuck ur you dayin here?'

'Not exactly the greeting I was hoping for to be honest.' She looked different, he couldn't quite figure out in what way but there was something about her had changed.

'Jist a bit ay a shock that's aw.' Tam tried to mask any knowledge he had of how dangerous it was for her to be anywhere near the Monkford.

'Yeah, but we're still friends aren't we?' She reached across the bar and touched his wrist. He pulled away awkwardly.

'Aye uv course we ur.' His eyes scanned the room's faces and the windows onto the darkened street, no sign of him.

'So whit ur ye dayin here Stella?'

'That's not a very nice welcome is it?'

'Am sorry, as a said, jist a wee bit surprised tae see ye that's aw.'

'Buy me a drink and I'll forgive you.' He poured a red wine while studying her. What was different, had she had a haircut perhaps?

'So how is it, working behind the bar?'

'Aye it's good, early days but Lina's keepin me right.' Stella took the wine glass, looking back with a smile.

'It suits you, you look like a barman, you have a presence.'

'Don't know aboot that, but it felt like the right thing tae dae. The brewery wur thinkin uv shuttin the place. That wid a made Lina unemployed and baith uv us homeless, so a decided tae get involved, try tae help. Ye know how it is, a suppose ye could say ma priorities huv chynged.' He began dipping glasses in the washer, while continuing to scan the room.

'You, alright Tam?'

'Am awright, you awright?'

'You seem a bit distracted that's all.' She looked over at the windows.

'Long story Stella.'

'I'm a good listener.'

'As a say, don't take this the wrang wye but am supposed tae be workin, a don't waant Lina thinkin am a slacker when av jist started.'

'I'm glad to see you're helping Lina, it's very commendable Tam.'

'Whit aboot you, how's things been it the firm?' He knew of course she had been in the safe house but felt it necessary to act dumb.

'You'll never believe what happened. Can you take a break?' He couldn't let Pat see her; that was a complication he could do without.

'Awright, through ye come.' He lifted the hatch and she followed him to the base of the stairs. As he passed a worried-looking Lina, he assured her he wouldn't be long. There had been a time when the current enthusiasm Stella was showing for going upstairs would have had his heart racing. Now though, his only concern was that she be kept away from Pat.

On entering the darkened living room he walked straight to the window looking down onto the street – the coast was clear for now. He watched her over his shoulder as she kicked off her heels, standing at the CD player. She looked much shorter out of her heels. He must persuade her to stay up here, out of sight. She unwittingly selected a Dean Martin CD from Lina's collection. He could have laughed at life's synchronicities if it wasn't all so bizarre.

'My dad loves Dean Martin, do you like him?' She moved to the sofa, patting the vacant cushion indicating she wanted him to join her.

'Av kind a gone aff em a wee bit recently tae be honest.' He sat next to her, still trying to figure out in what way she had changed since their last meeting.

'You awright Stella? Ye seem a bit, a don't know exactly whit it is, ye jist seem different.'

'Well I've been under a lot of stress recently with one thing and another,' she replied.

'How, whit's happened?'

'Strangest thing ever. A Police detective came to my place saying Campbell and I are in danger from whoever had originally abducted him.' Tam raised his eyebrows, feigning surprise.

'Turns out Campbell wasn't lying after all. I felt so guilty for doubting him in the first place. I had no idea why I would be in danger though, I was only trying to help him convalesce, you know that.' In that split second she avoided his eye in such a way that told him she had developed a physical relationship with Campbell.

'They let us pack a bag and then moved us both to a safe house. Complete fucking dump, we've been there since.' She drank two thirds of her wine in thirsty gulps.

'They said we have to stay put till they come back and tell us it's safe to leave. Neither of us have been able to contact family or anything, I couldn't even phone work, they took my mobile.'

'So did they tell you who you might be in danger from?'

'Not got a clue, Campbell was much better after you got him that stuff. Thanks again by the way I know you don't like him very much so I really appreciated you agreeing to help, you're a very kind person Tam.' Again, he considered his decision to agree to source the poison. There was no denying that part of him had wanted to do it for selfish reasons, to help facilitate his termination of the partnership with Pat. It had, of course been a waste of time on reflection.

'So where's Campbell noo?'

'He's still at the safe house.' Them not being told by Frank that the person they were in so much danger from lived on Tam's scheme explained her not having a problem with coming to the Monkford tonight, but it still didn't explain why she was here. He didn't want to seem rude but that was the question he wanted to ask.

'This wine's nice.' She passed him her now empty glass.

'Listen al get ye another boatel, bit a need tae get back tae ma work, kin ye chill here fur a bit an we kin talk efter ma shift?' He picked up the empty bottle from the coffee table, as he moved to stand she gently gripped his wrist.

'Tam what's up with you? You're being a bit funny with me.' He pulled his arm away and moved to the window, again checking the street.

'Am jist a wee bit confused that's aw, you turnin up oot the blue like this, especially when yuv been telt by the Polis no tae leave the safe hoose, whit's it aw aboot?' She looked back at him, pausing thoughtfully.

'Campbell's ran out of stuff.'

'Aw a get it noo, so yuv came here tae score fur yer new boyfriend is that it?'

'The stuff you gave him last time has run out, he's desperate, I wouldn't have asked you otherwise.' Tam spoke with his back to her, continuing to scan the street outside.

'That stuff wis supposed tae be helpin em wae ees cauld turkey, you need tae get em aff it, any mare'll be a death sentence fur sure.' He studied a group of people congregating around the bus terminus.

'Hang on a minute Tam, you're the one that gave him a bag

of smack big enough to keep a scheme out its nut for a holiday weekend.' She had a point. While it had been Pat who had procured the sizeable bag, Tam hadn't voiced his concerns over the quantity.

'A don't think gettin em any mare is such a good idea Stella, yuv no seen whit that poison dis tae people. It'll kill em, simple as that, it's a fuckin death sentence.' The only light in the room came from the street, casting a mixture of an orange glow and dark shadows. When he turned from the window to face her, he had to close and re-open his eyes so as to do a double take; he couldn't even nearly believe what he was looking at.

'This is what you want Tam isn't it?'

'Whit the fuck ur ye playin it Stella?' She was lying on the sofa and had removed her outer clothing, leaving only stockings and suspenders with no bra or pants.

'It's what you've always wanted, come on don't deny it.' Both her feet were perched wide apart on the edge of the low set coffee table. She was right, he was looking directly into the one thing that for weeks had blinded him as though he were walking in a sand storm.

'Well maybe it wis, bit things huv chynged Stella, av chynged.' He wanted to turn away but felt somehow transfixed.

'Just think of all those times you got so close, would be a waste never to get the job done right, don't you think?' She slid both hands slowly across her stomach, pushing her fingers downward. He felt a heavy sense of numbness, as though the thing he was staring at were capable of hypnosis. Like the dregs of a bath he was being sucked down and into the plug hole.

'Why did you always stop me?' he asked, wanting desperately to stem the blood from pumping out and into him.

'Doesn't matter about all that now, I've been thinking about it loads recently, It's here for you if you want it, I want you inside me now.' Her fingers slid downward and still his blood kept pumping outward as she moved her feet wider apart along the edge of the coffee table.

'A cannae dae it Stella, this isnae right.' He had forgotten about everything else, including Pat. His steps were tentative toward the sofa, not blinking once or taking his eyes away from it.

'What do you mean it's not right, of course it's right. I'll bet any money you've got a hard on that could crack concrete slabs, come on let's get it done once and for all, we've both got unfinished business.' He stepped in even closer, kneeling down on the floor so close the smell of her wafted up his nostrils.

'This isnae right Stella.' His hand reached up in autopilot, snapping back his belt buckle.

'Will you please stop saying that and just put it inside me now, come on you know it's what you want, it's what you've always wanted, it's what we've both always wanted.' She adjusted her position in preparation as he tugged at the buttonfly and his jeans fell to his knees compliantly.

'That's it Tam, here it is right here.' Her hand reached down, grabbing him firmly and steering his approach into proper alignment. He could feel her warmth on the end of him and her nails pulling at his arse cheeks but something was stopping his hip bones from relaxing into a push, not even a push would be required. All he needed to do was unclench his muscles and gravity would take care of the rest, he would fall downward and into her. She clamped on the back of his neck with both hands, pulling herself upward and corkscrew-licking his ear.

'This isn't just a one-off Tam, you can fill me up any time you want, day or night.' Her head dropped back on to the sofa and she touched his chin as he stared into her hazelnut eyes.

'I'll still pay for the stuff Tam, I'm not expecting it for free.'

There was a delay, a combination of him processing and then interpreting the actual content before in a flash he realised what this was all about. He pushed himself backward and onto his feet.

'Aw naw, no you as well fur fucks sake, please tell me yer jokin Stella!' She reached forward desperately, trying to pull him back down.

'What's the problem Tam? Here it is right here, this is what you've always wanted isn't it?'

'Aye maybe at wan time it wis, but no any mare, especially since yuv turned intae a junky bastard like yer boyfriend. Dae ye know whit that makes you Stella? Eh, it makes ye a fuckin prostitute, huvin sex wae men so ye kin score.'

'I don't see what your problem is Tam, you gave us the stuff in the first place and didn't even take any money that time. Well, I'm offering to pay you cash plus you get this as well, it's like a bonus.' He managed to release himself from her desperate gripping and climbed quickly back into his jeans. He moved back to the window looking on to the street.

'A jist cannae believe you uv all people huv ended up oan that shite Stella.'

'We've been locked up day and night in that place with nothing but a big bag of heroin for company, which was in case you had forgotten, supplied by you Tam. You're a total hypocrite, if anything it's your fault I ended up taking it in the first place. Campbell always seemed so relaxed afterwards, I was completely stressed out, I just wanted to relax for a bit, I was so freaked out, I was scared and I had no one.'

With hindsight of course he could now see the dangers of locking them up in a safe house with such a large quantity, but it hadn't even occurred to him that she would end up taking it as well. If he had known that was even a possibility he would never have agreed to source the stuff. He should have requested Frank intercept it. There had been so much going on he hadn't thought, besides with Tam being the supplier, notifying the Police might not have been such a great idea in any case.

He had buttoned his jeans wrong and while trying to fix himself scanned the darkness of the terminus, the shops, the street.

'It's a fuckin death sentence fur baith ay yees.' As he turned from the window, he stared at the empty sofa before running from the room.

241

After a frantic dash around the upstairs rooms it quickly became apparent that she was gone. Back in the living room, he stared down onto the darkened street with the lyrics of Dean Martin playing out in the background. The speed with which Stella had been consumed by the poison wasn't that much of a surprise. Growing up he had known many people who made that same transition, there was often little in the way of warning for family and friends.

As he pondered the hopelessness of her plight, he fingered the razor in the pocket of his jeans. Yet another name that could be added to the growing list of victims caused by his alliance with Pat. Nothing of any note on the street, so he returned to his duties downstairs in the hope Stella would return to the safe house.

'Everythin awright Tam?' Lina's face framed a worried expression.

'Aye nae bother, she wis jist tryin tae talk me intae goin back tae the firm, a telt er am done wae that place.' The image of what had been offered to him upstairs flashed across his mind's eye, forcing him to avert eye contact. The room upstairs with its dark shadows dancing in the orange glow from the street had given everything a sinister, somehow depraved ambience. It would have been the easiest thing in the world to just take it, but he also knew that something being easy doesn't necessarily make it right. He spent the next hour trying to distract the focus of his attention away from images of her gaping wound. The bar was getting busier. A voice travelled through the hallway from the Lounge and immediately his heart rate accelerated.

'Son you goet any decent red wine fur ma guest?' He turned to see Pat wearing a satisfied smile.

'It's awright Tam al get that.' Lina moved to locate and open a fresh bottle.

'Better make it a large yin Lina, cheers.' Pat waved Tam toward him. As he approached he looked over at Pat's usual table in the corner and saw Stella sitting on her own studying a crossword page.

'Kin ye believe oor luck son, a found er at the terminus waitin fur a fuckin bus. Noo we kin find oot fae her where the boyfriend is an take care a business wance an fur aw.' Lina placed Pat's drinks on the bar.

'A didnae know you knew her?' She nodded in Stella's direction, somewhat confused.

'Aye, dae ye no remember the night the bold yin here brought er back? A goet chattin tae er that night, nice lassie.' She didn't look convinced as she took his cashline twenty; Tam waited for Lina to move out of earshot.

'Whit exactly dae ye think yer playin it Pat?' This was the first time they had spoken since Pat's drunken confession about Paula, or since the memory of his mother's rape. He had prepared a speech, but struggled to remember how it began.

Coconut Badger! Coconut Badger!

'A telt ye, a need tae use her tae get tae the boyfriend, in case McGregor disnae get that CCTV. She said you widnae help er get mare stuff, is that right?' Tam briefly considered lying, but in view of the circumstances decided the time had come to be honest, there would be no more lies.

'Aye that's right, am no gettin anybody any mare ay that shite. A shouldnae uv geed it tae em in the first place, that poor bastard Campbell hus been through enough as it is.' Pat smiled with what looked like amusement, but his expression gradually changed as though something had occurred to him.

'You awright Tam? Is there somethin ye waant tae get aff yer chest?' Tam was unsure if perhaps the old man suspected something, in any case he had picked up on the shift in Tam's demeanour.

'Am no scared any mare.' As he spoke the words, Tam stared in and through Pat's deranged eyeballs. Not that long ago this action would have been comparable with staring at the sun.

'Whit's that yuv goet in yer poaket?' Pat asked.

Tam continued to finger the razor, refusing to break the stare.

'It's none ay your business whit av goet in ma poaket, it's ma poaket intit?'

Coconut Badger! Coconut Badger!

'Whit's up wae yoos two?' Lina returned with Pat's change, sensing the tension immediately.

'Och it's nothin sweetheart wur jist hivin a wee cerry oan, take wan fur yersel anaw.' She paused, studying both their faces before deciding she would leave the questions until after her shift and moved away to serve a thirsty punter.

'A heard you're gonnae be workin here full time son, that's good so it is. That means we'll be seein a lot ay each other.' Pat downed the whisky in one gulp, picking up the lager and wine. Tam remained silent, concentrating hard on not breaking eye contact. Within those few moments everything that had to be said was communicated silently between them. Pat now knew that Tam was no longer with him, so as a result he must be against him.

Tam continued to serve punters, while watching the old man's every move. Within an hour Stella was pissed and her relaxed manner indicated she was unaware of any danger. Pat passed the bar on his way to the gents, turning to face Tam with a conquering smile. He seemed to be enjoying himself even more than usual.

'It's alright by the way, your friend has agreed to help me.' Stella now had her jacket on, standing at the bar waiting for Pat to return. They were obviously leaving.

'Listen Stella a don't huv time tae go intae aw the details, but you're in serious danger if ye leave here wae him.' He was reluctant to give her a direct link between himself and Campbell's abductor. But unless she knew the truth she would leave.

'What are you on about, he's a total sweetie.' Smiling blindly she looked over toward the gents; it occurred to him that even if he was honest about her predicament she might not care. With her being pissed and cold turkey she would probably chain herself to the gates of hell if it meant securing her next fix. Tam lifted the latch and moved forward with an urgency that startled her, gripping her by the elbows.

'You've goet nae idea how much danger you're in right noo, as a said a cannae let ye leave wae him, It's fur yer ayn good.'

'Let go you're hurting me.' She wriggled, attempting to free herself.

'Besides, It's not for you to say who I can and can't leave with, thank you very much.'

'Right sweetheart, ready tae make a move?' Tam hadn't seen Pat approach but now found himself standing right next to him, within striking distance. Stella managed to pull herself from his grip and moved closer to Pat.

'Here whit ye geein the lassie a hard time fur?' Pat put a supportive arm around her shoulder.

'Where ye takin er?' Tam couldn't even imagine what Pat had in store for Stella, whether she gave up Campbell's location or not.

'We're goan back tae ma place tae listen tae some mare Deano, huv a couple a drinks, an then a said a wid get er some stuff later oan seen as you're bein a spoilsport.' Tam knew that the time had come. Although uncertain what would happen next, he knew one thing for sure. He wouldn't allow Stella to leave with him.

'Nah fraid not, the games up Pat, she's no goan anywhere.' He held Pat's eye steady, all the while thinking about Paula and his mother. Now that the time had arrived he almost felt relieved. It was as though everything had been building up to this moment.

'Exactly who the fuck dae ye think yer talkin tae son?' The volume in the room crashed from normal levels to complete silence within a heartbeat.

'Am fuckin talkin tae you, an am no yer son eether.' Those standing nearby discreetly shuffled back – even Stella had sensed something wasn't right and moved away slightly. Pat smiled back at Tam with a look that may have been fury, possibly even mixed with a little sense of pride.

'A know yuv been makin good progress, but yur way oot ay

yer league here am afraid tae say.' The Lounge was packed but punters moved back from the bar creating space around both men, akin to a playground fight. Lina had come through from next door, sensing something wasn't right, and there were even a few people out on the street peering in through the windows. The entire community seemed to be captivated by what was an unbelievable sight. It would seem that David was standing up to Goliath. Tam spoke directly to Pat, but raised his voice in such a way that everyone could hear what he had to say.

'A know everythin, an am tellin ye right noo that yer nothing but a durty fuckin liar.' Tam's chest pounded beneath him as he continued to finger the razor in his pocket. Pat looked first at Tam's face then at the hand in his pocket and finally scanned the faces of the shocked patrons.

'Jist calm yerself doon, you've obviously goet the wrang end ay the stick, c'moan we'll go ootside fur a quiet word an sort everythin oot.' Pat attempted to touch his elbow but Tam pushed his hand away firmly.

'Am no goan anywhere, whit av goet tae say needs tae be heard by everybody here, yer so-called friends an neighbours.' Pat's face was smiling in a casual but not untroubled way. Tam knew he had to get the rest of the Monkford on his side. Of the list of charges to be levelled at Pat, he decided to present his case starting with what he suspected the community would regard as the worst of them.

'Yer a fuckin grass!' The room collectively inhaled at those shocking words.

'Av goet proof that yuv been workin wae DCI McGregor fur years.' Tam knew what he had just said to a man like Pat would normally initiate a non-verbal response, and watched as Pat slid his hand into his pocket. The younger man took that as his cue and pulled the silver handle from his pocket in a flash. Twisting his wrist he extended the mirror-like blade and Pat stepped backward, palms outward.

'Hing oan a wee minute, easy does it, a kin explain everythin, yuv goet it the wrang wye roon son. McGregor's a bent copper so he is, he's the wan that works fur me!' Pat smiled; it was obvious to Tam he was going to have to keep the pressure on.

'That's bollocks Pat, yees work fur each other, he helps you, you help him, bottom line yer a fuckin grass.' Ultimately it was Tam's word against his and Pat knew it. Like a chess player, Tam scanned the board before him, considering the options available.

'And ye even telt me yersel it wis you that telt Paula the lies aboot me an Stella. Aw because ye didnae waant me an her makin a go uv it.' Tam lowered the razor to his side; it was still available to him but something was preventing him from lifting his arm to strike.

'A told ye Tam, that wisnae ma fault, you've messed that lassie aboot fur years, if it's anybody's fault it's yours. So whit if a telt her, a didnae know she'd go an top erself did a.' Pat seemed to be indignant, losing his temper almost. Tam watched the thick worm-like veins pulsing on his neck.

'Well maybe a did mess er aboot, but a telt ye that night that a waanted tae put things right wae er. Anywye that's besides the point, a wisnae even seein Stella. You made up lies, an then she killed erself, that's doon tae you ya twisted bastard no me.' Tam fondled the handle in his fingers. He could see Pat was getting angrier but that he also seemed to be calculating which way public opinion was leaning before deciding on his next move. Pat would be aware that Tam had previously lost his nerve when it came to the razor's usage. But of course that was before Tam knew what he knew now.

'An there's somethin else yees need tae know.' Tam stared hard at Pat as he addressed the collective.

'Ur ye there Lina?' He didn't take his eyes off Pat as he spoke.

'Aye am here, take it easy son, gonnae calm doon yer scarin me.' He could hear the fear in her voice as she peered over the heads in front of the bar.

'The night this place wis robbed, the reason ma Maw an Da left, this bastard wis behind it.' Of all the revelations, it was this that drew the most audible response from the locals.

'Is that right Pat?' Lina's voice was firm. Pat looked from Tam's face, to the razor, to the crowd, to Lina.

'A jist agreed that they could dae the joab, they wurnae supposed tae get violent—' There followed a gasp from the onlookers at this admission. '—It's the brewerys' money anywye intit, it's no as if it wis comin oot yer Maw an Da's poakets.' Pat looked again at the faces around the Lounge, most of whom he had known for many years. For the first time they were staring back in defiance, with a mixture of disgust and hatred. He knew in that instant that he was finished on the Monkford.

Tam felt himself being consumed by a white-hot rage. It rose up from his ankles filling every piece of him; he wanted desperately to open Pat's flesh but also knew somehow that if he did, it would change things forever. There would be no going back after that, he would become the man who slashed the legend and part of Pat's aura would be passed to him. It would mean always looking over his shoulder. The fury within was desperate to unleash itself but there was a blockage he couldn't reconcile. He let out a deep roar as his body shuddered, thirsty for revenge.

'A really waant tae hurt em bad Lina.'

'Please son don't dae it, you're too good fur that, ye don't waant tae end up like him dae ye?' The silence in the Lounge was the loudest Tam had heard in his life as he faced the black pupils of his one-time mentor. Just then he felt a soft and reassuring breeze touch the side of his face and it came to him. He would use Coconut Badger on itself. Reverse engineering the strategy in order to stop the blood thirst.

Buckaroo! Buckaroo! Buckaroo! Buckaroo!

Not to throw a saddle over his adrenal dump like previously, but to anchor it steadfast and maintain his control. He now understood that he had always had a choice. Supposed hard men like Pat were always having to prove something to themselves and others. But working men like his father and Archie, he now knew they were the real men, the real heroes. The endeavour and priority directed toward their families demonstrated a bravery and commitment beyond the comprehension of monsters like Pat. The Lounge was spinning around him ferociously as a battle between right and wrong was fought within. Part of him desperately wanted to lash out. Hatred and pain seemingly linked every one of his footsteps since the night of the robbery to this spot. But what of his mother's pain? His father's shame? Paula's innocence? Eventually the room slowed from its spin to a stop. He slipped the razor back into his pocket. Lifting the latch, he moved toward Lina.

Pat was silent in Tam's wake. There was a mumbling among the crowd. It was understood by everyone, including Pat, that Tam had delivered him into the hands of the community. They would now carry out whatever sentence they deemed appropriate.

'Ur yees gonnae at least gee me a start?' Pat addressed the collective.

'C'moan tae fuck, where's yer sense ay sport eh?' Some faces looked to Tam, but were met by an expression that indicated the decision wasn't his to make. Tam turned to the gantry and poured himself a single malt.

'Awright then, at least count tae ten.' As he spoke, Pat backed his way carefully toward the door. He removed and opened his razor, his signature tobacco-stained smile looking back at Tam. As Pat reached the door, Tam decided there was one last thing to be done and vaulted over the bar to the jukebox.

You're nobody till somebody loves you.
You're nobody till somebody cares.